"The authentically Southern Boyer writes with heart, insight, and a deep understanding of human nature."

– Hank Phillippi Ryan,
Agatha Award-Winning Author of *What You See*

"Boyer delivers a beach read filled with quirky, endearing characters and a masterfully layered mystery, all set in the lush Lowcountry. Don't miss this one!"

– Mary Alice Monroe,
New York Times Bestselling Author of *A Lowcountry Wedding*

"A complicated story that's rich and juicy with plenty of twists and turns. It has lots of peril and romance—something for every cozy mystery fan."

– *New York Journal of Books*

"Has everything you could want in a traditional mystery...I enjoyed every minute of it."

– Charlaine Harris,
New York Times Bestselling Author of *Day Shift*

"Like the other Lowcountry mysteries, there's tons of humor here, but in *Lowcountry Boneyard* there's a dash of darkness, too. A fun and surprisingly thought-provoking read."

– *Mystery Scene Magazine*

"The local foods sound scrumptious and the locale descriptions entice us to be tourists...the PI detail is as convincing as Grafton."

– *Fresh Fiction*

"Boyer delivers big time with a witty mystery that is fun, radiant, and impossible to put down. I love this book!"

– Darynda Jones,
New York Times Bestselling Author

"Southern family eccentricities and manners, a very strongly plotted mystery, and a heroine who must balance her nuptials with a murder investigation ensure that readers will be vastly entertained by this funny and compelling mystery."

– Kings River Life Magazine

"*Lowcountry Bombshell* is that rare combination of suspense, humor, seduction, and mayhem, an absolute must-read not only for mystery enthusiasts but for anyone who loves a fast-paced, well-written story."

– Cassandra King,
Author of *The Same Sweet Girls* and *Moonrise*

"Imaginative, empathetic, genuine, and fun, *Lowcountry Boil* is a lowcountry delight."

– Carolyn Hart,
Author of *What the Cat Saw*

"*Lowcountry Boil* pulls the reader in like the draw of a riptide with a keeps-you-guessing mystery full of romance, family intrigue, and the smell of salt marsh on the Charleston coast."

– Cathy Pickens,
Author of the Southern Fried Mystery Series

"Plenty of secrets, long-simmering feuds, and greedy ventures make for a captivating read...Boyer's chick lit PI debut charmingly showcases South Carolina island culture."

– Library Journal

"This brilliantly executed and well-defined mystery left me mesmerized by all things Southern in one fell swoop... this is the best book yet in this wonderfully charming series."

– Dru's Book Musings

Lowcountry
BOONDOGGLE

The Liz Talbot Mystery Series
by Susan M. Boyer

Lowcountry BOONDOGGLE

A Liz Talbot Mystery

Susan M. Boyer

HENERY PRESS

Copyright

LOWCOUNTRY BOONDOGGLE
A Liz Talbot Mystery
Part of the Henery Press Mystery Collection

First Edition | June 2020

Henery Press
www.henerypress.com

Trade Paperback ISBN-13: 978-1-63511-607-6
Digital epub ISBN-13: 978-1-63511-608-3
Kindle ISBN-13: 978-1-63511-609-0
Hardcover ISBN-13: 978-1-63511-610-6

Printed in the United States of America

For my readers...
Thank you for making my dreams come true. While this is a
dramatic chapter in Liz, Nate, and Colleen's story, rest assured, it
is not the last.

ACKNOWLEDGMENTS

Heartfelt thanks to...

...each and every reader who has connected with Liz Talbot.

...Jim Boyer, my husband, best friend, and fiercest advocate.

...every member of my fabulous sprawling family for your enthusiastic support.

...Lesa Dion, who appears with her husband, Dave, because she won a contest during the launch of Lowcountry Boomerang. I so hope you enjoy seeing your name in the book.

...Tracie Crane, Rachael Palasti, and Misty Partin, members of the Lowcountry Society, who appear as characters in this book. Writing y'all in was such fun! I hope you enjoy being a part of the story.

...all the members of the Lowcountry Society, for your ongoing enthusiasm and support.

...Gretchen Smith, for letting me tell her a story, and brainstorming garish Halloween displays with me.

...Rachel Jackson, Marcia Migacz, and Pat Werths whose sharp eyes find my mistakes when I can no longer see them.

...MaryAnn Schaefer, my able assistant, who handles All the Things with grace.

...Christina Hogrebe at Jane Rotrosen Agency for being the best sounding board around and for your ongoing encouragement.

...Kathie Bennett and Susan Zurenda at Magic Time Literary.

...Jill Hendrix, owner of Fiction Addiction bookstore, for your ongoing support. I can't imagine being on this journey without you.

...Kendel Lynn and Art Molinares at Henery Press.

As always, I'm terrified I've forgotten someone. If I have, please know it was unintentional, and in part due to sleep deprivation. I am deeply grateful to everyone who has helped me along this journey.

ONE

The dead are audacious sorts. Take my best friend, Colleen. I'm not saying she's brave. She is, of course, but you'd expect that, I suppose. The thing virtually all mortals fear most is death—either their own or someone else's. Colleen cleared that hurdle our junior year in high school, when she downed a bottle of tequila and went swimming in Breach Inlet. She's fearless, all right, but what I'm saying here is that Colleen has abandoned all sense of decorum. I've resigned myself to the fact that she'll forever be a teenager. But her behavior at times is more fitting that of a six-year-old.

By way of example, on a Monday morning in late October, Nate and I were meeting with a client, Darius Baker, and his attorneys, Fraser Rutledge and Eli Radcliffe, in their elegantly appointed offices. Rutledge & Radcliffe is one of the most distinguished law firms on Broad Street in Charleston, South Carolina. The furniture in that office is museum quality, the sound so utterly dampened by luxurious rugs you almost feel the need to whisper like you're in church. Colleen sat cross-legged like a child on the corner of Fraser's massive desk. In her ankle-length tangerine dress with Swiss polka dots, her long red hair loose about her shoulders, she brought to mind a big orange tabby cat.

Talbot & Andrews Investigations—that's the name of our PI firm—had an arrangement with Rutledge & Radcliffe. We didn't work for them directly, though they'd tried to hire us many times. But Nate, my husband and partner, and I had an open-ended contract, and lately, a sizable chunk of our workload came through

Rutledge & Radcliffe. In a switch, we'd referred Darius Baker to them recently when he had an unfortunate run of luck and a pressing need for a highly skilled local criminal attorney.

That particular morning, Darius, our celebrity client, had requested the meeting with both his legal and his investigative teams. Darius always covered his bases. The five of us, Nate, me, Darius, Fraser Rutledge and Eli Radcliffe, congregated in Fraser's office to put our heads together regarding the developing situation with Darius's long-lost love child. Let me tell you, between the colorful personalities present, the sensitive subject matter, and the unconstrained teenaged guardian spirit, it was a potentially combustible situation.

Fraser Alston Rutledge III may have been the most comfortable person in his own skin I'd ever met. A study in contrasts, he clearly came from very old Charleston money. His seersucker suit was light blue, his bowtie and suspenders navy. The oil painting on his cypress-paneled office wall featured him with his Brittany spaniels. But his gelled hair, spiked on top, was not a style favored amongst the South of Broad set.

Fraser sat back in his executive leather chair and gave Darius a look that called his common sense into serious question. "Mr. Baker, Eli and I have deliberated over the developments you outlined by telephone, but for the sake of ensuring we are all on the same page here, let me see if I have the details of your predicament straight."

Wearing jeans, a white button-down, and a navy blazer, Darius looked the part of a modern Lowcountry gentleman, which he was. His smooth skin was the color of fine milk chocolate. He wasn't quite forty, but he was completely bald. Darius closed his eyes, sighed, moved restlessly in his chair. "Fine."

Fraser said, "A suspicious fire wiped out Brantley Miller's entire adoptive family up in Travelers Rest back in March. In August, Mr. Miller contacted you online and indicated that he believed you were related. Subsequently, you ascertained that he is your son. He arrived in Stella Maris in September. Today is October 26. Mr. Miller is living in your home, and you have invested in his business venture with two other young men to grow *hemp* commercially." Fraser tasted the word "hemp," seemed to find it disagreeable.

"Last week," continued Fraser, "another potential investor in that enterprise, Dr. Murray Hamilton, a beloved local college professor, who is coincidentally the uncle of one of Mr. Miller's business partners, was murdered in his home over on Montagu Street and his house was subsequently blown to kingdom come, the remnants burned to a pile of ash. His nephew, one Tyler Duval—Mr. Miller's friend and business associate—has been questioned by the police, and Mr. Miller is concerned that Mr. Duval may be arrested at any moment. Am I in possession of all the salient facts?"

Darius flashed him a pained expression. "Yeah. Sounds like it."

Fraser leaned forward. "I would not be fulfilling my responsibility to you as a client of this firm if I failed to acquaint you with the many potential exposures you face here." He proceeded to hold forth for the better part of ten minutes, which he was prone to do.

Bored, Colleen commenced standing on her head. "I wonder if I can hold this as long as he can talk?" Through some magic of hers, her dress defied gravity and didn't flip over her head.

Eli, Darius, Nate, and I occupied the four deep leather visitor chairs in front of Fraser's desk. Nate and I were the only ones who could see Colleen, and we ignored her completely. We'd discovered this was often the best strategy. Colleen loved nothing more than to provoke me in front of others, make me respond to her and look like a lunatic to everyone else in the vicinity.

Fraser droned on, oblivious to Colleen's antics. "Eli and I have discussed this at great length. It is our considered opinion that you, Mr. Baker, and all of your interests, would be best served by keeping Mr. Miller and his friends—this *hemp* business and the recent untimely death of Professor Hamilton—at arm's length. Your own legal troubles are not that far behind you. To become embroiled in another murder case at this juncture would be highly imprudent—"

Darius raised both palms and shook his head until Fraser stopped talking. As a relatively new client at Rutledge & Radcliffe, Darius was unaccustomed to listening to someone else talk for such extended periods. He had little patience with Fraser's affection for the sound of his own voice. Darius looked at each of us in turn, wide-eyed and solemn, first Fraser, then Eli, then Nate, and then me. "I'm gonna be real with y'all."

Until recently, Darius was the star of a hit reality TV series, *Main Street USA*. He traveled to a different small town each week, sampled the local food, attended festivals and whatnot, chatted with the local folks, and offered colorful commentary. He was a character, is what I'm saying. And his character spoke in "down home, easygoing, funny, Southern black guy, with a bit of Hollywood," a patois that was his brand. Darius could no doubt turn that off if he wanted to. But it was rare for him to break character, even now.

Fraser sat back in his chair, raised an elegant eyebrow, and gestured magnanimously. "Well, by all means, Mr. Baker. Do be *real* with us."

For her part, Colleen came down off her head and settled back into a cross-legged pose.

Darius continued, "Now, I know y'all have my best interests at heart. And I appreciate that, I do. But we're talking about my son here. Brantley is my *son*. You feel me? Family is family. Now, I'm not stupid. I know he might've originally got in touch with me 'cause he was all excited about maybe he was gonna get himself some of my money. But we're gettin' to know each other. We're buildin' a relationship here. And he came to me for help. So I want to help. Now, can y'all help me help him...or not? 'Cause there's more than one high-dollar law office and more than one set a private investigators in this town."

Fraser's brown-and-gold-flecked tiger eyes went hard, but he was silent, an unusual situation to say the least. I liked Darius more all the time. He respected Fraser's abilities, or we wouldn't have been there. But Darius wasn't going to suffer Fraser's high-handed manner in silence either. I was torn because I agreed with Fraser's assessment if not his style.

"Darius," I said, "does it not worry you the teensiest bit that we haven't been able to rule out Brantley's involvement in the house fire that killed his entire adoptive family barely more than six months ago?"

"Naw," he said. "Uh-unh. I believe you tried your best to find something...*anything*...that would incriminate him in that horrible fire that killed that poor family, but you can't."

Nate said, "You make it sound unsavory—like we were trying to frame him, Darius. We're just doing our due diligence, trying to protect you. You and anyone else on Stella Maris Brantley becomes involved with."

Stella Maris is the island north of Isle of Palms where Darius and I grew up. He'd recently retired from the Hollywood high-life and moved home. Brantley, a son—now twenty years old—had shown up fast on his heels, thanks to the marvels of DNA testing and its use in ancestry research.

"I understand that," said Darius. "That's why I continued to pay your bill this last month while you went up to Travelers Rest and looked into all a that. But if I understand what y'all are tellin' me, you can't find one thing to tie Brantley to that fire."

"We can't," I said. "But that doesn't necessarily mean he's innocent. It may mean he's very smart." Brantley had turned up in our hometown out of the blue the second he learned his biological father was an international celebrity. Would he have come lickety-split if Darius had been a busboy? We'd never know. But I was keeping a close eye on him for the foreseeable future.

"Y'all just cynical," said Darius. "Probably comes with the job. But I refuse to think the worst a him. If y'all had come back and told me you thought he set that fire, even if you couldn't actually prove it, I could see sending Brantley packin'. But that's not what you told me."

"I am afraid I must agree with Miz Talbot and Mr. Andrews," said Fraser. "Best to err on the side of caution. Especially given this latest development."

"That's not a *development*," said Darius. "The fire over on Montagu has nothing whatso*ever* to do with Brantley."

"As far as you know," I said. "But he is connected to Professor Hamilton's death. That's the only reason you want us to get involved. Hell's bells—think, Darius. One brand-new son. Two fires involving deaths."

Darius said, "Brantley ain't got nothing to do with that professor's house catching on fire. If Sonny Ravenel thought for a second that he did, Brantley would be sitting over at the jail in North Charleston, just like I was for four long days and three long nights not very long ago. Sonny, he ain't shy about locking people up."

Sonny Ravenel was a good friend and a Charleston police detective. Back in September, he'd had no choice but to arrest Darius in the case of his high school girlfriend—Brantley's mother's—murder, but that's a whole nother story, and all behind us now, thank goodness.

"You've got to admit, it looks suspicious," said Nate. "Brantley and his buddies meet with the professor, Tyler's uncle, right?"

"That's right," said Darius. "They were there last Monday evening."

"They need money for their hemp business," said Nate. "The professor is skeptical. He doesn't give them any money. Then the professor dies and leaves a substantial sum to his nephew, Tyler Duval. And then Murray Hamilton's house explodes into flames, possibly destroying evidence."

What was the protocol? Was Murray Hamilton properly referred to as Dr. Hamilton or Professor Hamilton?

Colleen consulted the ceiling, the way she does when she's using the cosmic version of Google. "Professor Hamilton. Students would address him as Dr. Hamilton. Outside the classroom you use Professor to differentiate him from a medical doctor, though you'll hear it both ways."

Thank you.

"I never said it don't look suspicious," said Darius. "Of course it looks suspicious. I know all about suspicious, believe you me. If it didn't look suspicious, I wouldn't need y'all to help Brantley's friend out of this mess. Suspicious don't mean that boy killed nobody. And it definitely don't mean Brantley burned somebody's house down."

Colleen blew a stray lock of hair off her face, looked annoyed. "I tried to tell y'all...if Darius was in danger, I would know. Right now he's not."

As a guardian spirit, Colleen's mission was to protect the people of Stella Maris by safeguarding the island from developers and all such as that. Overpopulation was a huge risk for us, as the island was only accessible by boat. Colleen's primary method was to ensure the town council consisted of people who loathe the idea of condos and high-rise resorts on our pristine beaches. I held one seat on the council. Darius was the newest member, handpicked by Colleen for his conservationist views.

And he gave Brantley money to invest in this hemp project. Brantley doesn't need Darius out of the way as long as he's willing to hand him money. I threw the thought at her. This was how we communicated when others were around.

"You're awfully suspicious of Brantley," said Colleen.

And you could put my mind at ease once and for all where he's concerned if you'd simply tell me whether or not he lit fire to a house with his entire family inside or not. This was my problem. Colleen could often read other people's minds, not just mine. When she couldn't read a person, sometimes it meant they were just plain evil. Other times it didn't mean anything at all except Colleen wasn't privy to whatever was on their minds. But it always gave me pause when she couldn't read someone.

"Apparently that falls under the heading 'Information not Needed for My Mission.' It's not my job to solve your cases for you."

So you tell me. Frequently.

"But like I said," said Colleen, "if Darius was in danger...that I would know. And since I'm getting nothing on Brantley at all, I have to suspect that means he's harmless. I think I'd know if Darius had a firebug living in his house. *That* would be mission critical."

"Did I understand you correctly?" asked Fraser. "These boys believe they can make supercapacitors from hemp? Replace the graphene?" Skepticism drew an odd look on his face.

Darius said, "I don't think they're gonna make the supercapacitors themselves. They'll sell the stems to a manufacturing facility for that. Look, it's brand-new technology, and it's over my head too, to be honest with you. But what they tell me is the part used for these supercapacitors is normally waste. They'll sell the rest of the plant, the leaves and the flowers and so forth, for CBD oil."

"If that is indeed feasible, it would be quite lucrative," said Fraser.

"That's what they tell me," said Darius.

"And you invested how much in their proposition?" asked Eli.

"A hundred thousand dollars," said Darius.

"And yet they still needed money from Tyler's uncle?" I felt my face screw up in that expression Mamma is always warning me will cause wrinkles. "What for? They have the land, right?"

"Yeah, uh, Will Capers," said Darius, "one of the other boys—his grandfather owns a big farm over on Johns Island. A hundred and twenty-five acres. He's letting the boys grow there. But they're putting up greenhouses so they can grow year-round. Greenhouses cost money. They need some other equipment too. They're doing most of the work themselves. Few of Will's grandfather's field hands are helping out. They have to be paid, of course."

"Brantley met his partners at school?" A contrast to Fraser, Eli Radcliffe listened more than he spoke.

"Yeah," said Darius. "They're all agriculture majors at Clemson. Will Capers, he's in agri*business*. I guess you'd call him the mastermind of the project. He's the one with all the facts and figures."

"So it's Brantley, Tyler Duval, and Will Capers. The three of them?" I asked.

"That's right," said Darius.

"Did anybody else's family give them money?" I asked.

"Not cash money," said Darius. "But Will Capers's grandfather, he's heavily invested. Had to cost him something not to grow tomatoes or somethin' on that land."

Sea Island tomatoes in general were special. Mamma's were prize-winning. But Johns Island tomatoes were practically legendary.

"Indeed." Fraser cast Darius a thoughtful look. "What sort of agreement do the boys have with him? Let us assume they are wildly successful with this venture. They make millions of dollars. What is the landowner's share?"

"Twenty-five percent," said Darius. "And they pay me twenty-five percent a year beginning the third year they make a profit, until I'm fully repaid, plus five percent. I figured the first few years they'd need to reinvest that money back into the business."

"Five percent?" Fraser looked like he had a very bad taste in his mouth. "Five thousand dollars over four years, best-case scenario? That is your return on your investment?"

"Like I said..." Darius drew "said" out to five syllables. "He is my son."

Fraser closed his eyes, shook his head. "It is your money to do with as you please. I hope you are fully apprised as to the changing nature of the laws governing hemp farming, both at the federal and state level."

"It's my understanding that the recent changes are in favor of the growers," said Darius.

"It is a fluid situation, to be sure," said Fraser.

"How are they going to work a farm on Johns Island and go to class in Clemson?" asked Eli.

"Tyler and Will graduated in May," said Darius. "Brantley's a junior, but he's decided to take some time off. He's had a rough patch, with his adoptive family being killed in an *accidental* house fire and all. Now he and I are getting acquainted. I'm all the family he has. We need some time. That school's not going anywhere. While he's here, he's going to do a little farming. Won't hurt him a bit."

"Back to Professor Hamilton," said Fraser. "Did the boys meet with him just once?"

"Nah, the three of them were at his house a lot," said Darius. "He was real interested in what they were doing. Unfortunately, the last time they were there was the day before he died. That just looks bad."

"And when did the police talk to Tyler?" I asked.

"Sunday—yesterday," said Darius. "The medical examiner did a tox screen on the professor's body. Said somebody poisoned him with antifreeze. They think it was in some green vegetable juice. Another reason not to *ever* drink anything green right there."

"So they're looking at Tyler," I said. "What about the other boys?"

"Sonny has an appointment to see Will Capers and his

grandfather this afternoon," said Darius. "I imagine he'll get to Brantley soon enough."

"I will contact Mr. Capers and offer my assistance," said Fraser.

"Let me handle that, Fraser," said Eli. "I know Gideon Capers."

"Very well." Fraser eyed Darius pointedly. "We will attend to this matter unless and until your interests diverge from those of the boys. In the meantime, none of them speaks to the police without either Eli or me present. And no one speaks to the press but me."

"Fine by me," said Darius. "You can handle the press for me from now on, if you want to."

"Miz Talbot, Mr. Andrews," said Fraser, "do you have everything you need at present?"

I mulled that. Ultimately, Fraser and Eli were our clients. Through them, because Darius was their client, he was also ours. But we were being hired on behalf of Tyler Duval. He was also now our client. Because he was Brantley Miller's friend. Brantley wasn't technically our client, but he was the client's son, whose interests Darius would want protected. That was a lot of layers of clients.

The thing we bypassed when we took on business through Rutledge & Radcliffe was our contract directly with the client. This unsettled me. I preferred being able to ask questions like "Do you own any firearms?" of the people we worked for. It paid to be careful in our line of work.

"I think we're good," said Nate. "Can we get Sonny's meeting with the Capers moved? Have it here, in the conference room?"

Eli nodded. "Of course. I'll arrange that."

"But, Darius," I said, "you need to be prepared. If we chase this rabbit on behalf of Tyler Duval, we may well come up with something that incriminates Brantley."

"If you find out for sure he's killed somebody, or had any part in killing somebody, I'll drop him off to Sonny Ravenel myself," said Darius.

TWO

Tyler Duval lived in a carriage house behind a stately Charleston mansion on Rutledge, a few doors from its intersection with Montagu. It was less than a block from what was left of his uncle's house. He agreed to see me immediately. While Nate stayed behind at Rutledge & Radcliffe to coordinate with Eli on the meeting between Sonny and Will Capers and his grandfather, I zipped on over to meet Tyler.

I turned left off Rutledge, passed through a wrought-iron gate, and drove down a shady driveway between two Charleston single houses. The drive turned to gravel with a brick edge. It wound deep into the trees and ended at the edge of a lovely garden. I felt as though I'd traveled a long ways off Rutledge, farther than I should've been able to travel without crossing Ashley Avenue, to a secret sanctuary.

The carriage house was built from the same brick as the ivy-covered courtyard wall. Three large arches housed sets of black-painted-framed French doors that opened from the garden. A young man in his early twenties who must've been Tyler opened one of the doors and stepped into the courtyard. He was roughly six feet tall and fit, with close-cropped reddish-brown hair. His faded green T-shirt said, "Hemp Farmer" on the front.

I opened the Voice Memo app on my iPhone, tapped record, and spoke into it. "Initial meeting with Tyler Duval, Monday, October 26, 11:00 a.m." Then I slid it into the side pocket of my crossbody bag and climbed out of the car.

"Hey, I'm Liz Talbot?"

"Hey there." He started across the courtyard, and I met him partway. He extended a hand. "I'm Tyler Duval. Nice to meet you." His drawl held a bit more twang than your typical Charleston tones. His handshake was firm, and he had no trouble looking me in the eye. Freckles sprinkled his nose and cheeks.

"Are you from Charleston?" I asked.

"Naw, I'm originally from Birmingham, Alabama. Did you want to sit here in the garden or go inside?"

It was one of those bright, clear October days when the humidity was down and the air felt soft against your skin. It was a shame to go inside, really, but I wanted to get a look at how Tyler lived. "Inside sounds good."

"Would you like something to drink?" He turned and stepped towards the French doors, then stood back and gestured "after you" with his left arm. "I've got some fresh iced tea."

"That sounds lovely." I smiled, stepped into the small entry hall. I was having tea alone, in a secluded spot, with a man Sonny had questioned in a homicide-by-poisoning case. Had Tyler killed his uncle for his inheritance?

"Have a seat." He nodded to the right, to a living room with exposed brick walls, then headed left towards the dining area. "I'll be right back."

The living room was sparsely furnished with a brown leather sofa, a club chair, and an armchair with an exposed frame. There were no tables in the room, only a couple floor lamps. A wall-mounted TV hung across from the sofa. Nothing else adorned the walls, and there was nothing personal in the room—no magazines, no books, no photographs.

I took a seat on the sofa. After a minute, Tyler appeared with two glasses of iced tea and handed one to me.

"Thanks." Should I drink this or not? I didn't want to be rude, but I didn't want to be dead, either.

"I'm sorry I don't have a place for you to set your glass," said Tyler.

"Well, my goodness, I don't want to set it down." If he was a poisoner, he had no motive to poison *me*. I was there to help. And it wasn't green. I took a sip. Fresh brewed. "That's delicious."

"Thanks. Uncle Murray was a tea drinker. He made sure I could brew a pot and make a decent pitcher of iced tea." Tyler took the club chair across from me. "So...I guess Darius musta hired you. He said he was going to."

"That's right. He gave me a rough outline of what's going on, but I'd love to hear it from you. But first, if you don't mind, tell me a bit more about yourself. You're from Alabama?"

"Roll Tide." He grinned. "I went to Clemson for agriculture. But Alabama football, that's in my blood."

"How long has Charleston been home? Did you move here when you graduated?"

"My sister, Flannery, and I, we moved here to live with Uncle Murray when I was thirteen. Nine years ago. Our mamma was his sister. She passed, cancer."

"I'm so sorry to hear that."

"Thank you. Our dad, he was killed in a car accident when I was three. Uncle Murray was the only family we had left."

"His house—the one that was just destroyed—is that where you all lived?"

"Yeah. Uncle Murray lived there all his life. It belonged to his parents. I don't know if Darius told you. Uncle Murray was a history professor at College of Charleston. He liked living next to campus."

"Were you close to your uncle?" I asked.

"Very. I don't remember my dad at all. Uncle Murray, even before we moved here to live, he was the closest thing to a dad I ever had." A muscle in his jaw twitched. His eyes shone with unshed tears. He blinked, cleared his throat.

"I'm so sorry to intrude on your grief," I said.

"Naw, that's okay," he said. "I 'preciate you coming. I 'preciate Darius doing this. It's just unbelievable to me that anyone would imagine I would ever hurt Uncle Murray. The very idea is absurd. But Brantley, he felt like that police detective has made up his mind I did this, and now he's just looking for a way to pin it on me. I hate to think that's true. But I guess it's better to be prepared."

"I know Sonny Ravenel pretty well," I said. "He's not trying to frame you."

"I'm not suggestin' he would manufacture evidence against me. That's not what Brantley meant either. He was just saying the detective was only looking for evidence to support his theory."

"I gather you and Brantley are close."

"Yeah, we met his first semester at Clemson. I was a junior. He was interested in hemp, and that's my passion. I guess we bonded over that."

Imagine that. College students bonding over cannabis. An image of them smoking joints around a campfire popped into my head. "And Will?"

"Same thing. The three of us have been tight for a while. Been planning to go into business together when we all graduated for a couple years now. The plan was always to grow hemp, but then Will ran across the research for using hemp for supercapacitors. That's pretty much all any of us talk about. We're excited. But I guess other people don't share our enthusiasm for the details. We spend a lot of time together."

"This supercapacitor thing...that's a game changer?"

The air in the room shifted. I had the strangest feeling that Colleen was there with us, but I didn't see her. I glanced around the room. Being discreet purely wasn't her style. Where was she?

Tyler winced. "Yes and no. For the planet, it could be huge. Financially, for us, not really. The Chinese are flooding the market with cheap hemp right now. The money is in growing for flowers and buds for CBD oil. But using the hurd for supercapacitors, that's cutting edge. Everything okay?"

Caught scrutinizing the corner of the ceiling, I smiled, tilted my head in a signature ditzy blonde inquiring look. "What's hurd?"

"That's the woody core of the stem. The stem has two parts. The outside is used for fiber. That's where you get your rope and fabric and such."

"I honestly don't know what a supercapacitor is."

"It stores energy, kinda like a battery. Right now they don't store enough energy to compete with batteries. And they're made with graphene, which is expensive. But researchers have been successful using hurd and a hydrothermal synthesis process instead. It stores more energy and costs a lot less. This could be a huge step forward in green technology."

What was she up to? "But not one in and of itself that will make you and your partners rich?"

"It might make the folks making the supercapacitors rich. But hemp would just be raw material for them. For us, the money's in the oil. There's several things we could market the stem for. We'll multi-purpose the crop for sure. I call hemp a super crop. You can do so many things with it: make clothes, food, paper, CBD oil, all kinds of stuff. And now maybe supercapacitors."

He was clearly a hemp enthusiast. "Fascinating."

Tyler chuckled. "Naw, I get that's it's not fascinatin' to most people. I've lost a couple girlfriends talking hemp too much."

I laughed. He seemed like a genuinely nice guy—easygoing, personable. That didn't make him innocent. Was Colleen surreptitiously protecting me? Did that mean Tyler was guilty?

"All right." I spoke sternly to myself, focused on the interview at hand. I was probably imagining things. "So, you and Will graduated in the spring?"

"That's right."

"And the two of you got started on this venture then? On Will's grandfather's farm?"

"Well, yeah, but there was a lot we needed to do to position ourselves. We've been working on making contacts, sourcing seedlings, infrastructure, building our soil—all kinds of things. Our first field crop won't go into the ground until early spring."

"Did all that positioning earn you a paycheck?" I softened the question with a smile. They were farmers. The first crop wasn't in the ground. They couldn't be making money.

"The paychecks didn't start until last month. We all agreed that we'd pay ourselves a small salary when each of us was able to work on the farm full time. For me and Will that would've been June. But we didn't have the funding until Darius invested."

I'd gone to Clemson myself. By some standards, no doubt the tuition was a bargain, but it still wasn't cheap. Just then, I was imagining Mamma and Daddy's reaction if I'd suggested after college maybe I'd go into business with a couple friends, but we didn't know when we'd be getting a paycheck. That would've gone over about like a bouquet of cast-iron balloons.

"So beginning last month, your company—" I gave him a questioning look.

"BTW," he said. "It's each of our first initials. We drew lots for the order."

"BTW is paying you and Will a salary now?"

"Six hundred dollars a week each. It would be fifteen dollars an hour if we worked forty hours a week, but we work way more than that. Normally, this time a day on a Monday, I'da been at the farm for six hours already."

"And Brantley?" I asked.

"Honestly, he didn't want the money. Said he didn't need it—it didn't make sense. But since he's decided to take some time off school and work full time, Will and me insisted we pay him too. It's only fair. He got his first check week before last."

Darius, through his investment, was paying Brantley's salary, in addition to giving him a place to live and who knew what all else. "Is that your only source of income?"

"Naw, I tend bar nights and weekends at Minero over on East Bay."

I nodded. "I love their tacos."

"Man, their tortillas are the best."

"You asked your uncle to invest in your company?"

Tyler sighed. "I did. I've been telling him about our plans all along. He was always real supportive. But I never asked him for money until last week. We're working on getting electricity in the greenhouses, getting the irrigation in, getting them ready for winter. All that's expensive."

"When did you appeal to your uncle for help?" I asked.

"A week ago—last Monday night. The three of us were over at his house. It was a regular Monday night thing. Uncle Murray would cook for us." Tyler looked away. "He was a good cook. He grilled burgers that night."

"Take me through the evening," I said.

"We all got there about six. Uncle Murray was out on the patio getting the grill ready. We all had a beer, sat and shot the breeze. Then I went inside to check on the potatoes in the oven. Will came in and helped me carry out the stuff for the burgers—lettuce, tomato, mayo—all that. We ate outside. Uncle Murray asked us about the farm. He always does. He loves all the details. Loved them."

"And then you asked him for the money?"

"Yeah, I was just straight with him. Told him where things stood on the money end. And I asked him if he would consider loaning BTW enough money to get us through to first harvest. I figured we'd structure it just like the loan from Darius."

"What did your Uncle Murray say?" I asked.

"He said he'd love to help us, but he felt like there was too much exposure. Uncle Murray never was much of a risk-taker. He's fiscally very conservative. He saved his money, invested it. Most of what he had he made himself that way. Always taught me and Flannery to pay with cash. He was careful."

"Did you try to talk him into it?"

"Not really, *I* didn't," he said.

"Someone else did?"

"Brantley was like, 'You won't make a lot of money off it, but you'd sure be helping us out.' But Uncle Murray, he just said we were smart and we'd figure it out. He was sure of it."

Had Murray Hamilton ever told his nephew to get his mind on something sensible? That's what my daddy would've said. "And Will?" I asked.

Tyler shrugged. "He didn't have much to say about it."

"There was no argument?" I asked.

"Not at all."

"Did all of you leave together?"

"Yeah, about 9:30. We went back to my place to try to figure out what we were going to do. Without a cash infusion, we won't be able to make payroll past the end of this month. And then there's ongoing expenses, nutrients and the like."

"Who all is on that payroll besides the three of you?"

"Couple hands from Mr. Capers's farm. And they'd work for him if we couldn't pay them. It's really just the three of us that would be out a paycheck. I can manage fine on what I make at Minero. Just pick up a couple more shifts. Brantley doesn't need the money. But Will, the business is his only income."

"How did you plan to handle that?"

"Will had more investors to talk to, but for the time being, we were going to stop drawing checks, all of us. Minimize expenditures."

"You said you'd talked to your uncle a lot about the farm...aside from last Monday."

"All the time. Like I said. He was like a father to me and

Flannery."

"Did he ever express other concerns about the business?"

"Nothing I can remember. Uncle Murray was careful with his money and protective of me, I guess. He just felt like hemp was a risky business. Too many regulations still being passed. He said if you owned land and were already a successful farmer, it made sense to convert some of that acreage to hemp. But if you didn't already have the land, that was another story altogether."

"Will's grandfather's land...that didn't satisfy him?"

"Nah, he felt like I should buy land to farm, but not focus just on hemp. He wanted me to buy land further inland, where I could get more acreage for the money. Maybe around Florence."

"Seems like good advice," I said.

"It was." He tilted his head, shrugged. "I guess we've got our plans, and we want to do it our way. But Uncle Murray and me, we didn't argue about that. I wasn't mad at him and he wasn't mad at me."

"But him not investing...that left you in a tight spot, right? Your company needed money."

He winced, didn't say anything.

I waited. Most people will fill silence if you give them half a chance.

"We can find another investor," he said. "It just might take a while. Will's talking to half a dozen other people that want in. Hemp's hot."

Interesting. I wondered what possessed a person to want to invest in a start-up hemp farm. Seemed risky to me too. "But an investor would likely want a cut. Giving a piece of your business to someone...I'm guessing y'all would rather not do that. And now you don't have to, right?" I asked.

"I get what you're asking," said Tyler. "Uncle Murray is—he was—a wealthy man. Everything he had will be divided equally between Flannery and me. That's what the attorney told us anyway."

"You've already spoken to your uncle's attorney?"

"He contacted us. We're supposed to go in for a formal reading of the will Wednesday. We haven't, ah...Uncle Murray's funeral is tomorrow."

"How much money did you ask your uncle to loan the partnership?" I asked.

"A hundred thousand dollars."

"And now you'll make that loan yourself?"

Tyler flushed. "I reckon. I mean, I have no idea how long it takes to probate a will. It might be years before I have money from that, and honestly, I don't care. Look, I know how it looks. But I did not kill Uncle Murray. I love him and I miss him."

"Tell me everything you know about how he died."

He drew a deep breath, swallowed. "My sister went by to check on him last Tuesday morning. He'd missed class, and someone from the department called her. They couldn't get ahold of him. Flannery tried to call too, and he didn't answer. She found him in his bedroom, called 911, then tried to revive him. Flannery's a nurse."

"Did the coroner perform an autopsy?"

"I don't think they were going to," said Tyler. "Uncle Murray had been to the doctor a couple times recently. He'd had some stomach issues. Thought it was maybe the flu at first. But he also complained about his heart kinda racing and fluttering. Said he thought he might have an arrhythmia. His doctor had scheduled him for a series of tests. At first, they were thinking his death was related to an irregular heartbeat."

"What changed the doctor's mind about that?"

"Flannery." Tyler raised both his eyebrows. "She works at MUSC. I guess she knows some people. She wanted to know for sure, in case it was a genetic thing. But too, she didn't believe whatever was going on with his heart had killed him. She said his last tests were completely normal. Flannery was very upset. I think they agreed to do an autopsy just for her peace of mind."

"What exactly did they tell y'all about the cause of death?"

"They said he had a lethal amount of ethylene glycol in his system. Started asking if he'd been suicidal—that's a hard no. Checked his garage for antifreeze, but there wasn't any there. Uncle Murray went to the dealership for car maintenance. I doubt he knew where to put antifreeze."

"Did the coroner's office mention the antifreeze being mixed with anything?"

"Yeah, and this is the kicker. Green juice, like that stuff health nuts drink all the time. Uncle Murray wasn't a green juice kinda guy. But he'd been seeing someone. A new philosophy professor at the college. Annalise Mitchell. I guess you'd call her a free spirit. She had Uncle Murray doing all kinds of things he didn't use to. Had him on a jet ski, which is something I'd a never thought I'd see. Annalise is a green juice drinker from way back. She'd been trying without much success to get Uncle Murray to drink it, but then I guess she must've convinced him."

"How long had your uncle been seeing her?" I asked.

"She was new on campus. Just started this semester. I think they'd been dating since late August."

"Your Uncle Murray, was he a widower?"

"Naw, he never did marry. Uncle Murray was a bit of a character, kinda set in his ways."

"Was he ever serious about anyone?"

"Not that I know about."

"What about close friends? Who did he spend time with?"

Tyler gave a half chuckle. "His best friend was Pierce Fishburne. He's an economics professor at the college. Lives across the street from Uncle Murray. The two of them bickered constantly, but they were inseparable. Just like brothers."

"Can you think of anyone who had a reason to harm your

uncle?"

"Not a soul. Uncle Murray was just the nicest guy. I can't imagine anyone wanted to hurt him."

"But someone did."

"'S hard for me to believe."

"I'll need to talk to your sister." I leaned over, set my tea glass on the floor, and grabbed a pad and pen from my purse.

"Sure thing." He called out her phone number. "I'll let her know she'll hear from you."

"Thanks." I jotted down the number. "Where are your uncle's services?"

"Grace Church, over on Wentworth. Uncle Murray was a member there. We'll have visitation tonight at J. Henry Stuhr's downtown chapel. There's a reception in the church fellowship hall tomorrow after the funeral."

"One last thing. Have you and your partners had any major disagreements?"

Tyler looked away.

I waited.

After a minute he said, "I don't know if you'd call it major. I don't, not really. But Brantley and me, we want to keep things just us as much as possible. Will has big ideas. He's the one always having drinks with someone who wants to invest."

THREE

By the time I finished at Tyler's, I was feeling peckish. It was lunchtime, so I called Nate and we arranged to meet at the Blind Tiger. Before Sonny was assigned a new partner, it wasn't at all unusual for him to meet us for lunch or coffee. But since he'd been paired with Jeremy Jenkins, things had changed. Jenkins was a by-the-book type and maybe not my biggest fan. I took a chance and called Sonny. He was up for the Blind Tiger. Jenkins had taken his wife to New England to see the leaves. I was feeling lucky.

As I pulled into a parking space on Broad Street, my phone sang out the bridge in Miranda Lambert's "Mama's Broken Heart." I'd recently assigned the lines about lining your lips and keeping them closed as Mamma's ringtone.

"E-*liz*-a-beth," she said when I answered. "Do you have any idea what your father is up to?"

My mind positively reeled. "What's he done now?"

"He's getting three or four packages every single day. He won't say what's in them. He doesn't open them or anything. He just takes them out to his workshop in the garage. He's keeping it locked up."

"Can you tell where the packages are from?" I asked.

"A lot of them are Amazon packages. But he won't let me see the shipping labels, and some of the boxes aren't marked."

"Don't y'all share an Amazon account?" I asked.

"Well, I suppose we do. We have Prime," she said.

"Log in and look at the order history," I said.

"Now why didn't I think of that? I'll do that very thing. Thank you, darlin'. I'll see y'all Wednesday evening at dinner."

We said bye and all that, and I shook my head as I ended the call. There was no telling what my daddy was up to. The one thing beyond a shadow of all doubt was that it would be something Mamma purely would not like.

I stopped by the ladies' room on my way in to the Blind Tiger and scrubbed up good. Nate had already snagged our favorite corner courtyard table. Our waitress dropped off iced tea just as I slid into my chair. I pulled the hand sanitizer out of my purse and slathered on a generous dollop. You can't be too careful.

"What'd you think of Tyler Duval?" Nate asked when the waitress was out of earshot.

"Seems like a nice guy," I said. "Down to earth. I believe he loved his uncle. My first impression is he probably didn't kill him, but people are often not what they seem."

"Our jobs would be a damn sight easier if murderers were all transparently evil," said Nate. "He certainly had a powerful motive."

I perused the menu, which was pointless because I'd been looking forward to the steak fries since I'd left Tyler's house. "But did he have the only motive?"

"Let me guess." Sonny tucked into his chair. "Darius hired you."

"Technically we work for Rutledge & Radcliffe," I said.

"Naturally," said Sonny. "It's a wonder the City of Charleston keeps writing me a paycheck. Fraser Rutledge has y'all working all my cases for me."

"You're welcome." I closed the menu and offered him a sunny smile.

The waitress appeared to take our order. When she'd disappeared again, I turned to Sonny. "You think Tyler Duval killed his uncle?"

"Either him or one of his partners," said Sonny. "They all had motive. Tyler had a little more opportunity."

"Just because he had a motive doesn't mean he did it." As soon as the words were out of my mouth, I pondered why I was already feeling a bit protective of our new client. Tyler was young and vulnerable. My heart went out to anyone who didn't have a huge, noisy family who always had their back, even Brantley Miller, even if I did still harbor my suspicions of him.

Sonny lifted a shoulder. "I don't know how you work a case, but me, I start by investigating the people with motive."

"Fair enough." Nate raised an eyebrow at me. "We all want to get to the truth here."

"What can you share with us about the cause of death?" I asked.

"Someone spiked Murray Hamilton's juice with antifreeze," said Sonny.

"It was green juice, right?" I asked.

"Yep," said Sonny. "The stuff that was supposed to be so good for him."

"Was it fresh squeezed, or a commercial juice?" I asked.

"His girlfriend made it for him on Monday," said Sonny. "A pitcher of it. She told him to drink a glass every day."

"So the pitcher was in his refrigerator?"

"That's what she told us," said Sonny. "We didn't hear from the coroner that this was a suspicious death until late Friday. I went by there Saturday around two. Checked for antifreeze in the garage, couldn't find any. Was just about to go inside when I got a call in reference to another case. I walked back to my car to get a file. I was parked a block away. The house exploded right in front of me. I had a front row seat. All the evidence, if there was any, went right up in flames."

"Oh my stars! *Sonny.*" I grabbed his arm. But for the grace of God. Had Colleen intervened on Sonny's behalf? Prompted someone to make that call that sent him back to his car?

"Damn, that was a close call," said Nate.

"You're tellin' me," said Sonny. "Blew out the windows at the houses on each side. It's a miracle no one was killed."

"It's a miracle *you* weren't killed," I said.

"Yeah, trust me. That detail didn't escape my notice," said Sonny.

"How in heaven's name are we just now hearing this, nearly forty-eight hours later?" I asked.

"What do you mean?" asked Sonny. "It's been all over the news. Part of Montagu Street is still closed."

"But we had no idea you were nearly killed," I said. "For heaven's sake, Sonny, you're family. Blake—wait. Does Blake know about this?" Sonny had been my brother Blake's best friend since forever.

Sonny studied something over my shoulder. "He does. But—"

"How could he not have said anything?" I turned to Nate.

His eyebrows lowered. He gave Sonny a quizzical look. "I thought Blake and Poppy were out of town."

"That's right." I turned back to Sonny, whose face had gone blank.

Sonny shrugged. "You'd have to ask him about that." His voice was just a hair too nonchalant.

I knew right then something was up. "What's going on?"

"What do you mean?" Sonny looked all innocent. "Anyway, this case already has too many clowns in the ring—Jenkins and me, the fire department, SLED, and the ATF and the FBI are arguing federal jurisdiction. Welcome to the circus."

SLED stands for South Carolina Law Enforcement Division. Whatever was going on between Sonny and Blake, I wasn't going to get anything further from Sonny Ravenel. I made myself a mental note to call my brother. "What does the fire marshal have to say about what caused the explosion?"

"It's early yet," said Sonny. "But the house was leveled. They've ruled a few things out. The professor wasn't running a meth lab. There's no evidence of explosives. No plane parts in the rubble. No one in the area had any wayward fireworks. And the military denies it was a drone strike."

Sonny continued, "The gas company says there are no irregularities in the lines leading into the neighborhood or up to Murray's house. Our working theory...we've found evidence to support the theory that someone opened the gas valves on the stove, maybe the fireplaces too. Gas leaked into the house for a while, they don't know yet how long. Our perp put a large sheet of aluminum foil in the microwave and set the timer. When the microwave came on, the aluminum foil sparked and triggered the gas explosion."

"*Sonavabitch*," I said. "It's scary easy to blow up a house."

"We got very lucky," said Sonny. "Case like this in Indianapolis in 2012 killed two people, injured a bunch more, and damaged dozens of homes. If the gas had leaked longer before the timer on the microwave went off, or if an accelerant had been in the microwave, an entire neighborhood of homes, many of them historic, could've been lost."

I pondered that for a minute. "I wonder if we got lucky, or if someone who knew exactly what they were doing was careful to only destroy one house."

Sonny winced. "Hard to predict that kind of thing. Haven't run across anyone yet in this case who's a demolition expert."

"Where do you stand on collecting alibis?" I asked. "Looks to me like that'd be problematic for both the murder and the explosion. There's a fairly wide window of opportunity for both."

"Exactly," said Sonny. "Everybody had an alibi for some of the time. Nobody has one for all that time. And most of the alibis are provided by other suspects. It's a damn mess."

"Hard to imagine Tyler blowing up his uncle's house," I said. "That was his home for a long time."

"How'd you settle on him as a suspect?" Nate asked.

"The girlfriend, Annalise Mitchell. She told me the boys were there Monday night asking Professor Hamilton to invest in their hemp farm. He refused. They're strapped for cash. And now young Tyler is a multi-millionaire. Money." Sonny shook his head. "It's often about money."

I mulled Tyler's account of Monday evening. The waitress set a plate of steak fries in front of me. I inhaled deeply. The tender, savory steak with chimichurri smelled purely decadent. Nate's steak sandwich on focaccia and Sonny's pub burger looked equally delectable. We tucked into our food and conversation lagged a bit. This gave me time to process things. Food always helped me think.

After a few minutes, I said, "Love is also a common motive for murder. What do you know about the girlfriend?"

Sonny said, "It's not like she's his wife. Or his fiancée, or even his long-term girlfriend. She hadn't known him long enough to work up the passion required to commit a murder. My impression is it wasn't a serious relationship."

"She tell you that?" I delivered a bite of steak to my mouth.

"They'd only been seeing each other since August," said Sonny.

I pointed at him, took a sip of tea. "But she made him the pitcher of juice."

"Which anyone with access to the house could've poisoned," said Sonny. "I don't see Annalise Mitchell as a serious suspect."

"What about the other hemp partners?" Nate asked.

"I'm not done talking to them," said Sonny. "I'm nowhere close to making an arrest on this thing. They could've been in it together, all three of them. But I doubt that."

"Why is that?" Nate asked.

"Remember being twenty, twenty-two?" asked Sonny.

"Seems like yesterday," said Nate.

"Seems to me at that age, I thought I was the smartest bear in the woods," said Sonny.

Nate said, "Yeah, I guess most people that age are pretty cocky."

"Exactly," said Sonny. "Working as a team, trusting each other enough to work together on an elaborate murder conspiracy...that coulda happened, but I suspect their egos woulda been a hurdle."

"You're aware of Brantley's history, right?" I asked.

"I'm aware his adoptive family died in a fire," said Sonny. "And I'm no more a fan of coincidences than you are. Then again, there's not a common pattern to the fires. The one in Travelers Rest was a clogged dryer vent."

"So maybe he doesn't set fires for a thrill, but he's used them twice to cover up a crime," I said.

Nate said, "The suspicious thing about the TR fire is that the house had smoke alarms, but they failed to wake even one member of the sleeping family. They all died from smoke inhalation—not something else that the fire was designed to hide. But the fire on Montagu, that was almost certainly to destroy evidence."

I said, "I know you don't think they're connected, but—"

"Slugger, it's not that I think we can absolve Brantley. But we've beat this TR case to death. There's just no way to know for sure what happened there. The smoke detectors failed. The batteries were most likely dead."

"Here's why I struggle with this," I said.

Nate sighed, closed his eyes. "I know why."

I was undeterred. "We have smoke alarms in every single room of our house. And do you know what happens when the batteries get weak? No, you don't, because this only happens when you're out of town."

"I know." Nate nodded.

"The suckers start beeping at 3:00 a.m. They never beep during the day. Always between 3:00 and 4:00 a.m. And they beep until you change the batteries. I have climbed on a ladder trying to figure out which one was beeping at me countless times. I just don't understand how your smoke detector batteries go dead and you don't know it."

"I give you my word, I will change them all when we move the clocks back," said Nate.

Sonny laughed out loud. "This is great. I don't think I've ever heard the two of you bicker like normal married people."

"We're not bickering," I said. "And the point is, how could the Millers not know they had dead batteries in their smoke detectors unless someone put dead batteries in there on purpose?"

"We've been through all this," said Nate. "Brantley could have absolutely put dead batteries in every smoke detector in that house the last time he was home. He could've stock-piled lint cleaned out of the dryer screen between loads, stuffed it in the dryer exhaust, and waited for a fire to start. But what was his motive?"

"It could've been money. That was before he knew Darius was his father," I said. "The Millers weren't wealthy, but Brantley collected from the fire insurance and their modest estate might've looked big to him at the time. Or he could've just been mad at them. Maybe he's a sociopath."

"The problem with all of this," said Nate, "is there's just no way to know, and no way to prove any of it. It might've happened one of several ways. Bottom line. We'll likely never know if Brantley is an innocent victim of a tragedy or a very smart murderer."

"You know how much that torments me." An entire family had been wiped out—except Brantley, of course. It was a hard pill for me to swallow that we couldn't see justice served. I needed to know that if someone were responsible for their deaths, they were called to account.

"You've mentioned that a time or two," said Nate.

"Did Greenville County Sheriff's Office suspect Brantley set that fire?" asked Sonny.

"Not that they shared with us," I said.

"Back to Murray Hamilton," said Nate. "You said all three partners were there Monday evening?"

"Right." Sonny took a bite of his cheeseburger.

I was thinking they'd been pretty up front about that. Technically, they'd all had the opportunity to slip antifreeze into Murray's juice, but they'd've had to've known how obvious that would be. "And no one saw Professor Hamilton after that until the next morning when his niece found him?"

Sonny shook his head, swallowed, and sipped his tea. "I didn't say that."

"Who else saw him during that window?" I asked.

"Not who else," said Sonny. "Who came back?"

"What?" I asked.

"After Brantley, Will, and Tyler left at around 9:30, Tyler came back," said Sonny.

"Why?" I asked. Tyler had left that part out.

"He said he went back to tell his uncle he understood. No hard feelings about him not giving them the money," said Sonny.

"You have a reason to doubt what he says?" I asked.

"Right now I'm not taking what any of them tell me at face value," said Sonny. "But the bottom line is, Tyler was the last person to see his uncle alive."

"Are you sure of that?" I asked. "Murray Hamilton must've spoken to his girlfriend after the boys left. She knew they asked him for money. Did they speak by phone, or did she come by? Or did Murray go out to see her?"

"She says they spoke by phone," said Sonny. "Last time she saw him was at tea Monday afternoon."

"And you're willing to take her word for that?" I asked.

"Fair point," said Nate. "What makes her more credible than

Tyler?"

Sonny shrugged. "Only that I haven't been able to uncover a plausible motive for her to kill Murray Hamilton."

FOUR

I'd parked along Broad Street a few blocks away from the Blind Tiger. As soon as I was by myself in the car, I picked up the phone to call Blake, then stopped. Sonny acted real funny when Blake's name came up. My sister radar told me something was going on with him. But he and Poppy had left Friday for a four-day weekend in the Turks and Caicos.

Neither Blake nor Sonny was the type to pick up the phone to share. It just wasn't their way. Blake had evidently talked to Sonny from vacation, which was out of character, but given the circumstances of Sonny's close call, maybe...nah. Sonny would've told Blake that story over a beer when he got back. Something else was up.

I sighed. Blake and Poppy would be back late tonight. They were most likely in the air right now headed for a layover in Atlanta. Whatever was going on with my brother would have to keep until tomorrow.

Since Murray Hamilton's home had been reduced to a heap of rubble which was now crawling with members of every local, state, and federal law enforcement agency in the known universe, I decided to have a look at his office before someone cleaned it out. Who knew how long that might take? The college might need the space. Hopefully the alphabet soup gang would be busy sifting through ash long enough for me to see if his campus office held a clue as to who might've wanted him dead.

The History Department at College of Charleston was in

Maybank Hall, on the corner of Calhoun and St. Philip Streets. I parked in the St. Philip Street Garage half a block away and walked down the brick sidewalk dotted with palm trees.

An assortment of young adults headed to and from class, work, the library, the gym, Persimmon Cafe, Kickin' Chicken, Kudu Coffee & Craft Beer, or any one of a hundred other local eateries. Students at CofC did not lack for food choices. The stream flowed in both directions, some of them meandering, others scurrying. They wore athletic shorts, cargo shorts, leggings, and jeans with an array of sweatshirts, button-downs, T-shirts, and tank tops that in some cases seemed seasonally mismatched. It was October in the Lowcountry.

I crossed Calhoun, then turned right and walked alongside the tree-lined brick courtyard wall to the gate between Maybank Hall and the Robert Scott Small Building. Cougar Mall, the plaza between the two buildings, buzzed with activity. Palmetto trees reached toward the crystal blue sky. Bright blooms spilled out of large planters. I climbed the steps and walked past the large metal cougar statue, then bore left through the crowd towards the entrance to Maybank, a three-story pink concrete building.

According to the directory, Dr. Murray Hamilton's office was on the third floor. Regardless of what kind of lock I'd find on the door, there was no way I'd have an opportunity to pick it. People were everywhere, so I resorted to a simple pretext.

I climbed to the third floor and found the professor's office two thirds of the way down the brick-walled corridor. One of the black benches scattered along the hall sat conveniently right outside Murray Hamilton's door. I took a seat and pulled up the College of Charleston website on my phone. The phone number for the History Department's offices was two clicks away.

A woman with a cheerful voice answered. "History Department, this is Sally."

"Hi Sally, this is Flannery Duval, Professor Hamilton's niece?"

My tone was appropriately subdued.

"Oh, Miss Duval, we're just devastated...Professor Hamilton was such a special man. What can I do for you?" She was so distraught and so eager to help, I might should've felt guilty lying to her. But I had a job to do.

"We're having trouble locating my uncle's watch," I said. "It was special to him, a gift from my mother. He'd want to have it with him, I'm sure."

"Why yes, of course."

"The only place we haven't checked is his office. Could you look for me? See if maybe it's on his desk?" I asked.

"Certainly. Shall I call you back?"

"You know, I'm at the funeral home. I'm not sure how long this will take. I'll check back with you shortly to see if you've found it."

"I'll go look right now," said Sally.

"Thank you so much. I really appreciate your help."

I busied myself pretending to look something up on the internet with my phone. Traffic in the hallway started to thin. Class must've been starting soon. After a moment, a trim woman, maybe in her mid-fifties, with a dark brown bob approached the door and punched a combination into the keypad. She opened the door and disappeared inside. Discreetly, I slipped on a pair of clear vinyl gloves. Five minutes later, Sally came back through the door.

She spoke quietly to someone on her cell phone. "I'll make a note on her calendar as soon as I'm back to my desk..." She headed towards the stairs. Murray's office door was a heavy wooden affair with a door closer at the top that eased it shut. I caught the door just before it settled into the frame.

Watching Sally's retreating back, I slid inside the door and eased it closed behind me. I peered out the small slitted window in the door. It wasn't large enough for anyone to notice me in there unless they were checking to see if someone were there, which seemed unlikely. I verified my phone was set to silent mode and surveyed the room.

Murray's office looked as if it had been lovingly assembled piece by piece over many years. It was tidy, tastefully decorated, and filled to overflowing with books. Bookcases ran along each wall, broken only by the windows and the door. I scanned the shelves, which were filled with all manner of history tomes, textbooks, biographies, and political opinion books.

A comfortable sitting area anchored by a deep brown leather sofa and expensive-looking rug that might've been Persian stood in front of the left wall of books. Stacks of magazines sat on the coffee table and each end table. I flipped through them. Good grief. He had current issues of dozens of magazines. News magazines, political magazines from several perspectives, health magazines, *National Geographic*, *People*...the list went on. And they were all addressed to him. Murray Hamilton subscribed to a dizzying number of magazines. Was this a Publishers Clearing House thing? Did he know a child who sold magazine subscriptions for school? Or was he just trying hard to keep current? None of the magazines appeared as if they'd even been read.

I opened the mini fridge that occupied the space between an end table and one of the club chairs. No green juice here, only bottled water, a block of Vermont cheddar, and some leftovers in a glass dish with a plastic top. Looked like meatloaf and mashed potatoes.

Murray's desk was dark-stained wood, perhaps walnut, in a Shaker style. I sat in his leather high-backed chair. The desktop was neat, with only a calendar, stapler, pencil holder, and a framed photo. I picked up the frame for a closer look. This must've been recent. Except for the clothes, Tyler looked the same as he had that morning. His smile matched that of the young woman beside him with sandy-colored hair and freckles who had to be Flannery. Professor Hamilton stood between them, an arm around each. He looked distinguished, in a grey seersucker suit with a red bowtie.

Murray Hamilton favored his niece and nephew a bit, with hair that had once been reddish brown but was a softer color in the photo due to the streaks of grey. It curled a bit on the ends. He wore a thick mustache over a wide smile. Branches of a live oak tree framed the shot. They all looked happy. This family had been destroyed by someone's decision that their own needs justified taking a life. I prayed the family hadn't been shattered from within.

I snapped a photo of the picture.

A soft breeze riffled through the room. I jerked my head towards the door. It hadn't moved. I looked towards the windows—closed. "Colleen?"

I could feel her presence. "What exactly are you up to?"

No answer, and no further sign of her. Damnation. The last thing I need during a surreptitious search was a distraction. Where was I?

I looked under the desk. A power supply which I recognized as one to a MacBook was on the floor under the desk. Professor Hamilton had either used a laptop, which he'd taken home with him, or some manner of law enforcement had already been here and taken it. *Damnation.* I could've learned a lot by going through his computer.

The desktop calendar had notes scattered across October in a neat cursive hand. I took several overlapping pictures, then stood back and perused it. The first thing that jumped out at me was every day had the notation on the next-to-last line in the box: 4 p.m. Afternoon Tea. Tyler had said that Murray was a fan of tea. But I had lunch every day too, and I didn't note it on my calendar.

The second thing I noticed was Will Capers's name—not "Tyler and his friends" or "The Boys" or anything similar, but just Will Capers, with the note "8:30 @ TC" on October first, eighth, and fifteenth. What was that all about? Was Tyler aware his uncle had met privately with one of his business partners? Interesting.

Various names appeared in the weekday boxes with the time

notations 2:00 p.m. and 2:30 p.m. These must be students. Murray's office hours must've been between 2:00 and 3:00 p.m. Only two names appeared more than once: John Porcher and Dean Johnson. Could someone have snapped due to a bad grade? Seemed like people were coming unglued more and more often, for increasingly small reasons. Did one of Murray's students have an entitlement mentality?

Had he kept previous months? I slid the corners out of the leather pockets that kept them in place. Bingo. I slid each month to the top in turn and photographed January through December.

The Afternoon Tea notations started the second week of September, when it appeared only twice, on Tuesday and Thursday, followed by the name Annalise Mitchell. She was the woman Tyler had mentioned his uncle was seeing. The everyday entries began the following Monday, September 14. I definitely needed to speak with Ms. Mitchell.

I pulled open the center drawer. A clear plastic desk organizer with compartments for paperclips, staples, binders, and all the common office supplies was inside. I slid my hands underneath the drawer bottom and along the back. Nothing taped there. I moved on to the set of drawers on the left.

The top drawer held extra pens, two unopened packs of blue Paper Mate gel pens with a comfort grip, notepads, and notebooks. I leafed through them, but these were all blank. I checked the drawer bottom, then moved on.

The second drawer held disinfectant wipes, two bottles of hand sanitizer, cough drops, ibuprofen, mints, vitamin C supplements, and all such as that. Professor Hamilton was nothing if not prepared.

The bottom drawer on the left was the snack drawer. I spent long enough to make sure that there were no secrets among the granola bars, then moved to the drawers on the right. The top drawer was where he kept his current class rosters. There was also a list of seniors who were history majors. Nothing was impossible—Murray could've been killed by a disgruntled student, perhaps one who felt that a bad grade had damaged their GPA unfairly. I scanned the lists. Both John Porcher and Dean Johnson were in an advanced course on Reformation Europe. They were also both senior history majors. There were no notes by any of the names. Nevertheless, I took pictures of each list just in case.

The remaining two drawers held first-aid supplies, a change of clothes, and an umbrella. Nothing of interest whatsoever. I sat back in the chair and scanned the book-lined room. What had I missed?

A shadow crossed the window in the door. A faint clicking noise came from the other side. Someone was keying in the combination. As quietly as I could manage, I bolted across the room and ducked behind the couch. Had Sonny already been here, or was this him? ATF agents? FBI? SLED? Dear heaven, let it not be any of them. I'd be here for hours and would no doubt be discovered. How on earth would I talk my way out of this? What possible pretext—

The door opened. Someone must've pulled it closed because it clapped into the frame faster than the door closer would've operated.

I peeked out from behind the sofa.

Brantley Miller crossed to the front of the desk. What was he doing here? How had he known the combination? He stood with his back to me, looking at the calendar upside down.

I ducked back behind the sofa and slid my phone out beyond the edge and snapped a few photos.

A moment later, the door opened again. I waited a three count after it closed, then peeked out again. Brantley had gone. I climbed out from behind the sofa and crossed to the desk.

The calendar was gone too.

Well, well. I was on to Brantley Miller, but I couldn't help but feel bad for Darius.

When I got back to the car, I called Sally in the History

Department to check on the watch. If I hadn't've followed up, no doubt she'd've told Flannery at the funeral home later how sorry she was she couldn't find it. Sally sounded bereft that she couldn't help.

FIVE

The shiny silver Lincoln Navigator pulled into the spot beside my white Escape at J. Henry Stuhr's downtown chapel. A red brick building with white columns, the funeral home sat a scant three blocks down Calhoun Street from Maybank Hall. It was only 5:30, still thirty minutes until visitation started. The parking lot was mostly empty.

When the door to the Navigator swung open, my heart leapt. An older man, with curly salt-and-pepper hair under a tweed driving cap, a full mustache and beard, and wire-rimmed glasses climbed out.

He reached for the door of my car and the door unlocked. What the hell? He must have Nate's key fob. *Nate.* Where was Nate?

The man started to climb into the passenger seat.

I grabbed my purse, pushed my door open, and scrambled out of the car while I felt for the Sig 9 inside my bag. "Who are you? What have you done with my husband?"

"Slugger, it's me." Nate's voice.

I stood, heart pounding, mouth wide open in what must've been an unattractive expression, for a three count, processing what I saw.

"It's one of the new disguises I bought a few weeks ago," he said. "What do you think?"

I eyed him carefully, climbed back into the car, and closed the door. "I think it's a damn good one. What did you do to your face?"

He patted the area along his gum line. "Wax plumpers here. Changes the shape of my cheeks. And a bit of makeup."

"*Damnation*. You're lucky I didn't shoot you."

"I think it was a good investment," said Nate.

"Amazing." I shook my head.

"It's a trial run," said Nate. "I doubt it's necessary this evening, but I had some time to kill and wanted to see how it looked. I've got an artificial palette that even changes the way I sound."

"It's a fortunate thing you didn't stick that in your mouth earlier. Your voice is the only way I knew it was you." I was still marveling over the transformation.

"You look lovely," he said. "I did wonder if my date this evening would be blonde, brunette, or redhead." He took in my disguise. "Nicely done."

I fluffed my long curly copper-colored wig with golden highlights. "Why thank you. I feel like Colleen in this wig. I had some extra time on my hands too. No sense going home and coming back, so I went all out on the makeup." With green contacts, dramatic eyeliner, shadow, and fake eyelashes, Mamma would've looked twice before she picked me out of a lineup. I couldn't stop looking at my unrecognizable husband. "But you...that's incredible." I shook my head. "How did things go with Sonny and the Caperses?"

"We had things set up where I could listen from Fraser's office. From that standpoint, it worked the way we planned. But I didn't learn anything new from them."

"Anything interesting on the farm?" I asked.

"Nah. I put this getup on before I went out there, just in case. Spent some time with Gideon Capers. Told him I was looking for farmland to buy in the area. We got to talking. He showed me the greenhouses his grandson and his friends are building. Got plants in a few of them." He shrugged. "Not much to see out there. How was your afternoon?"

"Tell you about it later. We need to get inside. What's our cover story tonight?" I asked.

"Whatever it is, I guess I'm either your daddy or your sugar daddy."

"Hmm...how about my uncle?"

"You don't want a sugar daddy?" He lowered his voice, used a tone I was fond of hearing in the bedroom.

"Stop that." I slapped his shoulder, laughed. "You are freaking me out."

"We can't say we're with the college. Too many of those folks will be here, and even if they don't all know each other, they know of each other."

"Yeah, that'd be risky."

"How's this?" he said. "Murray was in a support group with us. We don't have to say what kind, just let people think what they want. Most people will be too polite to ask many questions about that sort of thing."

"That's good. I like it." The parking lot was starting to fill up. "We should go in."

I popped an amplifier in my right ear and Bluetooth connected it to my phone. Crowds could be difficult with the eavesdropping device. I could adjust the volume with my phone if need be. Nate opened a white plastic case and popped what I assumed was the artificial palette into his mouth, then climbed out of the car and walked around to open my door. He reached for my hand and helped me out. I smoothed the skirt of my black seasonless wool sheath.

"I do like that dress," said Nate with a slight lisp.

"This old thing?" I smiled up at my husband. The v-neck was modest enough to be decent for a funeral home, but it fit me well.

"Mmm, mmm, *mmm*," said Nate. "And you're sure you don't want a sugar daddy?"

I gave him quelling look. "Behave yourself."

"As you wish."

My second three favorite words. I smiled to myself. Working with Nate was a lot of fun. I especially enjoyed being incognito with him. There were far less entertaining ways to make a living. We were fortunate indeed.

Cars pulled into the lot from both Calhoun and Ogier Street. A few people who'd either parked in nearby garages or walked from campus crossed from the sidewalk to the parking lot.

I slipped a GPS tracker from my purse. "The red F-150 is Tyler's."

"Let me have that," said Nate. "You've got no business crawling under trucks in those heels."

I handed it to him. "I need to figure out what Will's driving. I'd love to get a tracker on him, and Brantley too." Brantley, we knew, drove a shiny new black BMW, a gift from Darius.

"I don't see Brantley's car," said Nate. "I'll come back outside in a bit."

We proceeded, a friendly distance apart, towards the side entrance. Tyler's truck was parked close to the building. As we walked beside it, I stopped and spoke loudly enough for the benefit of anyone who happened by. "Oh no, I've lost an earring. I think it's bounced under that truck."

I stood behind Nate, blocking the view from the parking lot. "I think I see it." He bent to attach the tracker to the back wheel well of the truck, then straightened. "Here you go." He faked handing me my earring.

"Thank you so much." I pretended to take it and put it back on my ear.

We made our way towards the building. I could not get over the way Nate looked. It wasn't that he'd never been incognito before—we both used disguises often—but this transformation was positively stupefying. In a jacket made of a darker tweed than his hat, with crisply pressed pants, he looked like a dapper older gentleman.

"Let me get that for you." He held the door for me, then nodded and smiled as a gorgeous, mature, voluptuous brunette with porcelain skin walked through the door behind me. I waited for him, letting her walk past. He started to close the door when a well-maintained blonde who was maybe fifty approached. He nodded and smiled and held the door for her.

Nate went to close the door again, and here came a redhead, her hair in one of those dos that require a weekly salon blowout. She was trim and wore an expensive-looking suit. She offered Nate a sad smile as he held the door for her.

He gave the parking lot a long look, as if to say, "Anyone else?" then closed the door and joined me at the top of a short stack of steps.

"You'd best be careful," I said. "All three of them gave you the once-over."

"You don't say?" There was the lisp.

I blinked, shook my head, then glanced at the video display. "Murray's family is in room C." I walked towards the second door on the left.

The setup was the same as the last time we'd been here, back in August. Three connecting parlor rooms formed an L-shaped area. The furnishings were traditional, with sofas and wingback chairs, along with a few scattered occasional chairs. The casket would be in the third room, the bottom of the L. We joined the line to offer our condolences to the family.

The three women Nate had held the door for were immediately in front of us. Behind us, the line was building fast. The conversations I could make out with the amplifier ran together in an overwhelming din. I reached for my phone and adjusted the volume and the directional setting.

"We came in just in time," I murmured.

"Appears the professor was quite popular," said Nate.

"Probably a lot of the faculty, some students."

I scanned the room. The woman who'd opened Murray's office chatted quietly with two other ladies in a corner. With my earpiece, I could easily hear them going on about poor Murray.

Ten minutes later, we approached the room with the casket. It stood on the far right between the United States and South Carolina flags. The brunette Nate had held the door for gazed at Murray Hamilton. I detested viewing bodies, but it bothered me less if it was someone I'd never met. Did this indicate a character flaw? Something about an unoccupied body disturbed me.

"Nice hair."

I jumped a little.

Colleen was behind me. "It bothers you because you're forced to face that it's a step in everybody's journey. At some point, we all leave our bodies behind. The soul moves on. That body no longer has anything to do with the person who once inhabited it. But like I keep telling you, it's the beginning of a whole new adventure. Look at me. I'm having a blast."

You startled me. What exactly have you been up to today, following me around all secretive?

"Secretive? Me?" She looked all innocent. "If you knew I was there, I was hardly being secretive."

You know exactly what I mean. If you were there, why? And why not show yourself?

She shrugged. "I was trying to be considerate—not distract you."

I squinted at her. Something was up, but this wasn't the time or place to get into it. *See if you can read Tyler or Flannery's mind, would you?*

"I'll give it a try, but you know I probably can't," said Colleen. "They've fine-tuned my abilities. If it's not related to my mission, I usually don't have access to what's on people's minds any more than you do."

Just try, please.

"Fine, okay." She stepped out of line and moved over to the spot past the casket where Flannery and Tyler stood in front of two burgundy wingbacks. She curled up in Tyler's chair.

The lovely brunette stepped in front of the siblings. Her voice was low, but with the amplifier, I could hear what she said as she took Flannery's hand. "I don't suppose your uncle mentioned me, but my name is Rose Kendrick. We'd been seeing each other for about six months. He was such a dear man. I had hoped—" Her voice broke. She raised a fist that clutched a handkerchief to her mouth.

"Of course," said Flannery. "Thank you so much for coming." Her voice was clear, soothing, and strong. She was trim, maybe an inch shorter than me, about five seven. Her multi-toned blonde hair was straight, shoulder length, and perhaps a bit more golden than mine, her eyes a bright blue. Her makeup, if she wore any, was applied with a light hand. In a well-tailored navy suit, she seemed mature beyond her years.

"If there's anything I can do for y'all, please let me know." Rose held out a calling card.

"Thank you." Tyler accepted the card with his left hand and slipped it into his shirt pocket. "We 'preciate that."

Rose clasped his right hand with both of hers, held it a moment, then nodded and slowly moved along. The line moved up, and Nate and I stood in front of the casket. Murray wore the same grey seersucker suit and red bowtie he'd worn in the photo on his desk with Tyler and Flannery.

"Hello." The blonde woman who'd come in behind Rose took Flannery's hand. "I'm Clairee Pringle?" She waited, like she was expecting her name meant something to Flannery.

Flannery smiled. "Thank you so much for coming, Mrs. Pringle. I know my uncle would appreciate your being here."

Clairee's brow furrowed slightly. "We were..." She lowered her voice to a whisper. "Quite close." She nodded slowly, widened her eyes as if to give the words weight, imply things.

Colleen let loose her signature bray-snort laugh. "This is interesting."

Nate and I exchanged a quick glance. How many women had Murray been seeing aside from Annalise Mitchell, the "girlfriend" Tyler had told me about?

Clairee cut her eyes at Rose Kendrick's retreating back. "That poor dear must be delusional, bless her heart. Either that, or she's an opportunist out to get something from your uncle's estate. Do be cautious, you hear?"

"Yes, ma'am," said Tyler. "We will. Thank you."

The woman took Tyler's hand with her left, but didn't let go of Flannery's with her right. "Murray was so proud of you both. If there's anything I can do for either of you, don't hesitate to ask."

"Thank you." Flannery offered her a sad smile.

Clairee was slow to let go of them. Finally, she released them and moved on, giving way to the redhead, whose face had turned pink. She stared after Clairee for a long moment.

"Well, I have just never." The redhead turned back to Flannery and Tyler. "Those two have a lot of nerve, parading in here and introducing themselves at visitation, no less. I'm Alice. Alice Vaughn. I regret we're finally meeting under such sad circumstances." She extended a hand to Flannery.

"Yes ma'am." Flannery nodded. "Thank you so much for being here. Were you—"

"Well, of course I'm here. Where else would I be? Now tell me, what can I do to help you with the reception tomorrow?"

"We have everything covered," said Flannery, "but thank you so much for the kind offer."

"Are you certain, dear?" asked Alice. "This isn't my first rodeo. I've buried three husbands, you know."

"Oh." Flannery's composure slipped, her eyes widening. "I'm

sorry to hear that."

Alice waved a hand. "Nonsense. They're all better off, and so am I. Murray, though...." She sighed. "Such a lovely man. I've no doubt he would've been my number four. But here we are. So very sad."

"Indeed," said Flannery. "We miss Uncle Murray very much."

"Of course you do, my dear," said Alice. "He was a gentleman and a scholar. They don't make them like that anymore."

"Thank you for saying so, ma'am," Tyler said.

"*Tyler...*" Alice clutched her pearls, blinked, and shook her head. Then she took his hand, dropped it, and folded him into a hug. "You're so much like him."

She held onto Tyler, squeezing him tight.

He twisted his head, looked at Flannery for help. His arms hung in the air above Alice for a few seconds before he patted her on the back lightly several times. "Thank you, ma'am."

She gave him a final squeeze before stepping back, holding him at arm's length. "I bet you'd like my granddaughter, Juniper. When you've had time to grieve properly, I'll introduce you."

"Oh, I—" Tyler started.

"Now, now, this isn't the time," said Alice. "I'll be in touch. Do let me know if you need help with anything. Now...where did you want me to sit?"

"I'm sorry?" Flannery looked a bit panicked.

"At the service tomorrow," said Alice. "Would you and Tyler prefer to be alone on the first pew? I certainly understand if that's the case."

Someone had to do something to help that poor girl. *Colleen...*

"Oh, all right." She disappeared from the chair, then popped in behind Alice and tapped her on the shoulder.

"Yes?" Alice turned. "What is it? I'm in the middle of—"

Colleen pushed her gently.

"Take your hands off me." Alice searched wildly for whoever

pushed her. "What in the world—"

Of course, no one could see that someone had their hands on her except Nate and me, so she came off like she might be Not Quite Right. Nate and I stepped quickly into the spot she'd vacated in front of Flannery and Tyler, who exchanged a glance before reaching out, Tyler for Nate's hand, and Flannery for mine.

"I'm so sorry for your loss," I said.

"Hi there," said Nate, his word choice as foreign as the rest of him. He was definitely in character. "We were friends of your uncle's. I'm Manfred Wright. This is Miss McGillicuddy."

"Thank you for coming." A look of relief settled onto Flannery's face. "We appreciate it. I know my uncle would too."

"Of course we're in shock," I said.

"Yeah, we are too," said Tyler.

"Are you all with the college?" asked Flannery.

"No," I said. "We were part of a support group that your uncle attended."

A confused look passed over both their faces.

"At the college?" asked Flannery.

"No, no," said Nate. "We met at a church not far from here."

"I see," said Flannery, who looked like she didn't see at all.

"We just wanted to offer our condolences," I said.

"Pay our respects. Murray was a great guy. He'll be missed." Nate nodded, stepped away.

"Thank y'all for coming," said Tyler.

I scanned the room for Colleen as we walked away. The crowd had grown. An assortment of academics, students, and well-dressed Charlestonians stood chatting in small bunches all around the adjoined rooms. A few people took spots on the furniture, perhaps waiting until the line subsided. Too many people were crammed into the space.

My claustrophobia clawed at me, urging me to bolt for the exit. I bit it back. Some of these people no doubt had colds, or worse. I reached into my handbag for my hand sanitizer, slathered on a layer, and offered it to Nate.

"I'm good," he said.

I caught sight of Colleen across the room. She gently, but firmly, pushed Alice towards the door. Alice looked flummoxed, maybe a bit drunk. Some people averted their eyes, others stared. Finally, Alice threw up her hands and strode quickly towards the door, muttering under her breath.

"That was quite something," said Nate. We negotiated our way through the crowd to the far side of the room and found a spot against the wall to observe the mourners and those who came to offer comfort.

Nate said, "I couldn't make out what the brunette and the blonde had to say, but I gather all three women claim to be Murray's significant other."

"That's the gist of it. The brunette's name is Rose Kendrick. The blonde is Clairee Pringle. Do you see either of them?"

"No. They musta either gone to the ladies' room or they've left," said Nate.

"They seemed to not know about each other, the three of them, or about Annalise Mitchell, either."

"Murray Hamilton was a ladies' man," said Nate. "All right. Good for him."

I raised an eyebrow at him. "You think a man needs four women?"

"No, ma'am." Nate shook his head emphatically. "I do not. It's all I can do to keep up with one. But you do have to admire a gentleman of Murray's age who just sucks the marrow out of life."

I rolled my eyes, shook my head at him.

Nate inclined his head across the room. "Brantley's in line. Will's with him."

I pulled out my phone and opened a new subscription app that made Department of Motor Vehicle lookups much easier. It was expensive, but Nate had convinced me it was worth it. Tonight, I was happy we had it. I did a search on Will Capers. "You're looking for a brown Jeep Wrangler."

"I'll go tag him and Brantley. You okay here?"

"Sure."

"Be right back." Nate headed towards the door.

Brantley Miller was a good-looking young man, no one could say otherwise. He was maybe six feet tall and fit, with light caramel skin, bright blue eyes, a fashionable amount of stubble that wasn't quite a beard and mustache, and a movie star smile. He had an angelic look about him, which was part of what troubled me. Looks were so often deceiving. Though I was in disguise and he couldn't have recognized me, he caught me looking his way and gave me a little nod and a grin. Was he flirting with me? Regardless of my hair and eye color, I was too old for him. And I was wearing my wedding band and engagement ring.

What was he up to? I could not wait to talk to him. I finally had something on him he couldn't glibly explain away. I had pictures of him standing in front of Murray's desk. I had pictures immediately before that, with a desk calendar, and pictures immediately following with no desk calendar. Brantley had some explaining to do. He was into this far deeper than he'd told Darius, no doubt.

What had Darius told him? He'd said Brantley had asked for his help. Why would he do that? If Brantley was involved, surely he wouldn't ask for more investigators. Or was that a sly way to deflect suspicion? Had Brantley asked for "help" when what he really wanted was more money? Had he framed it to Darius that he needed money for an attorney for Tyler, hoping for a check, but getting Fraser, Eli, Nate, and me? I nodded to myself. That felt right.

The two young men were roughly the same height. They both had a lean, sinewy look that seemed appropriate for farmers.

Darker complected than Brantley, Will had a more clean-cut look. His hair was close cropped and he was clean shaven. Dressed neatly in pressed khakis and a blue button down, he called to mind a Boy Scout. They stood quietly in line waiting their turn to speak to Tyler and Flannery.

A striking woman of a certain age with shoulder-length red hair excused her way through the door. Her gaze swept the room and settled on a gentleman standing by himself against the wall across the room from me. He looked younger than his solid grey hair, beard, and mustache would've suggested. His hairline was slightly receded. Dark-framed glasses stood out on his face. He was dressed similarly to Nate, in a tweed jacket and khakis.

The redhead moved with purpose towards him. "Pierce, I'm so sorry to be late." She placed a hand on his arm.

Pierce Fishburne. Murray's best friend, the economics professor.

"Annalise." His nod did nothing more than acknowledge her presence. He seemed tense, but I wasn't close enough to read his expression.

"Have you been through the line?" she asked.

"No," he said. "I'll wait until the crowd dissipates."

"All right then." Annalise took her hand off his arm.

He looked off past her, like maybe he was hoping she'd go away.

"I wish you'd talk to me," she said.

"What is there to discuss?" His voice was bitter. "My best friend is dead."

Did he blame her? He certainly didn't seem to like her much.

"You shouldn't bottle things up so," said Annalise. "It's not healthy."

"Excuse me," he said. "I think I'll get in line after all."

He crossed the room and went out the door, apparently searching for the end of the line in the hallway.

Annalise bit her lip, watched him go.

I crossed the room and took the spot Pierce had recently vacated. "There's a draft over there."

Her lips turned up in an imitation of a smile, but she didn't speak.

"I'm Suzanne McGillicuddy," I said. "A friend of Murray's. I don't think we've met."

She offered me a hand. "Annalise Mitchell."

"Ohh...." I nodded. "You're Murray's girlfriend, right?"

"I suppose you'd say that," said Annalise. "We were good friends, anyway. We really hadn't known each other that long."

Interesting. With three other women jostling for the title of girlfriend, the one he'd told his family about was hesitant to claim it.

"Would you excuse me?" she asked. "I see someone I need to speak to."

"Of course."

"Nice to meet you."

"Likewise." I watched as she approached Sally from the History Department and her group.

A flurry of hugs and sympathy followed. When they settled, Sally, the woman who'd opened Murray's office, said, "Oh, Annalise, how are you holding up? Your house wasn't damaged in that awful explosion, was it?"

"Thankfully not," said Annalise. "I was very lucky. Well...in that regard, anyway."

"I heard it could've taken out the whole block," said the elegant black woman in the charcoal grey dress.

"I heard that too, Benita." Annalise stared at someone who was making his way through the crowd to the front of the line.

He was maybe thirty, dark hair with a bit of wave. He wore jeans and a button-down collared shirt. "Excuse me," he murmured as he stepped in front of one person, then another.

Tyler's jaw set when he saw him.

Relief and aggravation played tug of war on Flannery's face.

He stepped up to Flannery, placed a hand under her elbow, and kissed her on the cheek. Then he took the place beside her and looked up to greet the next person in line.

"Flannery deserves so much better," said Benita.

The other women made noises of agreement.

"Just you wait," said the woman with the British accent. "I'll bet good money that Keith Laurens had a hand in Murray's death."

Annalise said, "Now, Emma, that's just loose talk. He's Flannery's husband, and she's been through enough. Let's not wish that on her."

"I didn't say I wished it," said Emma. "I'm only saying that's the most likely scenario, whether we like it or not."

SIX

We were starving by the time we got out of the funeral home, so I called us in an order at Acme Lowcountry Kitchen on Isle of Palms. Acme has nine different varieties of shrimp and grits on the menu. My favorite was the Lowcountry—sautéed shrimp in tasso gravy with onion, sweet peppers, and corn—but Nate loved the BBQ—sautéed shrimp over a fried grit cake with bacon, scallions, smoked gouda, and BBQ sauce. We always sampled a bit of each other's.

Because we were incognito, after we parked, I climbed in with Nate. No sense in making the ferry crew wonder who the strangers driving our cars were. Word would've gotten around to Mamma via the Stella Maris grapevine before we made it home, and she'd worry we'd been carjacked or some such disaster.

We rolled down the windows to enjoy the warm evening air. I pulled out the hand sanitizer, rubbed a big squirt onto my hands and forearms, and offered it to Nate. He held out his hand in submission, but made a face that said he was humoring me. Whatever. I was only trying to keep us both well.

We dug into our takeout. After a few minutes, Nate said, "Man, the Amelia Ruth II is gorgeous. Be even nicer when we can sit up top."

The Amelia Ruth II was the island's brand-new ferry. The Amelia Ruth had met with an unfortunate end related to our last case, but that was a whole nother story.

"Yeah, it's too pretty of a night to be cooped up in the car," I said.

"Wanna make out?"

I looked at my husband and burst out laughing.

"That was not the reaction I was looking for," he said.

"Finish your dinner," I said. "We'll discuss making out when I don't feel like I'm cheating on you with an old man."

He sighed. "As you wish."

"Where'd you get those names?" I asked as I forked a bite of grits, gravy, and shrimp. "Manfred Wright and Suzanne McGillicuddy?" Normally we used our middle names—Thomas and Suzanne—along with Mamma's maiden name, Moore, when we needed an alias.

Nate shrugged. "In this getup, I didn't feel like Tommy Moore. I was listening to the oldies station earlier. 'Do Wah Diddy Diddy' was playing. By Manfred Mann. It stuck in my head, I guess, but I didn't want to use Mann as a last name. Too obviously made up. And my grandmother used to watch reruns of *I Love Lucy*. You look a little like Lucille Ball with all that red hair. Her mother—on the show—was Mrs. McGillicuddy. The names just came to me."

"They suited us," I said.

"I'm happy you approved," he said.

I laid my head back on the headrest, looked up at all the stars scattered across the velvet night like so many diamonds. "Murray Hamilton was a good soul. Something about his joie de vivre reminds me of Gram."

"I can see that," said Nate. "They were both free spirits."

"What was it you said?"

A shooting star crossed the sky. "Look—did you see that?" asked Nate.

"I did...you said he was a marrow sucker."

"That's my impression."

"Gram was like that. She was just always finding the joy in every moment, creating joy for everyone around her. Murray, he took over raising Tyler and Flannery. Made a home for them. It's easy for folks to get lost in that—the everyday routine of it. But Murray, he seems to have held on to the essence of who he was."

"I see what you mean," said Nate.

"It's just such a damn shame someone extinguished that beautiful soul."

Colleen appeared, sitting cross-legged on the hood of the Navigator, a look of dismay and outrage on her face. "You know better than that. Souls don't get extinguished by mere mortals. Flesh can only snuff out flesh. Your immortal soul and mine and Murray's and every other soul ever to be belongs to God."

Rhett bounded down the front steps to greet us at home. We pulled both cars into the garage and our golden retriever followed. When I rounded the back of the Escape, he was sitting at the bottom of the steps that led to the mudroom. He barked once and tilted his head.

"What's the matter, boy?" Nate chuckled.

Rhett barked again with emphasis.

"It's us, buddy." I walked over and ruffled his fur, baby-talked him a little. He seemed mollified, but he didn't bring a ball or try to get us to play.

"I think he's trying to tell us to get cleaned up," said Nate.

Rhett barked again in agreement. He followed us upstairs as if to see that we got out of our ridiculous costumes. I'd barely stepped into the bathroom when my phone sang out "Mama's Broken Heart."

"He hasn't ordered a single thing on our account," Mamma said without preamble when I answered the phone. "He must've set himself up a private account. Why on earth would he do such a thing?"

"Mamma, I don't have a clue."

"I need you to get to the bottom of this," she said. "There's just no telling what he's gotten into."

"Mamma, please don't put me in the middle—"

"Elizabeth, need I remind you about the pygmy goats? I have the image indelibly engraved on my temporal lobe of one of those devils standing on my Duncan Phyfe dining room table—my grandmother's table, Elizabeth—eating mashed potatoes."

"I remember the goats, Mamma."

"Then for heaven's sake, find out what he's up to and put a stop to it. I may not even want to know. You don't have to tell me. Get whatever's in those packages out of my house and don't even mention the contents unless I need to call an attorney. It can't be any more difficult than chasing down and photographing fornicators."

I sighed. "I'll check into it, Mamma."

"Oh, thank you, darlin'. I can't tell you how much I appreciate it. My nerves just can't take his nonsense right now."

"Is everything all right? You feeling okay, Mamma?"

"Goodness gracious, of course. I'm fine. I'm just not in the mood for any of his foolishness. I've barely gotten over the swimming pool debacle. I'm not of a mind to start taking medication for my nerves on a regular basis."

"All right, Mamma. I'll talk to him."

"Well, don't tell him I told you to." She sounded scandalized. "You wouldn't violate a client's confidentiality. I should think your own mother's would be infinitely more sacred."

"Of course, Mamma."

Twenty minutes later, I settled in at my desk in the room that served as my office, our living room, the library, and the place where we set up our case boards, knocked around theories, and discussed each client, victim, and suspect. I opened a case file and set to profiling Murray Hamilton and the people closest to him.

Nate set a glass of wine on my desk. "I opened a bottle of the Land's Edge." Pricier than our normal weeknight wine by a long shot, a case of Land's Edge had been a gift from a grateful client.

I looked up from the screen. Thank heavens he looked like my husband again. He leaned in and kissed me on the neck. I inhaled the medley of scents: him, the woodsy soap he liked, and a good pinot noir.

He smoothed a lock of hair behind my ear, then took his wine and settled into the sand-colored sectional in front of the wall of windows looking out on our front porch.

"I haven't had a chance to tell you yet what happened in Murray's office." I brought him up to speed.

Nate was quiet for a moment, rolled his lips out and in, considering. "Well, that is unfortunate. Looks like you were right about young Brantley. He is clearly not as innocent as I'd hoped. You want to talk to him, or you want me to?"

"Oh, I cannot wait to get ahold of him."

"What I figured."

"I've generated the case file," I said. "I'll be ready to set up the case board in a minute."

"That was fast," said Nate.

"A lot of the people in Murray Hamilton's orbit are college students or recently graduated. They have small electronic footprints. Brantley, we've already got everything there is on him. They're all so young. Keith Laurens is barely thirty, and he's the oldest one in that bunch."

"Where do he and Flannery live?"

"Radcliffborough. Lovely Charleston single house on Warren Street."

"That's high-dollar real estate. How long have they owned the property?"

"Two years. The sale closed a month before they were married. There's a mortgage recorded, but the amount is substantially less than the value of the property. They made a sizable down payment. Keith doesn't come from money. His parents are solidly middle-class, but my gut says Murray gave Flannery and Keith the down payment."

"If so, perhaps Tyler was angry that Murray helped Flannery and not him."

"Could be," I said. "My instincts tell me Tyler isn't our killer, but we can't rule him out just yet either."

I saved the case file, picked up my wine glass, and walked over to the corner by the fireplace. I attached Murray's photo, a cropped version of the picture on his desk, to the top of the case board.

"There's something I haven't had a chance to share with you too," said Nate.

I picked up a marker, then turned back to him. "Do tell?"

"Those three women at the funeral home?"

"Yeah?"

"They're predators. Every one of them gave me her phone number. The brunette was in the hall when I went out to put trackers on Brantley and Will's cars. She introduced herself, gave me one of her calling cards. Told me to call her sometime and maybe I'd like to buy her a cup of coffee.

"Then the blonde caught me just outside the door. She wrote her number on one of the programs. And the redhead—the one Colleen bounced out of there—she was out in the parking lot. She made me put her number in my phone."

I chuckled. "Even in that getup, you are quite the catch. At least we know how to get ahold of them."

"Desperation could've morphed into anger. Gives them all a motive."

"We have no shortage of suspects." I started a list on the case board. "Our first possible narrative of the crime is that Tyler Duval poisoned his uncle to get his inheritance. He needed the money. Murray wouldn't give it to him." Of course, this was the theory we hoped to disprove, but we'd go where the facts took us.

"And he may have been angry because Murray did apparently give a sizable sum to Flannery for a house," said Nate.

"Or, scenarios two and three, would be that Brantley Miller or Will Capers killed Murray so Tyler would inherit the money to save their business." I added their names to the board with the motive "money." "What about Will's grandfather?"

"Gideon Capers?" Nate mulled that. "No reason to rule him out. He had a financial motive. And there could've been a conspiracy involving two or more of the partners in BTW and/or Gideon Capers. They all share the same motive."

"I'd say the two of them most likely to be involved are Brantley—he took that calendar for a reason—and Will."

"What makes you suspicious of Will?" asked Nate.

I studied the ceiling. "Something Tyler said about Will wanting to bring in a bunch of investors. He and Brantley want to keep things just them. And the fact that he was on Murray's calendar by himself. If he met with Murray without the others...that seems like he was going behind their backs."

"Yeah, something doesn't smell right there," said Nate.

"That brings us to Flannery Duval and her husband, Keith Laurens. He owns a pedicab company, by the way, over on Pinckney."

"I wonder how business is," said Nate. "Perhaps we should make Keith a priority."

"Based on the things the women from the History Department were saying?"

"That, and any guy who's late to the funeral home when the man—who for all intents and purposes raised his wife—dies and she's greeting guests...that guy has character issues."

"Agreed. That was bad form. There could've been extenuating circumstances, I guess."

Nate made a face that said he wasn't buying that. "Do we have any reason other than motive to suspect Flannery?"

I moved Keith Laurens up on our list of suspects. "Not so far. I need to figure out the best way to approach her. She and her husband could've conspired, I suppose. But Tyler said she's the one who insisted on an autopsy. If she was trying to get away with murder, that's not her best move."

"Unless she thought something would trigger one eventually and she was trying to look innocent."

"Yeah." I rolled that around in my head. "She is a nurse."

"How about the girlfriend?" asked Nate. "The real one?"

"You're thinking maybe she found out Murray was seeing three other women?"

"'S possible, I suppose," said Nate. "Probably shouldn't rule her out. Just because Sonny hasn't found a plausible motive doesn't mean she didn't have one."

"She was talking to Pierce Fishburne earlier this evening for a few minutes. Murray's best friend. He was definitely either mad at her or he just doesn't like her. Could be he blames her for Murray's death."

"What about him?" asked Nate.

"Pierce? Hard to see a motive. But with Tyler and Flannery the only family Murray had, friends would be even closer to his inner circle." With every case we worked, we started with the victim, looked at the people closest to them first, then worked our way out in a spiral. Statistically, you're most likely to be killed by someone you know, and most likely to be at home when it happens. I added Annalise Mitchell and Pierce Fishburne to the list of suspects.

Nate furrowed his brow. "There was no mention of Rose Kendrick, Alice Vaughn, or Clairee Pringle on Murray's calendar?"

"Not that I saw," I said. "I took photos though. I'll go over them again, but my sense is it was mostly work stuff. He probably had a calendar in his phone for personal appointments. The exception was his daily afternoon tea with Annalise Mitchell. She was his girlfriend, according to Tyler, and had him doing all manner of things out of character. Those things weren't on his calendar. No other dates with Annalise. Just the teas."

"But he had meetings with Will on there, you said."

"He did," I said. "Could just be as simple as he was sitting at his desk when he agreed to the meeting."

"Murray's phone was likely in the house when it blew up, but we should confirm that."

"When the coroner's office took his body, there wasn't an obvious crime. Unless it was in his pocket, they probably didn't take it, but I'll check." I added that to my list of things to follow up on. "It could be his calendar was backed up to a cloud. Flannery would probably know. But if any of these three women killed Murray, their motive would've been anger or jealousy. They found out about Annalise Mitchell."

"So it would seem," said Nate.

Rainbow ribbons of light swirled over one of the club chairs. Colleen popped in with a burst of silver stars. This evening's sundress was a soft blue. She turned to Nate. "How was that for a warning? The rainbow? You asked me for a warning...that I was about to appear?"

"I appreciate the effort," said Nate. "That was a decided improvement."

"Were you able to read Flannery or Tyler?" I asked.

"I was." She sounded both surprised and proud of herself. "They're both sincerely mourning. Neither of them was glad to be rid of their uncle."

"That's not necessarily exculpatory," said Nate. "People often regret a murder."

Colleen shrugged. "I can only tell you what I get from them. Neither of them was thinking, 'I sure wish I hadn't a killed Uncle Murray.' That's the problem with me reading minds. People don't necessarily think about what you want them to while I'm there. I can't change their channel to a different topic. Flannery was fretting about her husband, Keith, not being there. She was pretty upset with him."

"He showed up later, after you escorted Clairee to the parking lot," I said. "What else crossed their minds at the funeral home?" I asked.

Colleen bray-snorted exuberantly. "They both thought their uncle was a Casanova. Those three women came as a shock. Neither of them was aware their uncle was seeing anyone besides Annalise Mitchell. They were both relieved when I hauled Clairee Pringle out of there. She's a piece of work. And she's got her cap set on you now." Colleen looked at Nate. "They all do."

"Did you get anything else from them?" Nate asked.

"Nah," said Colleen. "They're all pretty focused on landing a man. They were working it. You're not the only man they gave their numbers to, you know. But you were the pick of the crowd." She laughed again.

"If Murray was seeing three other women," I said, "what's to say there weren't four of them, or five? Maybe not all at the same time, but recently?"

"Good point," said Nate. "An unknown disappointed lover is a possibility."

I added a line to our case board. "Then there were two students who appeared on Murray's calendar more than once since the start of the semester. Could be an indication of some sort of issue. John Porcher and Dean Johnson."

"It's early in the year for any kind of angst over grades," said Nate.

"They're senior history majors. They've likely spent a lot of time in his classes. Could be some slight...who knows?" I said.

"Probably a good idea to talk to them anyway," said Nate. "They could know things."

"And the same thing with Murray's colleagues in the History Department," I said. "I was able to match some of them I saw tonight to profiles on the college website. Three of them in particular seem to be good friends of Annalise's. Benita Brooks is the department chair. Emma Thatcher, the Associate Chair. Sally Abbott is the Administrative Coordinator—she's the one I spoke to this afternoon. None of them rise to the level of suspects, at least not at this point, but we should talk to them."

I added our universal unknown subject and stepped back to look at our list of suspects. We both mulled it for a few minutes.

Suspect	Motive
Tyler Duval	Money
Keith Laurens	Money
Brantley Miller	Money
Will Capers	Money
Gideon Capers	Money
Conspiracy/Two of More of the Above	Money
Flannery Duval	Money
Conspiracy/Flannery & Keith	Money
Annalise Mitchell	Jealousy/Anger
Pierce Fishburne	Unknown Motive
Rose Kendrick	Jealousy/Anger
Alice Vaughn	Jealousy/Anger
Clairee Pringle	Jealousy/Anger
Unknown Lover	Jealousy/Anger
John Porcher	Anger/Revenge
Dean Johnson	Anger/Revenge
Unknown Student	Anger/Revenge
Unknown Subject	Unknown Motive

"That's a lot of viable suspects in the murder of a bowtie-wearing, tea-drinking college professor." I took my glass of wine and curled up on the sofa by Nate.

"Almost certainly not a random thing," said Nate. "The killer had to have access to Murray's house. But it could be someone we just haven't run across yet."

"I've got to go," said Colleen. "I'm meeting Blake and Poppy at the airport."

I scrunched up my face at her. "Why?" Colleen routinely protected all the members of our town council—me; Daddy; Grace Sullivan, my godmother; John Glendawn, who owned The Pirates' Den, the island's favorite restaurant and bar; Robert Pearson, a friend and local lawyer; Darius; and Lincoln Sullivan, our mayor. Colleen did not normally offer her protection to my brother, the town's police chief. And what would Blake need protection from?

"That's classified," said Colleen.

"But—" She disappeared in a spray of rainbow-colored stars.

"I knew something was up with Blake." I looked at my watch. It was after 11:00. They should be landing any minute.

"When's the last time you spoke to him?" asked Nate.

I thought back. "Same as you. Last Wednesday night at Mamma and Daddy's house. Everything seemed fine. They were excited about the trip."

Nate shrugged. "I'm sure everything's fine. Don't borrow trouble."

"Colleen wouldn't be headed to meet them unless there was trouble."

Nate gave me a long look. "You want to go welcome them home? We don't have time to get to the airport, but we could meet them at the houseboat."

"Nah. They could end up going to Poppy's apartment. They'll be tired. Whatever it is, I guess Colleen has it covered. I'll catch up with Blake tomorrow. Something else I need to do tomorrow is start scanning social media for last week. It could be someone from out of town witnessed something or even snapped a photo."

"Seems like a long shot," said Nate. "Montagu...it's not like it was South of Broad."

"There are historic homes on Montagu," I said. "The one at 60

Montagu was built around 1800 by Theodore Gaillard, Jr., a planter and merchant. He didn't live there long. Beautiful yellow house—it's huge, close to 10,000 square feet, with formal gardens. Anyway, in 1851, Washington Jefferson Bennett bought that house. He was in rice and lumber. His daddy was a governor. Robert E. Lee himself visited the family in 1870, about six months before he died—was there for several days. I understand he stepped out onto the second-floor portico to speak to a crowd that gathered."

"My apologies. I mean to cast no aspersions on fair Montagu. The painters are coming by in the morning to give us an estimate on the exterior of the house. Do you want to be here, talk to them?"

A familiar pain gnawed at my stomach. "Nah, no need in tying up your time and mine too. Did they give you any idea, any range what this would cost?"

"Guy I talked to figured it would take two coats," said Nate. "And there's a lot of trim work. He estimated between fifteen and eighteen thousand, but he said not to hold him to that until he takes a closer look."

Sweet reason. This could end up costing more than twenty grand.

"Is that more than you expected?" asked Nate. "I can get a few more estimates."

"I just...I worry. I love this house so much. You know I do. But it's a money pit. We've got to paint. We don't have a choice. It won't be long before we need a new roof, and the AC—"

"You worry way too much," said Nate. "I've told you. There's no need for you to stew about money. We've got this. Let me deal with the painters. Hey, have you checked the GPS trackers to see where our three young entrepreneurs went after the funeral home?"

"Damnation. I was starving and my head hurt from wearing the earpiece in a crowd. I haven't checked it yet." I moved to the desk and opened the tracking app. Three dots appeared on the screen: one blue, one red, one green. "Looks like Tyler's at

Flannery's house." I clicked on the history icon. "He went straight there after J. Henry Stuhr's."

"What about Brantley and Will?" asked Nate.

"They went for a drink at the Thoroughbred Club. Maybe more than one. Will's still there. Of course. Murray wrote on his calendar that he was meeting Will at 'TC.' The Thoroughbred Club. Must be Will's hangout. Looks like Brantley's on his way back to the ferry dock."

"Well, you won't have to go hunting him in the morning to talk to him."

"I've been thinking about that. I have something on him. I could just confront him about the calendar. But if he really is enough of a sociopath that he killed his adoptive family, he's not going to crack over a little petty theft."

"That may be true," said Nate. "But so is the reverse. If he falls apart over being caught stealing Murray's calendar, perhaps he's not a psycho after all."

I pondered that. "Maybe. Or maybe he's just that smart."

SEVEN

Brantley agreed to meet me at The Cracked Pot for breakfast at eight. I wanted to get him out of Darius's house to a place where he felt a bit less sheltered. And I had a powerful craving for biscuits, grits, and sawmill gravy. Moon Unit Glendawn's redeye gravy was exceptional, to be sure, but she made as fine a sawmill gravy as my Mamma, which is saying something.

I called ahead and asked Moon to hold the back booth for me, something she was loath to do during the morning rush. When I walked through the door at 7:45, my brother, Blake, was at the counter sipping coffee, no doubt waiting for his standard breakfast order. I inhaled slow and deep, savoring the heady aroma of pancakes, country ham, hash browns, gravy, and all manner of other delicious breakfast items. If Moon Unit could bottle the fragrance of The Cracked Pot, she'd be a wealthy woman overnight.

"How was your trip?" I dropped onto the stool beside Blake.

"Aww, it was fabulous." Blake grinned wide, joy bubbling off him. My brother was not given to bubbling. "Beautiful resort."

I studied him closely. Why had Colleen gone to meet him and Poppy at the airport? "You sure look happy. Everything okay?" I asked.

He looked at me like maybe I was speaking in tongues. "I just got back from a trip to the Caribbean. Everything's fine, except I wouldn't've minded staying a few more days."

I gave him a long, measuring look. There was something he wasn't telling me.

Moon Unit set a platter loaded with eggs over medium, country ham, grits with redeye gravy, and biscuits in front of Blake, then refilled his coffee cup. "Sweetie, if you don't want that booth, I've got customers waiting." She raised an eyebrow at me.

"Let's talk later," I said to Blake. "I'm going, Moon. I'd like sawmill gravy this morning, please."

"And two ham biscuits to go." On cue, Colleen popped in. She propped her elbows on the counter directly across from Blake and amused herself by getting right up in his face with a goofy grin.

No one but Nate and me could see Colleen in her default setting, which was ghost mode. But when it suited her purposes, she could solidify, and then she could eat. Since she passed on, Colleen had the appetite of a farmhand. The catch was it was against the rules for her to appear to anyone else who'd known her while she was alive. Consequently, I ordered a lot of takeout.

"And two ham biscuits to go, please," I said.

Moon Unit shook her head. "I will never know how you eat the way you do and stay so fit. You don't have an eating disorder, do you?"

"No, Moon. I don't have an eating disorder."

"Well, there's no shame in that, you know," said Moon. "A lot of women suffer from it, and it's no wonder, the way Hollywood pushes these unrealistic role models on all of us. Have you taken a good look at Sarah Jessica Parker? I am telling you, it's not healthy. There's probably a program over at the church—"

"*Moon.*" I tilted my head at her. "I am fine. May I please have my eggs scrambled with cheese?"

Colleen bray-snorted, slapped the counter.

Blake shook his head and swallowed a chuckle. They were having a fine time at my expense, let me tell you.

Moon Unit blinked, rolled her eyes, and propped a hand on her hip. "How many times do you reckon I've scrambled your eggs? Have you ever had them *without* cheese?"

"I'll be in the booth," I said. "I'm expecting Brantley Miller."

Moon Unit lifted her chin, gave me a knowing look. "I knew it. It's true, then?"

"What's true?"

"A little bird told me he's been growing marijuana over on Johns Island," said Moon.

"Hemp," said Blake. "It's completely legal, Moon. Lucrative too."

"I'm just tellin' you, that's not what Tammy Sue Lyerly was tellin' over at Phoebe's Day Spa," said Moon.

I left Blake to explain things to Moon Unit and slid into the back side of the booth. Colleen took the spot opposite me in the pink gingham-backed booth and commenced fiddling with the wooden pegs in the brainteaser puzzle on the table.

"Would you leave that alone?" As soon as the words were out of my mouth, I knew she'd gotten me. I closed my eyes.

Colleen laughed until she couldn't catch her breath.

I rubbed the tension out of my temples, opened my eyes, and gave her my best quelling look. At least she'd put the puzzle down.

Brantley came through the front door and scanned the room. He smiled, waved to me, and headed in my direction.

"I've got work to do. Would you please try not to be a distraction? Like yesterday?" I asked Colleen. "There's two ham biscuits in it for you."

"Seriously? You'd hold food over my head?" She huffed.

"Slide over," I said under my breath as Brantley approached.

"I'm sorry?" He really did have a beautiful smile. So did Ted Bundy, I understood.

Colleen moved over towards the window and went to sulking.

I waved a hand dismissively to Brantley. "Talking to myself. How are you this morning?"

"I'm good." He took a seat across from me.

"Have you had breakfast here yet?"

"Yeah, Darius and I've been here several times. Don't try to order cold-pressed juice or a smoothie."

Was he toying with me? "Do you like cold-pressed juice?"

"Seriously?" Colleen cast me a scathing glance.

"I do, I—wait now...just because I like juice doesn't mean I poisoned Murray Hamilton's." He looked flustered, offended.

"Why, I never said you did." I offered him my sunniest smile. Did he have a guilty conscience? It couldn't be both ways. He was either a sociopath who wanted to play cat and mouse, or he was a kid with a guilty conscience, or he was neither, but he was smart enough to know I was suspicious of him.

Moon Unit approached with my coffee. She set the mug in front of me and turned to Brantley. "Brantley." She nodded hello, all cool and businesslike, without a hint of a smile. "What can I get you this morning?" Her chilly reception was very un-Moon. Apparently Blake hadn't convinced her Brantley was growing a legal crop.

"So much for Southern hospitality," said Colleen. "Poor guy can't catch a break."

Hush up. I glared at her. *I need to focus.*

"I'd like a Western omelet, please, with hash browns," said Brantley.

"Coffee?" asked Moon Unit.

"Yes, ma'am, please. And orange juice."

She looked at me. "You want me to bring your breakfast with his?"

"That'd be great, thanks, Moon," I said.

"Um-hmm." Moon spun and disappeared.

Brantley placed his forearms on the table and leaned towards me. "Do you have any leads yet?" He wore a hopeful look.

I looked directly into his eyes. "So Darius told you he'd hired us—Nate and me—to look into Murray Hamilton's death on behalf of Tyler Duval?"

He held my gaze. "Yeah, of course. I asked him to help."

"Is this what you had in mind?"

"What do you mean?" he asked.

Moon Unit dropped off his coffee and orange juice and disappeared without comment.

"I mean, did you expect, when you asked Darius for help, that he would hire us and Fraser and Eli, or were you hoping for another check?"

Brantley sat back on the bench, his face twisted into a scowl. "I was grateful for any help I could get. Tyler's in a bad spot. He's my friend."

"Did it occur to you that maybe you're in a bad spot too?" I asked.

"Because we needed money for our business, or because Detective Ravenel might think I had a motive to kill Tyler's uncle? Or because his house blew up and some people seem to think I'm a fire bug?"

I shrugged. "Take your pick."

He tightened his lips, shook his head the tiniest bit, and rolled his eyes. "Of course I know we could all be considered suspects before this thing is over. I hear you're a good investigator. Maybe you can figure out who really killed Murray Hamilton. Then again, maybe you've already made up your mind."

"If I'd made up my mind, we wouldn't be having this conversation," I said. "But I'll tell you one thing, and you'd better take it to heart. The people in this town are my family. Some of them I'm maybe closer related to than others, but these are my people. I care quite deeply about each and every one of them. And I will do whatever I have to do to protect them, and I make no apologies whatsoever for that."

His blue eyes went misty. "I came here to find all the family I have left in this world. And I make no apologies for that, either."

Something grabbed my heart and twisted it.

"Feeling good about yourself?" Sarcasm dripped from Colleen's words.

Oh, good grief. Was I being unfair to this poor adopted orphan? Maybe. Or maybe he was accomplished at manipulating emotions.

I softened my approach. "You don't have any extended family back in Travelers Rest?" I knew the answer to this. I'd talked to every member of the extended Miller family.

He swallowed hard, shook his head. "They don't want anything to do with me."

"Why is that?"

"They were nice enough to me growing up. My mom, her name was Charlotte, by the way, she made sure everyone knew I was just as much her child as Luke and Lisa were. My parents didn't think they could have children. Not long after they adopted me, Mom finally got pregnant. With twins. But her and my dad—his name was Mike—they never for one second let me think I was any less important to them than my brother and sister. And they made sure the rest of the family never treated me differently, even though some of them probably hated the fact that there was a mixed-race child in the family. They hid that well enough.

"But after the fire...my grandparents, my aunts, uncles, cousins...I guess they're suspicious types, like you. Oh, they never accused me to my face of setting that fire. They just..." He wiped at a tear that slid down his face. "They let the police chief and the fire chief know they thought it was mighty strange I was the only one left. I grew up in the kind of family everyone wants—big, rowdy, supportive. That fire cost me everything that mattered."

The part of me that cherished my own sprawling family ached for him. But my suspicious nature had served me long and well. And that part of me had a hard time getting around how the people who knew Brantley best were suspicious of him. Still, grief did funny things to people. But I couldn't trust a hundred percent I wasn't being played. Last time I'd tried talking to Brantley about what happened, he'd been far less forthcoming. Had I worn him down to where he'd decided to open up to me, or was this a calculated bid to get me to let it go? Sweet reason, I was getting so jaded.

Moon Unit approached with our breakfast. "Here you go. Can I get you anything else?"

"No, thanks." Brantley averted his face.

"I'm good, Moon, thanks," I said.

She whirled away. I was unaccustomed to this quietly efficient version of Moon Unit Glendawn.

"I'm starved." I picked up my fork and Brantley followed suit. I mopped up all the gravy I could fit on a bite of biscuit and savored the first bite. For a few moments we ate in silence.

Colleen, who typically drooled over my food while I ate, studied something I couldn't see beyond the ceiling. Normally when she did this, she was asking for or receiving guidance from above.

Who do you have to talk to to get access into his head? I threw the thought at her. She must've had someone more important on the line, because she ignored me.

"That stuff's not healthy. You know that, right?" Brantley looked at my breakfast platter like maybe he was afraid of it.

"I don't eat like this all the time," I said. "Usually I have yogurt and fruit for breakfast. But sometimes I need comfort food. Things cooked the way my mamma cooks them."

Brantley's eyebrows crept up his forehead. "My mother would've never let me eat gravy. She'd say that's like digging your grave with your fork. She did make some fine grits now. She put a little club soda in hers to make them fluffy." He offered me a small smile.

"My mamma does that too." I forked another bite of grits and eggs. "What did your parents think about you growing hemp?"

He shrugged. "At first, they were worried because it's often mistaken for marijuana." He threw a wry smile over his shoulder, in the general direction of Moon Unit. "Some people just don't understand it's a legal crop with a lucrative future. My parents were scared I could get into trouble. But after they talked to a couple of my professors about the upside, the future for hemp-based products, they were excited for me. My dad especially. He loved his garden. He had a farmer's heart, I guess you'd say."

"Did they meet your business partners?" I asked.

"Oh yeah. I had the guys over all the time. My house wasn't that far from campus. Mom would feed us. They loved that."

"What did your parents think of Tyler?" I asked.

"They loved Ty. Mom especially. And Luke really liked Ty." Brantley took a deep breath, looked away.

"Will?"

His tone changed. There was just a hint of defensiveness in his voice. "Yeah, of course they liked Will. Dad liked to knock around ideas about growing tomatoes with him."

"But what?"

Brantley shifted in his seat, tilted his head to one side then the other. "They liked him fine."

His tone and body language indicated his parents were less fond of Will than Tyler. I gave Brantley a look that said, *Really?*

"Will just overdoes the technical jargon. Sometimes he doesn't know when to quit talking. Not everyone wants to hear all the minute details, you know what I mean?"

"I can see that," I said. "I understand the three of you spent a lot of time at Murray Hamilton's house. Was he interested in the minute details?"

"He was. Ty was like a son to Murray. Murray was excited about what Ty was excited about."

"Were you surprised, then, that Murray refused to get involved financially?" I asked.

Brantley winced. "Not surprised, really. You'd have to know

Murray, I guess."

"What do you mean?"

"Murray was a great guy—I liked him a lot. But he was...my mom would've called him eccentric. People my age would say he was extra. Also, he was tight with his money, except when he wasn't."

"How was he 'extra?'"

"He liked those striped suits, the ones with the puckered material..."

"Seersucker?"

"Yeah—seersucker suits, with bowties. And pastel shirts. Sometimes suspenders. And loud socks with saddle shoes or two-toned loafers."

I shrugged. "Seersucker and bowties aren't uncommon here."

"Every day?"

"Maybe that's a little less common." I tried to recall ever seeing Fraser Rutledge in anything other than a seersucker suit with a bowtie.

"And he was paranoid as hell about the government."

I felt my brows furrow and immediately smoothed them. "In what way?"

"Murray was convinced Big Brother watched everything we did and kept track in some master computer in a compound under a mountain somewhere. He was always warning us about social media. Hated it. Said it was part of a government conspiracy to monitor us."

"Interesting," I said. "Was he worried about the government cracking down on hemp growers?"

"Not specifically," said Brantley.

"Then I'm not clear on how all this relates to him not investing."

"He was just a strange bird. Not much he did surprised me. But what he told us was that hemp was a risky investment right now. And yeah, part of it was the government was still passing all kind of regulations. He wanted Ty to grow corn for biofuel, organic vegetables, and allocate some land for hemp."

"Did he object to Tyler being in a partnership with you and Will?"

Brantley shrugged. "Not that he ever said, or that Ty told us. He always made us feel welcome at his house. We were over there at least once a week."

"Did you ever meet with Murray one on one?"

Brantley's face took on a confused look. He shook his head. "No. Why would I?"

"Then why did you steal his desk calendar?"

Brantley froze, his fork partway to his mouth with a bite of omelet. He looked at me wide-eyed, his guilt as plain as day.

I waited.

Brantley set down his fork and took a long drink of juice.

I tilted my head at him, raised my eyebrows.

He stared at his plate. "How—"

"I have photos," I said. "Would you like to see them?"

He looked away, shook his head. "No thanks."

"What was on the calendar you wanted to hide? I assume, whatever it was, that you wanted to hide it from the police detectives investigating Murray's death."

"It wasn't me."

"I have pictures, remember? Let me show you." I reached for my phone.

"No," said Brantley. "I mean, it was me who took the calendar. It wasn't me who—it wasn't my idea."

"You took it for someone else?"

He sighed, nodded.

"Who?"

"It's not what it looks like."

"Lookit," I said. "I am three seconds away from calling

Detective Ravenel and giving him these pictures. You'd better come up with a real good reason why I shouldn't. Fast."

"Ty. We took it for Ty."

"Tyler Duval asked you to steal his uncle's desk calendar?"

"*No,*" said Brantley. "He didn't ask us to do that. We did it for him."

"Who is 'we?'"

"Will and me."

"Why?" I asked.

"We just thought as much as we were at Murray's house, and me with the connection to the fire in Travelers Rest...we thought it would cast suspicion on all of us. It would be bad for Ty."

"But Tyler was Murray's nephew. He lived in that house for years. He was there all the time. Murray wouldn't put every time Tyler came over on his calendar. Or even every time all you boys came over."

"We didn't know what he put on his calendar and what he didn't. We just felt like it would be better for Tyler if we did away with the calendar."

"Just the calendar?" I asked.

Brantley winced. "I was going to get his laptop, but it wasn't there."

"You keep saying 'we,' but I didn't see Will. Was he waiting for you in the hall?" I asked.

"Yeah. He was keeping an eye out. In case someone came."

"Where is the calendar?" I asked.

"I burned it. That's what Will thought we should do."

"Do you do everything Will tells you to do?" I asked.

Brantley made a face like he'd just taken a bite out of a lemon. "Of course not."

"Will's the one with the agribusiness degree. Is he the head of the group?"

"No, we're equal partners. No one's the boss."

"What happens if you disagree?" I asked.

"We vote."

"Did you vote on swiping that calendar? On destroying evidence? Because you're the only one who destroyed evidence."

Brantley looked like his breakfast wasn't sitting right. "No," he said softly. "Ty doesn't know about that. Will said he didn't want to worry him. That we should just take care of it."

"And by 'we,' he meant you."

"Looks that way."

"How did you know the combination to the door?" I asked.

"I asked Ty if he knew it. Told him I'd left a sweatshirt there and wanted to get it."

"You'd been to Murray's office before?"

"Only once. I went by there with Will a couple weeks ago to drop off a copy of a study on using hemp for crop rotation. When we were at Murray's that Monday, we'd gotten to talking about that. Murray seemed interested. He was great to bounce ideas off of."

"Did you look at the calendar after you took it?" I asked.

"No," said Brantley. "I mean, I glanced at it. Not much there aside from afternoon tea with his girlfriend. We all knew that was a standing four o'clock appointment."

"So you didn't see the entries where Murray met with Will at the Thoroughbred Club the three consecutive Thursday evenings before his death?"

A stupefied look washed over Brantley's face. "No, I—the Thoroughbred Club is Will's hangout. He meets investors there. I didn't know he was meeting Murray, but we were hoping Murray would invest, so I guess it makes sense."

"Does it make sense?" I squinted at him. "Seems like Tyler would be the person most likely to convince him. Seems odd to me that Will would meet with Murray without the rest of you, but especially strange that they'd meet without Tyler."

Brantley shook his head. "You'd have to ask Will about that."

"Oh, trust me. I plan to do that very thing. Do you have any idea how badly you have left yourself exposed, taking that calendar and burning it?"

"I hadn't thought about it that way. I just wanted to help Ty." He put his hands to his temples, closed his eyes. "I was so stupid. The last thing I need is more trouble. Darius is going to..."

"Darius is going to what?"

Brantley shrugged. "So far he's given me the benefit of the doubt. This could be the thing that makes him decide to wash his hands of me."

He looked thoroughly miserable.

And for the first time, I felt like he'd given me the whole truth about something. I'd caught him off guard, and his response had been unprepared. Maybe he wasn't a naturally smooth liar. Maybe he was trustworthy, a kid who'd been through a horrible ordeal. Maybe he didn't set that fire after all.

"Brantley..." I gentled my voice, looked deep into his eyes. "Did you set the fire that killed your family? Did you disable those smoke alarms?"

"No, I did not." The words came out wrapped in anguish.

"Do you have any idea who did?"

"No one did it. It was a horrific accident," he said. "No one had a reason to kill my family. They were good people—beloved, even, in the community. They had no enemies."

"But the smoke detectors—"

He shook his head. "That I can't explain. They had to have been defective. Dad changed the batteries twice a year—spring forward and fall back. I never knew him to miss doing that. Sunday, March 8, we switched to daylight savings time. That was ten days before the fire. Those batteries shoulda been real fresh."

"You received an insurance settlement for your parents' house, right?" I asked.

"That's right. For the house, the contents, and..."

"For your family."

He nodded.

"What did you do with that money?" I asked.

"There was no mortgage on the house. I decided not to rebuild it. I tried to give the money to my grandparents, but they wouldn't take it. My grandmother...she said she didn't want anything to do with it. She called it blood money." He looked like he felt sick. "So I put it in the bank. When we needed money to start building greenhouses, I invested some of it in the business."

"How much?"

"Fifty thousand dollars."

"Does Darius know that?"

"Of course."

"Did any of the others invest cash money?"

"Nobody else has any to invest."

"Then you own a bigger share of the business, right?"

"No, we each own thirty-three and a third percent of the business. The money I put in is a loan to the company. BTW will pay me back same as Darius. After we make a profit."

"Who keeps the books, handles the money?"

"We have an accountant who does all that."

"Whose accountant?" I asked.

"Will found them. It's McIntyre and Thompson. They're in West Ashley."

"Listen to me," I said. "Don't do anything else just because Will tells you to. Make sure all three of you are in on everything, and everyone agrees. And don't break any more laws. And whatever you do, don't invest more money in BTW. Not until all this is sorted out."

"Are you going to tell Detective Ravenel I took Murray's calendar?"

"No," I said. "You are. You're going to tell him exactly what you told me."

Of the three partners, Will Capers was the only name on that calendar. Why would he want to hide the fact that he met with Murray? Or had he, actually? I hadn't witnessed Will taking the calendar. I hadn't seen him anywhere around. I had only Brantley's word that Will was involved in the calendar theft at all. I was going to have to ponder exactly how far I trusted Brantley Miller.

Above the din of customer chatter, I heard the front doorbells jangle. Blake headed out the front door. *Damnation.* I'd have to chase him down.

Later, Colleen wolfed down her ham biscuits as I drove towards home.

"What were you up to in there?" I asked.

"Praying."

"About what?"

"For Brantley," she said. "He's been through so much. He needs someone in his corner."

"Looks to me like Darius is in his corner."

Colleen nodded thoughtfully, chewed a bite of biscuit. After a minute she said, "Darius could be swayed. You can be very persuasive."

"If Darius is in danger, he should be swayed," I said. "He should distance himself from Brantley if he's capable of this awful thing, whether we can prove it or not."

"A—I've told you repeatedly Darius is not in danger. That I would know about for sure. And B—Look me in the eye and tell me you're still convinced Brantley murdered his family," she said.

"I'm not convinced of that," I said. "I never *said* I was convinced of it. I had my doubts, for sure, but maybe I have fewer doubts since our conversation this morning."

"Then maybe my prayers have been answered. Give Brantley the benefit of the doubt. If all you mortals would just give each other the benefit of the doubt a little more, the world would be a better place."

"And more trusting souls would get cheated, robbed, and murdered."

"I didn't say be stupid," said Colleen. "Sometimes you know people are bad, there's no doubt."

"The problem, Colleen, is that bad people are often very good at hiding behind masks of fake virtue."

EIGHT

Grace Church Cathedral occupies the corner of Wentworth and Glebe Streets. While the church was consecrated in 1848, its U-shaped compound was built over time. The sanctuary is a neo-Gothic affair made from stucco over brick. It has survived all manner of calamity, from war to hurricanes.

A lovely courtyard—The Garden of Remembrance—occupies the middle of the church complex. Rising above it is a reinforced concrete tower with a tall Gothic window above glass doors. The remaining interior and exterior walls of the columbarium are made up of 12 x 12 niches, the final resting place for many church members. The columbarium also serves as Grace's bell tower.

Murray Hamilton's cremated remains were to be interred into one of the niches inside the bell tower at 1:00 p.m. in a private service for family only. At least that was the announcement at the end of Murray's obituary on the J. Henry Stuhr and *The Post and Courier* websites.

Manfred Wright escorted Miss McGillicuddy to the funeral and the reception that followed in the fellowship hall. Nate and I wanted to observe Murray Hamilton's friends and family a bit more closely. People tended to be much more guarded in front of private investigators when they knew we were around. Nate wore a nice but baggy dark grey suit he'd bought at the Salvation Army store a while back to add to his growing incognito wardrobe. My black pantsuit had come out of my own closet.

We arrived early to observe the interment service from a

respectful distance, in a corner beneath the roof of the cloister—the covered walkway that connected the sanctuary to the parish house. At 12:45, Clairee Pringle, Murray's blonde friend, approached the bell tower. She looked the part of a respectable Charleston matron in a tasteful black suit and low stacked heels.

A dark-suit-clad gentleman from Stuhr's intercepted Ms. Pringle and spoke to her in quiet tones. She straightened, turned, lifted her chin, and retreated across the courtyard in our direction. Rose Kendrick, Murray's brunette friend, arrived just in time to observe this bit of drama from a spot on the opposite end of the walkway from us. Like Clairee's, Rose's funeral attire was elegantly subdued. She made no attempt to approach the columbarium.

As Clairee reached the portico, she looked Rose up and down, then raised her chin higher still and averted her gaze in a perfect non-verbal show of Southern female contempt. Clairee took a spot on the walkway halfway between us and Rose. Rose raised a shapely eyebrow, but otherwise ignored Clairee. Rose kept her gaze focused in the direction of the columbarium.

"I hope neither of them is armed," murmured Nate.

The door behind me opened, and I glanced over my shoulder. Alice Vaughn, Murray's redhead girlfriend, came out of the parish house decked out in a dramatic, full-skirted, calf-length black dress that looked like it might've been made out of silk organza. It had a stiff upturned collar and three-quarter sleeves with wide cuffs and pearl buttons. With it she wore a triple strand of pearls, black stockings, pumps with ambitious heels, and black leather gloves. The ensemble was topped off with possibly the largest hat I'd ever seen. It was a wide-brimmed affair, tilted low over her face, with a stack of tulle bows, each one larger than the one above it. The bows were encased in a bubble of netting with its own train that fell past Alice's shoulders. The hat had just the suggestion of a veil—enough net to reach her nose, but so loosely woven as to be a mere fashion statement.

Owing to the veil and the tilt of the hat, she had to crane her neck backwards to see where she was walking, which was convenient because otherwise I wouldn't have known who was under that hat. Alice Vaughn looked like a royal widow sent from central casting.

She flushed as she took in Rose and Clairee, then donned a haughty expression and walked as briskly as her heels would allow down the walkway. She turned right into the courtyard and made for the door of the columbarium. The tall gentleman from Stuhr's stepped into her path, a few feet away from the glass doors. Alice had to lean way back and look straight up to talk to him.

It was bound to happen.

She gave a muffled cry as she tipped over backward.

Either Clairee or Rose gasped. The other barked a little laugh.

Nate sprang in Alice's direction, but the Stuhr's gentleman caught her before she fell and settled her back onto her feet.

Nate relaxed. "Women ought to have to pass a driver's test to wear shoes like that in public."

"I think her problem is that hat," I said.

The gentleman from Stuhr's leaned low to speak to Alice. Because we were headed to the funeral, which would no doubt feature organ music, I hadn't worn my earpiece. I couldn't make out what he said to her.

Whatever it was, she ignored it and tried to move past him.

But he was tall, with long legs and arms, and she was unsteady on her feet. He moved gracefully in front of her and again spoke quietly to her.

She raised her voice. "Murray Hamilton and I were practically engaged. This is an outrage. I will have you know—"

He leaned closer, said something right next to her ear.

She straightened, spun around, and tottered back down the walk. Ignoring us, Clairee, and Rose, Alice made a beeline for the sanctuary, no doubt to try to crash the front row.

"It's a shame Colleen couldn't be here," I said.

"I'd say our friends from Stuhr's have things under control," said Nate. "Can you imagine the stories they could tell? Probably have to sign non-disclosure agreements."

"That lisp is...quite effective," I said.

At 1:45, people started arriving for the funeral service. The sanctuary at Grace Cathedral is an imposing space. A series of tall arches create a dramatic, soaring ceiling. Two rows of arched stained-glass windows line the left and right walls. A dramatic, larger stained-glass window fills the space above the altar.

Nate and I took seats one row back from the front on the left, behind Alice Vaughn, but far enough over to see around the hat. She sat by herself on the front row. When Clairee Pringle sat down right beside her, Alice swiveled her head so fast her hat went askew. She shot poisonous darts at Clairee with her eyes. Clairee crossed herself and bowed in prayer.

I glanced discreetly around just in time to see Rose Kendrick find a place a few rows back from the front on the right. Steadily, the church filled with mourners. Just before the family was to come in, a lithe young woman in a short, sleek black dress above what appeared to be army boots strode to the front and sat to Clairee Pringles's left. Both Clairee and Alice cast quick, appalled glances in her direction.

At 2:00, Flannery, Keith, Tyler, and Annalise walked up the aisle and took seats in the first pew on the right, the one reserved for family. Flannery and Tyler were red-eyed but composed. They'd linked arms, seemed to be holding on to each other. Keith wore a nasty expression that seemed to dare anyone to criticize him. Annalise, in a simple black sheath, was elegant and restrained. She dabbed her eyes occasionally with a white handkerchief.

Clairee and Alice pivoted their heads in the direction of the family pew, but due to the angle, I could only imagine the poison darts they were no doubt shooting at Annalise with their eyes. One or both of them made indignant noises.

It was a lovely, traditional Episcopal service. We stood to sing "Morning Has Broken," accompanied by the organ. Alice's lungs must've been healthy, because she projected quite well. Unfortunately, she also sang so far off key it was a distraction. Perhaps to drown her out, Clairee turned up her own volume.

Alice took that as a challenge and sang louder still.

Clairee also had vocal fortitude and raised her voice even further.

By the end of the hymn, the choir members were stealing glances in their direction and the rector wore a strained look. Alice and Clairee glared at each other. Well, Clairee glared. It was hard to read Alice's expression. She'd adjusted her hat.

When the rector asked that we be seated, they both took their own sweet time settling back into the pew, then tilted their heads up at the rector, no doubt with innocent expressions. He smiled patiently and nodded at them, then proceeded with the responsive reading from the Book of Common Prayer.

A lay reader read from the book of Ecclesiastes, Chapter 1, and another read the twenty-third Psalm. We got all the way through the New Testament reading from Romans, Chapter 8, Verses 37-39, followed by Tyler's heartwarming words about his uncle, and Pierce Fishburne's touching, emotional tribute to his best friend of more than thirty years.

It wasn't until we finished singing "Take My Hand, Precious Lord," right before the Rector began his procession to the middle of the congregation for the reading from the Gospel of John, that the young woman with the black hair—the one who'd sat by Clairee—stood and raised her hand.

"Excuse me?" she said. "Hi. I didn't get my turn to talk?"

Clairee and Alice straightened, turned to stare at her, and shrank away from her in near identical pantomimes of abject horror. They both clutched their pearls.

The rector peered at her over his glasses. "I beg your pardon." He consulted something on his lectern. "Were you on the program?"

"No sir," she said. "I didn't know how to get on the program. But I wanted to stand up for Murray."

Nate and I looked at each other. This had to be one of Murray's students.

The rector turned to Flannery and Tyler. They exchanged a glance, then Flannery nodded.

The rector said, "Very well, please come forward and introduce yourself." His tone was reticent. He no doubt sensed trouble.

A wave of murmured conversation and rustling of programs and hymnals rolled through the crowd.

The young woman made her way to the front and climbed the two steps to the lectern in front of the choir that Tyler and Pierce had spoken from. She sported more in the way of piercings and tattoos than your average college student, not that there's anything wrong with that. She nodded her thanks to the rector, then to the assembly.

She leaned in to the microphone. "Hey, y'all, I'm Unity Maeve Sinclair? I haven't known Murray too long, not nearly as long as most of you, probably. We met over at Forte Jazz Lounge on King Street? Murray loved jazz and I did—I do—too. I just wanted to say how sad it makes me that most of y'all abandoned poor Murray in his later years. Shame on y'all for that."

The rector drew back, straightened.

"Well, look at that," murmured Nate. "Another girlfriend. Murray, you old dog."

Discreetly, I glanced around. All eyes were glued to Unity Maeve Sinclair. Some faces wore shock, others confusion.

Unity warmed to her topic. "None of y'all seem to know the most important things about him. Murray had a spiritual epiphany late in life. He'd awakened to the Universe. Murray Hamilton was a spiritually enlightened man. Much more enlightened than any of you sitting here. Murray was a devout Zen Buddhist atheist."

Several women gasped.

"I declare, I have just never." Clairee clearly meant to be heard.

Alice, not to be outdone in any regard, stood and shouted, "This is an outrage. A sacrilege."

More murmuring ensued, louder this time.

The rector turned, said something over his left shoulder, and raised his chin and nodded to the choir.

Unity persisted. "And I don't think Murray would appreciate—"

The opening strains of "Take My Hand, Precious Lord" rang out from the organ. The choir hopped up and broke into a rousing reprise.

Unity was still talking, but no one could hear her over the choir. The rector motioned for the congregation to stand and he joined in the singing. Gradually, the congregation joined in as well. One of the lay readers walked over and whispered something to Unity.

She recoiled, looked angry, indignant.

He said something else. Two gentlemen from Stuhr's joined him as backup. Unity stepped towards them and they parted as she threw her arms wide, clearing her way. She glowered in the general direction of Tyler and Flannery, then stalked down the main aisle. The gentlemen from Stuhr's followed her out.

The rector was a pro from way back. He didn't miss a beat, continuing with the Gospel and the homily. He made sure to mention how Murray was christened at Grace Church, had been a member since he turned twelve, and had rarely missed a Sunday his entire life. We made it the rest of the way through the service without further incident, except for Alice's continued off-key singing. Clairee gave up trying to drown her out.

Later, as we made our way to Hanahan Hall, I scanned the

crowd. "Something tells me Unity won't make the reception. No doubt she's long gone. I'll track her down later."

"It'll be interesting to see what Annalise Mitchell has to say about all these other women," said Nate.

"I've got a meeting with her tomorrow afternoon," I said. "I didn't want to trouble her or Flannery either one until after the funeral."

"I'm not so sure I agree with Sonny about Annalise," he said.

We climbed the steps and entered the vestibule of the parish house. Hanahan Hall was a large, light-filled room lined with rows of tall windows. To our right, the windows overlooked Glebe Street, the ones to our left, the courtyard. Below the windows, dark-stained wainscoting circled the room. Light grey acoustic panels hung above the wainscoting, dampening the noise of the gathering crowd.

In the far corner of the room, Tyler, Flannery, and Keith greeted guests. A long-skirted buffet table stood in the middle of the room, piled high with food—everything from cheese straws to tea sandwiches to bite-sized tomato pies to miniature corn fritters to bacon pimento cheese tarts to a cheese and fruit display. Nate and I got glasses of iced tea from a corner beverage station to blend in, then took up positions on opposite ends of the room.

From a spot by a window overlooking the courtyard, I surveyed the guests. Many of the same folks we'd seen the evening before were here, but there were a few new faces. A pale Annalise stood with a cluster of ladies from the history department. Benita Brooks, the lovely black lady I'd seen with Annalise the night before—the History department chair—touched her arm, seemed to be comforting her. Emma Thatcher, the dark blonde, put a hand on Annalise's other shoulder while Sally Abbott, the brunette who'd opened Murray's office for me, offered earnest condolences. The women seemed to be holding Annalise upright, in the way friends so often do.

Rose Kendrick had apparently found someone she knew. She passed in front of me with an older woman who brought Queen Elizabeth to mind. "I just don't understand it," said Rose. "Murray told me he was a deacon at First Baptist."

"That is quite odd, my dear," said her friend. "You heard what the rector said. Murray Hamilton was a life-long Episcopalian. I taught him in Sunday school myself." The women passed out of earshot.

Apparently, Murray took the sampler's approach with religion as well as women. Good grief. I searched the crowd for Clairee and Alice, and spotted Alice's hat near the center of the far wall. Hell's bells—Clairee was with her. Had the two of them bonded after Miss Unity Sinclair's unseemly public display?

I recognized John Porcher and Dean Johnson from the photos I'd pulled in their profiles. They both cleaned up nice, in pressed slacks and button-down shirts. Both were clean shaven. John Porcher was average height, with short cropped blond hair. Dean Johnson was a couple inches taller. His dark brown hair touched his collar.

They made their way down the buffet line, piling plates high. John nodded towards the opposite side of the room and Dean followed him in that direction. I slipped my earpiece out of my purse, turned my head so that my ear was towards the window, and popped the device in. After adjusting the volume to the crowd noise, I headed in their general direction, scanning the crowd like I was looking for someone else.

They made their way back to the front end of the room. It was less crowded here as most people were either fixing plates or waiting to speak to Tyler, Flannery, and Keith. They moved to a spot next to the last window near a corner and set their tea glasses down on the windowsill. Both of them focused on their food. I walked on by and stopped a few feet away, turned my back to them, and found Nate in the crowd. He must've felt my eyes on him because he turned my way. He nodded, then moved to the other end of the room. I sipped my iced tea.

After a few minutes, possibly around a bite of food, in a low voice, either John Porcher or Dean Johnson said, "I still say we're in the clear."

"What are you, stupid? You think she's going to keep her mouth shut?"

"We don't even know for sure if she knows anything. Even if she does, why would she want to get involved? She's probably scared."

"She's probably already told the police everything."

"If she had, we'd know it. You can bet on that."

"Maybe. If that's the case, we still have time to shut her up."

Ever so nonchalantly, I glanced over my shoulder, smiled, and waved at someone I pretended to recognize a few feet from where the two millennial geniuses scarfed down food and argued.

"Whatever the hell you're talking about, I want no part of it," said Dean Johnson, the dark-haired one.

"Better think that through." John Porcher oozed arrogance. "What would you do if you lost your scholarship? Go to work at the Piggly Wiggly like your daddy?"

My hand itched to smack him. I pretended to look for something in my purse.

"You shut the hell up," said Dean.

Having identified who was who in the conversation, I faced the other direction again and waved to another stranger.

"I'm just saying we both have a lot to lose here," said John. "We need to stick together. Fix the problem."

"I'm leaving," said Dean. "We shouldn't have come. It's not right."

"Would you just calm the hell down?" said John. "I just want to talk to her. We're not going to have another opportunity to strike up a casual conversation. I just want to see how she reacts to us. If she recognizes our names."

"Do what you have to. I'm outta here." The clank of a dish on a hard surface exploded through my earpiece. He must've set his dish beside his glass in the windowsill. Dean strode past me and out the door.

A moment later, John made his way through the crowd towards where Annalise stood with Sally, Benita, and Emma, the ladies from the history department.

I didn't dare risk following him. He'd no doubt notice that. But I wasn't close enough to hear the conversation through the crowd, even with my earpiece. I did have a clear view of Annalise's face. She was composed, but you could tell she'd recently been crying. From my Apple watch, I texted Nate: *Annalise*.

He texted me back: *Roger that*.

John Porcher stood at Annalise's left elbow, presumably waiting for one of them to acknowledge him. His back was to me. Beyond where the women clustered, Nate—or rather Manfred Wright—moved in close but kept his focus elsewhere.

Benita Brooks said something, looked at John. All the ladies turned to him.

John must've said something.

Annalise's expression hardened, her lips pressed tightly together. I'd've been willing to bet my mamma's pearls she knew exactly who and what he was. She practically seethed.

After a moment, he nodded, turned, and walked out through the vestibule. His expression was grim.

Clearly John and Dean had been discussing Annalise. What exactly did they think she may have told the police? Had she? Could they possibly have conspired to kill Murray? Why? And exactly how did they plan to shut Annalise up?

NINE

We needed to keep Annalise safe, but we weren't quite ready to turn John Porcher and Dean Johnson over to Sonny. That would've created problems for us—we almost certainly wouldn't've had access to information he turned up until after the case was closed. Sonny didn't have the manpower to put her house under surveillance just to see if Porcher and Johnson tried something. The problem was, neither did we.

We'd parked in the garage on the corner of Wentworth and St. Philip. Nate climbed into the backseat of the Navigator and commenced climbing out of the Manfred Wright disguise. I opened the back and pulled out his navy blue and grey gas company uniform and work boots.

I opened the passenger-side door to the backseat and laid his change of clothes where he could reach them. He put the makeup remover wipes back in the large compartmentalized case on his lap and reached for a bottle of alcohol and a cloth. "Anything I can do to help?"

"Nah," he said. "I've got this."

"I'm going to drive the area, see how close we can get," I said.

"Roger that."

I hopped in the driver's seat, adjusted it, and started the car. I pulled out of the garage and made a left onto Wentworth. Montagu was only one street over, and Annalise's house was within easy walking distance. But it might seem odd to anyone who happened to look out the window that a gas employee walked from a parking garage on Wentworth. We needed Nate to appear and then quickly disappear.

Montagu was closed between Rutledge Avenue and Ashley Avenue. I pulled to a stop on Ashley as close as I could get to Montagu, in front of the Galliard House. I pulled out my amplifier and swapped it for a Bluetooth earbud that was paired to Nate's, giving us a private two-way audio channel without having to use our phones or wires. Another expensive piece of equipment he'd recently purchased. No time to think about that now.

I handed him his earpiece. "Let's do a comm check when you reach the corner."

"All right. How do I look?" He settled a gas company cap on his head.

I scrutinized my husband. "Turn sideways. The other way. Looks like you got all the makeup. You're good."

We both scanned the street. When nothing was coming in either direction, he scrambled out of the car and quickly shut the door. At the corner, he said, "Test, one two."

"I read you." I watched as he turned the corner on Montagu.

After a few minutes, he said, "No sign of Sonny. Things are pretty quiet here. Couple techs at the explosion site. Headed up her steps."

"Copy that."

Moments later, he said, "Good afternoon, ma'am. I'm sorry to bother you, but as a part of the investigation into the explosion across the street, we've identified a potential problem with your gas connection. I'm going to have to ask you to pack a bag as quickly as possible and move to another location until we clear things up."

"Oh...oh my goodness. Are you sure there's time to pack?"

"Yes, ma'am, if you hurry," said Nate. "I'm very sorry for the inconvenience. I'll wait here while you get your things. I'll need to verify you've left. Safety protocols."

"I'll be quick. I'm parked around back. You'll see me pull out of the driveway in a teal Prius."

"Will you be staying with family, or will you be needing our complimentary hotel room?" Nate asked. We knew Annalise didn't have local family, but she might opt to stay with a friend.

"Where?"

"Ordinarily, it would be a budget accommodation. But due to the unique circumstances, I've been authorized to offer you a room at Charleston Place."

"The Belmond?" I could hear the skepticism in her voice. I'd been certain this was too unbelievable—that it would cause her to question the entire pretext.

"Yes ma'am. Like I said. Unique circumstances. But we have to go *now*."

"Very well. Yes. I'd like a room, please." The door closed.

"She's probably calling the gas company office right now," I said.

"She'll think about it," said Nate. "But she'll be too worried about the house blowing up to stop and take the time."

Ten minutes later, Nate said, "Here comes the car out the driveway. She's rolling down her window."

"Ma'am...would you sign here please? This just verifies I've told you the house isn't safe. You can't return until we've notified you that it is, and you'll be staying at the Belmond, where we can reach you."

We had an electronic signature tablet with a stylus, similar to what you signed nowadays everywhere from Dillard's to the doctor's office. It was generic but looked official. People felt better when they had to sign something.

Nate said, "Thank you, ma'am. If you'll just give them your name at the Belmond, they'll bill us directly."

"What about my neighbors?"

"The problem is limited to your house at the moment," said Nate. "If we identify further problems, we'll notify the property owners involved."

"But—"

"We've already cleared most of the homes on your block. I'm going to finish checking the rest of them right now."

"All right. Thank you."

Seconds later, the Prius turned right on Ashley Avenue.

Nate said, "I need to make a quick call to the Belmond."

Nate knew somebody at the Belmond who could be relied upon to discreetly assist with the occasional investigative situation requiring luxury accommodations.

"Meet me around back?" I said.

"As soon as I get a camera on the front door," said Nate. "They'll most likely try the back, but best to be sure."

I climbed out of the Navigator and opened the cargo space. We were short on time, and it was faster to set up a mobile hotspot than break into Annalise's house and hack her Wi-Fi password. Everything we'd need was in three of the plastic totes we kept in the back. I grabbed a mobile hotspot router, an all-weather power strip with extension cord, a Ziploc bag, and a wireless night-vision camera.

When I had everything in a backpack, I cut through the yard of the Galliard house, which sat on the corner facing Ashley Avenue— not to be confused with the much prettier Galliard-Bennet house a block down on Montagu. Though Nate had said things were pretty quiet at the crime scene, Sonny or any one of a dozen agents could arrive at any moment. Better for me to slip in the back way.

The Galliard house was a massive structure built in the early 1800s. Once the home of a wealthy merchant, the two-and-a-half-story pale green wooden house standing on a high stuccoed basement had long since been converted to condos. Double-tiered piazzas overlooked the yard I trespassed through. Had any of the residents been porch sitting at that moment, I'd've smiled, waved, and told them a story about my dog who'd pulled the leash from my hand and run this way. A small parking lot, accessed from Montagu, ran across the back. Thankful I'd chosen the pantsuit, I climbed over a low wall and onto Annalise's driveway. From there I walked into the backyard.

Her home was a lovely white Victorian with grey trim and pink shingles in the eaves. The front porch wrapped all the way around to the back, with a second-story piazza above on the side next to the driveway. I surveyed the back of the house and the yard. The way the neighboring houses were situated on their lots combined with the trees and shrubs made Annalise's backyard quite private, which was a fortunate thing. I climbed the steps to the covered wrap-around porch.

First things first. An outdoor electrical outlet was conveniently located near the edge of the porch. Great—I wouldn't need the extension cord. One less thing to attract attention. I attached the power supply to the hotspot, plugged it in, and turned it on. Its battery life was only twenty-four hours. We couldn't count on results that fast. I slid the device, which was square and about the size of two decks of cards, into the Ziploc bag and sealed it except for a small opening for the cord. I slipped the device under a nearby wicker chair.

My watch vibrated with a text from Nate: *Headed your way.*

A minute later, I heard footsteps on the porch. He appeared from around the corner. "How we doing?"

"Hotspot is live. I just need to find a place for the camera. I was thinking about that bottle tree." The metal sculpture tree mimicked the shape of a crape myrtle, with glass bottles inverted on the end of each limb. The bottles were mostly blue, with a few other hues mixed in. The tree was in the center of a planting bed surrounded by glossy-leaved paper plants.

"I think I can make that work," said Nate.

I picked up my backpack, descended the steps, and approached the tree, tiptoeing carefully around the plants. "If we attach it here and point it up, the angle is perfect. It'll blend right in with these bottles. No one will ever see it."

Nate pulled a clear plastic zip tie from his pocket and reached for the camera. I opened the device control app on my phone and pulled up the feed for the camera he'd installed on the front of the house.

"Front camera looks good," I said. "The way it's angled, it covers a good part of the side porch. But any one of these windows is an access point. You think we should put a third camera on that side of the yard?"

"I can get it with this one, I think. Let's see what it looks like."

"I'll check the other side." I stepped out of the planting bed and around the far side of the house. There was no side entry here, and the windows were too high off the ground for college kids to easily access. If we'd been dealing with professional burglars, we might've added cameras to this side of the house as well.

I scooted back to the backyard, where Nate was stepping out of the bed around the bottle tree. "Neither of those two impressed me as ambitious enough to climb into those windows. They'd need a ladder." I pulled my phone back up and tapped the icon for the second camera. The back porch was centered perfectly in the frame, with a clear view up the side porch.

Both cameras had motion detectors and would begin recording if activated. I set the alarms to alert me. "All set," I said.

As we headed towards the driveway, I glanced at the Galliard house. Still no one on either piazza—at least the end I could see.

"Hold up." Nate put a hand on my arm.

I stopped and turned my head, looked down the driveway in the direction we were walking.

Keith Laurens walked up the sidewalk from the direction of Ashley Avenue, his eyes fixed on Annalise's house. We took a few steps back, further into the shadows. Keith disappeared from view as he passed in front of the house. I pulled out my phone, opened the surveillance app, and brought up camera one, which covered Annalise's front door.

Keith walked up the steps. He raised his hand to ring the bell, then hesitated. He lowered his hand, then turned as if to leave. Stopping at the edge of the porch, he ran a hand through his hair. I zoomed in. His expression was pensive. He spun around, approached the front door again, and rang the bell.

"Come on," said Nate. "Let's get out of here. We can replay this in the car."

I slid the phone back in my pocket. We both scrambled over the wall and dashed through the neighboring yard back to the Navigator. As soon as we closed the doors, I pulled my phone back out.

"What do you suppose he's up to?" I asked.

"Probably no good." Nate leaned in to see my screen. I rewound the feed until I saw Keith ringing the bell.

He waited. He paced. He rang the bell again.

After another minute, he pounded the door frame with a fist, then turned to go. We only had video, no audio, and I couldn't read his lips, but it looked like he was cussing a blue streak.

What exactly was Keith Laurens's urgent business with Annalise Mitchell?

TEN

We had dinner on the deck. It was a fine October evening, the kind when the sky melts into a deep blue and the air is silky on your skin, the temperature so perfect you want to sleep outside. I'd boiled and chilled some shrimp that morning after my run. It was quick work to throw together Cantina salads—tossed salads topped with a shrimp, pico de gallo, cocktail sauce, and avocado mixture.

Nate carried out a bottle of Santa Margherita Pinot Grigio in a chiller, opened it, and poured us each a glass as I set our salads on the table overlooking the Atlantic. We typically drink red wine—Pinot Noir or red blends. Nate loves a good Cabernet or a Malbec, and I have a particular fondness for Italian reds. But with the shrimp salad, the Pinot Grigio was perfect.

"To the lovely chef." Nate lifted his glass. "Cheers."

"And the sommelier." I clinked my glass to his.

We tucked into our salads, enjoying the sound of waves meandering to shore and crashing on the sand. After a few moments, Nate said, "We have quite a lot to process with this case. I think we'd best take the night off, clear our heads. Get a fresh start in the morning."

"Sounds like a good idea," I said. "Annalise is safely ensconced on the eighth floor of the Belmond. No one else is in any danger of coming to harm or being arrested this evening, as far as we know anyway."

"It'll keep," said Nate. "This salad is delicious."

I smiled. "Thank you. I'm happy you like it. We need to eat

light this evening. Who knows what all Mamma will fry up tomorrow night."

Nate's eyes widened with a look of alarm. "It'll be tasty. All of our arteries may clog, but we'll be happy pill poppers."

I reached for the breadbasket.

"Oh, that's dessert," said Nate. "But come to think of it, maybe we'd best skip that."

I peeled back the cloth napkin. "What is it?"

"I had some extra time today. We had four bananas that had gotten overripe." He shrugged. "I found a recipe for banana bread in one of your cookbooks, made a few alterations to it."

"Mr. Andrews, your talents are many."

"Nonsense. It's probably not any good."

I sliced off a bite and popped it into my mouth. I typically wasn't a banana bread fan, but this was delicious. "What did you put in it?"

"Bourbon."

I laughed. "Of course you did. It's delicious."

"You'd best finish your salad before you have dessert."

"Fine. You've been avoiding telling me what the painters said all day."

"Now, darlin', *avoiding* is not the precise word," he said.

I lifted an eyebrow. "Oh, really? Well, what exactly would the precise word be?"

"Let's just say I've been awaiting the exact right moment to share good news."

"Good news? What, they think we don't need to paint after all?" I squinched my face up, set down my fork.

"No, as we suspected, we're in serious need of a paint job. But the good news is, we got far enough ahead of it that there's no rot anywhere on the house—none of the siding or trim or anything needs to be repaired. They'll do two coats of a really good paint, and we won't have to worry about it for another decade."

"How much?"

Nate winced. "Twenty thousand dollars." He picked up his wine glass and drank.

"*Damnation.*" I knew it. "We can't afford that. I thought they said fifteen thousand."

"Well, now, I did mention he said not to hold him to his ballpark estimate, which was actually between fifteen and eighteen thousand."

I took a long drink. "Like I said, we can't afford that. We're going to have to get another quote."

"Slugger, I've gotten five quotes. There's not anyone else who has nearly the references these guys do. Please stop worrying about the money. We will work this out."

I managed the finances for our business as well as the household accounts. I knew what was there. "But we won't. Because we don't have that kind of money to spare. There has to be someone else."

Nate sighed. "In the interest of full disclosure, I haven't finished telling you everything they found."

"What do you mean?" I asked. "You said there was no damage."

"There's no damage to the *house*."

"There's nothing else to paint," I said.

"That's true." Nate rolled his lips in and out, nodded. "But the painters took a stroll out to the beach while they were here. Unfortunately, they found some rotted supports on the walkway during the trip. Honestly, I'm aggravated I didn't find that myself."

My stomach clenched into a tight fist. What were we going to do? I had trouble catching my breath.

In a burst of white light, Colleen appeared. She stood at the top of the deck stairs, looked from me to Nate, poised for action. "What's wrong?"

"Dammit, Colleen," said Nate. "I've asked you not to do that."

She looked at me. "Are you all right?"

"I'm fine."

"Call me suspicious," said Colleen, "but I don't believe you. Alarms go off in my head when you're in trouble."

"She's not in trouble," said Nate. "And this is a private conversation."

Colleen looked at me. "Well, that's just rude."

"*Colleen.*" Nate and I both spoke at once.

"All right, already!" She waved her arm dramatically and left in a poof of blue smoke.

Nate leaned in, put a hand on my arm. "Listen to me. This has got to be done—the painting, of course. And we have to replace the walkway. It's not safe. I'm going to get us some quotes on that. The painters found the problem, but they won't fix it, naturally. But I can't have you stressing out over this. I have the money."

"No." I shook my head emphatically. "We have a household budget. We both contribute to it and we pay our joint bills through our household account. Gram left this house to me. I will not let it become a financial burden to you."

"This is my home too now, right?" he said gently.

"Of course it is, but we agreed..."

"What did we agree on?" Nate sat back, gave me a look that said maybe he was losing patience. "We agreed that we would each keep separate accounts for our personal use, and we opened a household account for joint expenditures. We never agreed that we couldn't contribute from our personal accounts to our joint account. I'm sorry, Sweetheart, but that's a little bit crazy. You fret about money all the time. I'm far more worried about the effect of *that* on your health than I am anything else."

"And I worry that you don't fret nearly enough about money," I said. "Look at everything you've spent in the last two months—the Navigator, for starters. We didn't need to spend that kind of money on a car."

Nate raised an eyebrow. "*We* didn't."

"*Ooooh!*" *We* were married, weren't we?

"You can't have it both ways, darlin'. You can't insist we keep our finances separate, then complain about how I spend my money."

"You're spending money you don't have." I'd had this nagging worry for at least a month.

"I am doing no such thing," he practically shouted at me. Had he ever raised his voice to me before? My husband's even temperament was one of his most reliable qualities.

Rhett came running up the steps, gave a quick bark, as if to say, "Hey guys, what the heck's going on here?" He looked from Nate to me, then came over and stood by my chair.

"Then I don't understand," I said. "We take equal cuts from the agency, and most of that goes into our household account. Do you have a side job I'm unaware of?"

"Of course not." He rolled his eyes.

"Then we'll soon be bankrupt, the way you've been spending money lately."

"The *hell* you say."

"Every time I turn around, you've bought a new gadget. You replaced everything we lost when the Explorer blew up and then some. You're spending money like it's your job. Where exactly is this money coming from if you're not going into debt?" Now I was getting loud.

Rhett went to barking.

Nate started to say something, bit it back, closed his eyes, and looked away. After a minute, Calm Nate was back. "We're scaring the dog."

I reached over, put my arms around Rhett. "Shhh. It's okay, boy."

Nate said, "Look, I'm a saver. I always have been. Now, my parents won't win any child-raisin' awards, and that's a fact. But they did teach me the miracle of compound interest. They started me a savings account when I was born. Taught me to save part of my allowance every week. They matched what I saved. That stopped when I graduated college, but I kept right on saving. I have a nest egg. There is no sensible reason why we can't use that for unexpected household expenses."

I took a deep breath, let it out long and slowly. That sounded perfectly reasonable. What was my problem?

Nate leaned in, took my hand. "We're in this together, right?"

"Of course we are."

"Then let me help," said Nate. "This is *our* home now. It's just as much my responsibility as yours to keep things up around here."

"When you put it that way...I'll think about it." I gave him a little grin.

"There's my girl." He grinned back at me. "Be an awful shame to waste such a good dinner." He picked up his fork.

Neither of us said much as we finished our salads. I wanted to be reasonable, truly I did. But I also wanted to maintain my sense of self-reliance. And I damn sure didn't want us to go into debt. But, if Nate had saved the money, why couldn't he spend it however he liked?

I inhaled deeply, filling my lungs with salt air. I purely hated to argue with Nate. And we almost never did.

"Let me clear this." Nate stood, gathered our plates. "Why don't you soak in the tub for a while? It's been a long day."

"I love that idea so much."

He leaned down and kissed me, spoke in that velvety, leathery drawl that undid me. "Holler if you need help scrubbing your back."

An hour later, I'd soaked the stress out. Why did I let myself get so worked up? I had the best husband a girl could ask for. And he was offering to help me solve the one problem that had me worried silly. What was wrong with me?

I creamed my arms and legs within an inch of their lives, then did my face routine and brushed my hair while the moisturizer soaked in. Wrapped in my fluffy lime green robe, I padded to my walk-in closet and chose a little black lace nightie that was Nate's particular favorite. I slipped it on, lit the candles, turned on a playlist I'd named "A Little Romance," and arranged myself on the pile of pillows at the top of our bed. "Seven Days," by Kenny Chesney played softly.

Nate came through our bedroom door and stopped short. A smile crept up his face, his eyes glowing with appreciation. "Why, Mrs. Andrews. You are quite the fetching sight. I'm going to grab a quick shower. Stay right there."

For the first time in a while, I had the dream that night. The one where a monstrous hurricane is about to make landfall on Stella Maris. The ferry has sunk in the storm. Inexplicably, Nate and I are rushing towards the marina with two children, one a blonde little girl named Emma Rae—like my gram. We board a boat that is somehow ours when a huge wave washes Nate overboard.

I jerked awake, crying, sat straight up in bed, and reached for Nate.

"Liz?" He bolted awake. This had happened before. He must've realized I'd had the dream again. He took me into his arms. "We're all right. It's all right. Shhhh." He stroked my back.

After a moment, he laid back in bed, taking me with him, resting my head on his chest. "I'll never let anything hurt you."

"It's worse than that," I said. "The storm takes you."

"I'm not going to let that happen."

"Promise me?" I said.

"I give you my solemn oath."

ELEVEN

The next morning, Nate, Rhett, and I ran our usual five miles on the beach. As with most days, it was therapeutic, clearing my head of the cobwebs of sleep and invigorating me for the day. And as always, the rhythmic roar, crash, and retreat of the surf soothed away any lingering anxiety. As we ran past the marina, where my brother's houseboat was docked, I remembered I needed to talk to him. And then I remembered my promise to Mamma. *Hell's bells.* I needed to talk to Daddy before I left for Charleston.

Over a breakfast of Nate's Bourbon Banana Bread with whipped cream cheese, Nate and I chatted about the day's work.

"Oh." He took a sip of coffee. "I forgot to tell you. John Porcher and Dean Johnson tried to break in at Annalise Mitchell's house last night."

"You forgot to tell me?" I set down my coffee, gave him my best *What the hell?* look. "How exactly did that escape your recollection?"

"It wasn't particularly earth-shattering. We knew that would happen, just like the sun coming up in the east. The alarm on my phone went off at five after three. I didn't want to wake you. Didn't see the point. I called Charleston PD and reported it. Said I was a neighbor. Unfortunately, by the time the patrol car arrived to check it out, they'd given up. Burglary's a lot harder than it looks."

"What do you think their plan was? They had to see her car wasn't there."

He raised an eyebrow. "It was an odd hour for a surprise house cleaning."

"I'm glad we got her out of there," I said. "We need to prioritize those two."

"Agreed. I plan to spend the day on them. I need to do a deeper dive on their profiles, then head to campus."

I had an interview that morning with Flannery Duval, followed by one in the early afternoon with Annalise Mitchell. "I may have time to do a bit of surveillance on Keith Laurens."

"Are you sure he won't be at the house when you meet with Flannery this morning?" Nate asked.

I shrugged. "If he sees me, I'll just slip into a simple disguise. I'll have to take my bike. I can't very well do surveillance on a pedicab by car anyway."

I wasn't going incognito to meet with Flannery and Annalise, but I chose my outfit with care. I wanted both women to know I was a private investigator, of course, but for that detail to slip their minds while we chatted. I needed them to see me as a friend, open up to me. I chose a muted red-and-white boho-inspired tiered maxi-skirt with a serviceable white button-down. The combination was feminine, not overly dressy or formal, but still in the ballpark of businesslike. I added tan leather sandals embellished with puka shells, a simple silver chain with a shell charm, and small hoop earrings, then headed down the stairs.

"Sweetheart?" I called to Nate as I came downstairs.

"In here," he answered from the office. I found him on the sofa with his laptop. He hardly ever used his office on the second floor.

"I'm off," I said.

"You know, I'm thinking maybe I'll head into Charleston with you after all."

"You mean follow me? Take the same ferry?"

"I was thinking I'd just go with you. It's a pretty day. I'll maybe do background from the courtyard at Kudu. That puts me right by campus."

I scrunched up my face at him. We'd be so much less productive with one car between us. "Why would you limit what you can get done that way?"

He shrugged. "Just seems simpler. It'll lower our carbon footprint for the day."

I heard Mamma in my head preaching about wrinkles and focused on smoothing out my face. "You know I'm a tree hugger from way back, but seriously, we have to do our jobs."

"And I think we can get them done just fine with one car."

I widened my eyes, drew a deep breath. "We can try that if you want to. But I've got to run by Talbot's Treasures before I head to the ferry dock."

"Want to take your car or mine?" He stood, put his laptop in his backpack.

"Well, if we're worrying about our emissions, I guess we'd best take mine. My EcoBoost engine is much more environmentally friendly than that tank you drive."

"Let's go." He smiled wide.

My husband was up to something, just as sure as azaleas would bloom all over Charleston in the spring.

Talbot's Treasures was in an old red barn out on Marsh View Drive, south of Heron Creek. It was as far from Mamma's house as you could get and still be on Stella Maris. That was by design—hers.

Daddy's favorite pastime bar none is aggravating Mamma. It's his way of keeping her attention focused on him, just where he wants it. When he'd started talking about early retirement, she foresaw her future, realized she was headed straight for a nervous breakdown with him home all day, and got us all busy figuring out how to keep him occupied and out of her hair.

Blake, Merry, and I had a stroke of brilliance one night while discussing Daddy's second two most favorite pastimes—hanging out in flea markets and cussin' at the stock market prognosticators on cable news channels. We renovated the barn, which had belonged to a farm in Gram's family, installed a concrete floor, had it air conditioned, and turned it into Daddy's own personal flea market. It was Mamma's retirement gift to him, and he loved it—his off-site, supersized man cave.

He rented booths to a few of his cronies and the occasional crafty housewife. Daddy occupied a double booth by the front door with a recliner, a sixty-inch TV, and a desk with a computer. He had three tables set up, and occasionally Mamma would clean out a closet and send a box of junk over for him to sell. Daddy also let Ray Kennedy, a friend with a hard-luck background, sell solar panels and a few random products, such as bee pollen and Japanese weight loss sunglasses, from one of the tables on occasion.

Nate and I found Daddy in his recliner, ankle crossed over a knee, eyes glued to the TV. Chumley, his faithful basset hound, lounged by his chair. At first, I thought there must've been drama in the stock market, because Daddy didn't look up when we came in through the glass double doors. He studied the TV intently.

I was just about to open my mouth to say hey when he hollered out, "Alexa, order me a Puff-N-Fluff dog dryer."

Chumley barked a confirmation.

"Puff-N-Fluff dog dryer ordered." The electronic reply came from the grey speaker on his desk with a teal flashing light.

Nate said, "Well, this can't end badly at all."

"*Daddy.*" This explained all the packages.

"Tutti," said Daddy. "Hey, Nate. Y'all come on in." He climbed out of his recliner.

A look passed between my husband and my daddy. Daddy nodded.

Nate rubbed the back of his neck.

What was that all about? I looked from one to the other. "What exactly is going on?"

Nate said, "I'm curious, Frank. Puff-N-Fluff dog dryer? How exactly does that work?"

I cut my eyes to Nate. Had he just changed the subject?

He gave me an innocent look that said, *What are you talking about?*

Daddy said, "Carolyn says the hound dog here smells bad, even after he's had his bath. She pitches a fit if I bring him inside and he's the least bit damp. This thing here, you put it on the dog like a coat, and you plug a hairdryer into it. It blows up great big, like a balloon, and dries the dog off. It works like those old-timey hair dryers women used to use with the caps that would blow up great big around their heads?"

"I think I know what you mean." Nate nodded, wore a studious look.

What the actual hell?

I glanced at my watch. I smelled something afoot, but had no time to suss it out.

"Daddy, where did you get that thing?" I asked.

"Well, it'll come from Amazon," he said.

"No," I said. "*That* thing." I pointed towards his desk.

"What thing?" he asked innocently.

"The Alexa." I tilted my head, gave him a look that said, *You know full well what I'm talking about.*

"Ponder gave it to me," he said. "Somebody gave it to him, but he didn't want it."

Ponder was Daddy's cousin and a whole nother story. "What on earth did you want it for?" I asked.

He shrugged. "Well, I didn't, really. But come to find out it's pretty handy. I just tell it what I need and two days later it shows up on the porch."

"Who set this up for you?" My daddy was not technically proficient by anybody's definition. I was constantly having to run over here to fix his computer.

Daddy still wore that innocent look. "Ponder did. Didn't take but a few minutes. You ought to get you one."

"No, thank you. What all have you ordered with this thing?"

He held up his palms, made a face. "Aside from the hound dog's dryer, mostly just a few Halloween decorations."

"Halloween. Decorations. Since when have you been interested in Halloween decorations?"

He gestured with his right hand. "We've got these new neighbors. Folks that bought the Brewton place next door? The McKenzies, Raylan and Joetta."

"Right." Nate nodded, as if that explained everything.

I cut him a look.

Daddy said, "They have a hound dog too, pretty little red and white named Daisy."

"Uh-hunh." Nate kept nodding.

Daddy looked at me. "Your mamma really likes her. Ask her."

I closed my eyes. The translation was that somehow Daisy had gotten on Mamma's bad side. "Daddy, what do the McKenzies have to do with you ordering a pile of Halloween decorations through Alexa?"

"Oh, oh...right. They've gone all out decorating the yard. Your mamma was admiring it. I wanted to surprise her. She's going over to the day spa to get her hair colored this afternoon. She'll be there four hours. Who knows what all she gets done over there?" He raised his brows, looked to the side. "I'm going to decorate the yard while she's gone."

"You going to do that yourself?" Nate asked.

There was no way on God's green earth that was going to happen, and Nate well knew it.

"Ponder and Ray are going to help me," said Daddy.

This, of course, meant that Ponder and Ray were going to decorate the yard while Daddy watched and gave direction.

I looked at my watch, sighed. "We've got to go. We'll miss the ferry. I'll see you tonight at dinner." I walked over, unplugged the Alexa, picked it up, and carried it out with me.

Daddy followed me out, protesting mightily.

TWELVE

Once we were on the ferry, I called Blake.

"Listen, I've got to go into Charleston, and I'll be gone all day," I said. "Please check in with Daddy. He's got Ponder and Ray Kennedy decorating for Halloween while Mamma's at Phoebe's getting her hair done."

"Halloween decorations? They haven't done that in years. Since we were kids." Blake had a smile in his voice, like he was looking forward to seeing them.

I felt my face screwing up in confusion. "Right," I said. "And if you'll remember, Mamma always did that."

"I guess she did." He sounded completely untroubled by the potential for disaster.

"Blake? Does it not concern you the slightest bit that Mamma has no idea—and neither do we—what he has planned? It could be anything—"

"Oh, for heaven's sake, Sis. How bad could it be? Today's the twenty-eighth. Whatever it is won't be up but four days."

"Have you forgotten the pygmy goats?" I borrowed Mamma's line.

Blake laughed. He sounded quite jolly. "Well, Halloween decorations don't usually involve livestock, so we should be safe on that count."

"Blake, one of us needs to check on him, and I can't."

"I'm tied up today too," he said. "Maybe Merry can swing by there, but I think you're overreacting. Stop worrying so much. I'll see you at dinner."

I stared at my phone after I ended the call.

"Everything okay?" asked Nate.

I stared across the inlet, watched a pod of dolphins breach the surface. "I hope so. Something is definitely up with Blake, but he sure seems unconcerned about Daddy's Halloween decorations."

Nate shrugged. "Maybe we're worried over nothing. You want to call your sister?"

"There's no point," I said. "Whatever he's up to, she'd just encourage him. What was all that about back there?"

"What do you mean?"

"You and Daddy, giving each other baseball signals?"

Nate laughed. "Slugger, you're imagining things."

I dropped Nate a few blocks away at Kudu, then headed towards the Duval-Laurens residence. Warren Street is a short lane that branches off King Street and runs four blocks towards the Ashley River before dead-ending into Smith Street. Most of Warren is one-way and shaded by a canopy of live oaks. Flannery Duval and Keith Laurens lived in the third block.

I parked on the street by the crape myrtle in front of the cream-colored Charleston single house with black shutters and a teal door. Charming window boxes burst with colorful mounds of pansies and violas, English ivy cascading over the sides.

I opened a voice memo, stated the date, time, and Flannery's name, then slid my phone into a side pocket of my crossbody bag. Then I climbed out of the car and approached the house.

Flannery must've been watching from the window. She opened the door as I was climbing the grey concrete steps. "You must be Liz Talbot," she said. She wore a long grey jersey cardigan with matching pants and tank. If she had makeup on, it was minimal. Her golden blonde hair fell straight and sleek to her shoulders. I could see a bit of Tyler in her. She had a few of his freckles. Flannery Duval was a natural beauty.

"Hey, yes, I am. It's nice to meet you. You have a lovely home." I followed her onto the porch.

"Thank you. We love it here." She closed the door to the street and led me across the piazza to the front door of the house. The home's entry hall had been incorporated into the center section of the lower piazza. Was this the original design? It appeared so.

The home had lovely heart of pine floors and white-painted craftsman woodwork. The bones were clearly old Charleston, but the historic charmer had been updated. The walls were a crisp white, the space uncluttered. Flannery had chosen sleek modern furnishings that gave the space a light and airy feel.

"Let's talk in here." She led me to the front room and took a seat on a grey leather sofa.

I took a white upholstered side chair to her left. "I'm terribly sorry to intrude on your grief."

"I appreciate that," she said. "But honestly, I'm happy to talk to anyone who's looking into Uncle Murray's death. Maybe you can get to the bottom of what happened. I feel like I owe it to him to do everything I can. He raised us, Tyler and me. But one thing I can tell you for sure is that my brother had absolutely nothing to do with Uncle Murray's death." Her Alabama drawl had a husky quality.

"Tyler mentioned that you were suspicious from the start," I said. "Would you tell me why?"

"Of course," she said. "Uncle Murray had been feeling off for a week, maybe more. His stomach was bothering him. He did have some arrhythmia, too, but he just had a full workup—stress test and everything—six months ago. I had them run every test known to man on him. Uncle Murray was getting older, but I was proactive about his health. His heart was strong."

"I'd say it's a good thing you insisted on an autopsy," I said.

"Think carefully. When did he first complain of stomach issues?"

Flannery looked off to her right, as if searching her memory, then consulted her phone. "A week and a half before his death. Friday, October ninth. He saw the doctor that morning, said he'd been sick the night before."

"Any idea what he did the day before? Thursday?" I asked.

"Uncle Murray's kept the same schedule for years. He had morning classes five days a week. Virtually every day, he had lunch with Professor Fish—Pierce Fishburne. Tyler and I call him Professor Fish. They had a system. Thursdays were Asian food. Their Asian spot right now was Xiao Bao Biscuit. Uncle Murray loved pad Thai. He'd be back on campus by 1:45 and have office hours from 2:00 'til 3:00. The only new thing is he had tea with Annalise every day at 4:00. That started right after they started dating. Some days they had tea at her house, some days they'd go to Twenty-Six Divine, over on King Street. I'm not sure which it was that Thursday."

I said, "Since we now know he was poisoned, did you think maybe someone tried to poison him earlier, but they had the dose wrong?"

"I'd be willing to bet that's exactly what happened. And I spoke to his doctor, Dr. Whatley. I can get you his contact info if you'd like to speak with him."

"That'd be great, thanks," I said. "What did he say?"

"He agreed that it was entirely possible."

"Do you have any thoughts on who might've had a motive to kill your uncle?"

She grimaced, stared at the window for a moment. "I've given this a lot of thought. I've racked my brain. Everyone loved Uncle Murray. If he'd been hit over the head or stabbed or shot, it would still be hard to imagine, but at least you could say it wasn't premeditated. But poison...that's not something someone does in a moment of rage or whatever. That's calculated. The only motive I can think of is money, and the only people who stood to gain aside from Tyler and me are his two partners, Will Capers and Brantley Miller."

"How well do you know Annalise?" I asked.

"Oh, she's a sweetheart. She's one of those people. I just met her in late August, but it feels like I've known her for years."

"Were she and your uncle serious?"

Flannery tipped her head sideways. "You'd have to ask her if she was serious. I think he might have been."

I nodded, rolled my lips in and out. "But...what about those other women who showed up at the funeral home? The funeral?"

She rolled her eyes, looked at the ceiling. "Oh my stars. You heard about that. Before Uncle Murray started seeing Annalise, he was dating. He'd joined a couple of those services—Our Time and eharmony. All I can think of is these are women he met through those. The three older women, anyway. The young one that showed up at the funeral—did someone tell you about her?"

"Yes, they filled me in." Of course, I hadn't been to the funeral. Suzanne McGillicuddy had attended.

Flannery shook her head, grinned. "It sounds like he met her in a jazz club. I wouldn't put it past him. Uncle Murray was a character. But none of this was serious. He was having fun. Believe me, if he'd been serious about anyone, he'd have introduced her to Tyler and me. We met Annalise after he'd been dating her a week."

"He seems to enjoy the company of women," I said. "Were you surprised he never married? Was there ever anyone serious?"

She looked thoughtful. "I think for a long time he didn't date or anything because he was focused on his job and raising us. Over the years he dated a few women from church, but nothing serious. They mostly chased him, not the other way around. He spent a lot of time with his best friend, Professor Fish. He's an economics professor. He lives across the street from Uncle Murray, has for thirty years. The two of them just always had each other."

"Do you know what prompted your uncle to join the online dating scene?" I asked.

Flannery nodded. "Emma Thatcher. She's another history professor. British lady—I just love her to death. Anyway, maybe next to Pierce, Emma was Uncle Murray's best friend. *She* joined eharmony, found someone, and got married about eight months ago. I think it inspired Uncle Murray."

"You mentioned he'd dated women at church? He attended Grace Church on Wentworth, right?"

She gave a little eye roll, nodded. "His entire life. You might have heard that the girl at the funeral said he was a Buddhist or something. He wasn't."

"I wonder why she'd say such a thing..." I mused.

Flannery chuckled. "Uncle Murray. He worried a lot about the government...Big Brother, all that. His strategy to defeat the machine was to be in every database. He joined *everything*. He was a card-carrying member of the NRA and the Coalition to Stop Gun Violence. He donated to the Republicans and the Democrats. He was on the rolls at several churches. He thought all this would confuse Big Brother. Whatever churches those women went to, Uncle Murray probably told them that was his religion. But trust me. He was an Episcopalian."

"I bet he got a lot of junk mail." Just then I was remembering all the magazines in his office.

"Enough to start a side business in recycling paper," she said.

We laughed together. After a moment, I said, "So, back to Annalise...is there any reason you can think of why she'd want to harm your uncle? Any possible motive at all?"

"None. I mean, yes, I'm pretty sure Uncle Murray was in love with her. I think it was mutual. But it was a very new relationship. It's not like they'd been dating for years and he'd scorned her. Nothing like that." She winced. "I mean...you see this sort of thing in movies, but you never expect to encounter it. I guess it's possible she's some sort of psychopath. You know—people who kill for the thrill of it or whatever. But if she is, she hides it very well."

The way all psychopaths do. "Was there anything new going on in your uncle's life? Did he mention being worried about anything, change his routine?"

"He wasn't worried about anything I can think of…except, okay, yeah. He was concerned about security. There'd been a few break-ins in the area. He worried over the state of the country in general—the decline of civil discourse. Just felt like things were getting out of hand. That was why he was putting in a new security system when he was killed. How's that for irony?"

"He was doing this himself?" I asked. "Or an alarm company was doing it?"

"Oh, no. Once he decided he needed a security system, there was no one he'd trust to do it for him. He was maybe paranoid about other things, not just the government. I suggested he call ADT or one of the other national companies. He threw a fit. Said he wasn't giving anyone easy access to spy on him in his own home— listen to his conversations, all that. Anyway, he researched the best systems, ordered everything, and he was installing the cameras, motion detectors, glass breaks, door and window sensors—all of it."

"How close was he to being finished?" I asked.

"He had the cameras installed. And there was a DVR in a closet upstairs that kept ten days' worth of recordings. I told the police about it. In fact, I think they were going to check them out, see if the cameras had caught someone going in or out. But then the house blew up."

Sonny Ravenel had conveniently forgotten to mention these cameras. I made myself a mental note to take that up with him at my earliest opportunity.

"Do you know where the cameras were?" I asked.

"He installed one pointed at each door, inside and out, and a few windows downstairs that he thought were easy access points," said Flannery. "He hid them in things—smoke detectors, knickknacks on shelves."

"Just the access points?" Unless there was a camera pointed at the refrigerator, it was unlikely it had captured incriminating evidence. The sad truth was, the person who poisoned Murray's juice was most likely someone he invited into the house, not an unexpected intruder. Still, the cameras would definitely have told us who did and didn't have the opportunity to kill Murray Hamilton. Unless Annalise—who had no discernible motive—had killed him, the poison was added to the juice while it sat in Murray's refrigerator.

"That's all he told me about," said Flannery. "Uncle Murray wouldn't have wanted cameras—even ones he installed—on him in his house. The government could've hacked them." She gave a little smile.

"Do they know what caused the explosion?" Of course, I knew the working theory, but I doubted anyone had shared that with Flannery just yet.

"I suspect it was a gas line thing, but no one has told us for sure."

"Who all knew about the security system?" I asked.

"Just Tyler and me," she said. "Uncle Murray might've mentioned it to Annalise, I'm not sure."

"Did you mention to anyone that the police might check the footage from the security system?" I asked.

"I did tell Tyler." She looked at her lap.

"And your husband, Keith? Did he know about the security system? That the police planned to review all the comings and goings at your uncle's house?"

Flannery's eyes widened, just for a split second, her head turning sharply just an inch before she caught herself. "Well, yes, Keith's my husband. I'm sure we discussed it in passing. The security system was Uncle Murray's latest project. As to the police checking it, I don't recall mentioning that to him." She smoothed a hand through her hair.

"Did you have an opinion about your brother's latest project—the hemp farm?"

She gave a little facial shrug. "I agreed with Uncle Murray, I guess. I would've liked to've seen Tyler buy some farmland and grow several crops—diversify. But I'm happy with whatever makes him happy."

"Does your brother have the money to buy farmland? Enough to make a living off?" I asked.

"No," she said. "But Uncle Murray would've helped him out. Got him started."

"Do you think so? That would've been an awful lot of money." I handed her an opportunity to tell me that Murray had given her the down payment for her house.

"Absolutely." She didn't elaborate.

"But he declined to invest in the hemp farm…"

"That's true," said Flannery. "I guess he had his reasons."

"Did he share those with you?" I asked.

"No," she said. "Tyler told me what he said."

"How did Tyler react to that?"

She held up an open palm. "He just said they'd find the money another way. Will was talking to investors."

"So he wasn't angry?"

"Not at all."

"Even though he must've known that your uncle gave you and your husband a substantial sum as a down payment on this house?"

She flushed. "Of course Tyler knew that. I'm curious how you did. Uncle Murray was always generous with us both. Yes, he helped Keith and me out. He knew this house was a sound investment. He would've helped Tyler out if he'd felt the hemp business was also a sound investment. Apparently, he didn't feel that way. But Tyler wasn't angry about that, not in the least."

I switched gears on her. "Your uncle must've been technically pretty savvy to install that security system by himself."

"He was." She nodded.

"So, he had a computer, smart phone...?"

"He did. He had a laptop that he carried to the office every day. An iPhone, an iPad. I guess that's it."

"Any chance he would've backed up his calendar, contacts, emails, data, all such as that, to the cloud?"

She laughed. "No chance at all. Again, the government. Uncle Murray was very serious about his privacy. He backed up everything to hard drives in his media closet."

"Do you happen to know the login to his Apple ID?"

"No," she said. "And you can bet it was unhackable."

"As far as you know, all his electronics were in the house when it exploded?" I asked.

"I would imagine so. He would've brought everything home with him Monday evening."

"Do you know if anyone had a key to your uncle's house?" I asked.

"Tyler and I both did," she said. "I think Professor Fish did too. It's possible Uncle Murray gave a key to Annalise. Only people who loved him and would never have hurt him."

Just then I was thinking two things: Flannery's husband, Keith, could easily have accessed her key. And way too many people were killed by the people they loved most in the world.

THIRTEEN

I picked up Nate at Kudu. "Want to try some Asian soul food for lunch?"

"Sounds interesting," he said.

I headed down Vanderhorst and made a right on Coming. Five blocks later I turned left onto Spring Street. Xiao Bao Biscuit was on the corner of Spring Street and Rutledge, in an old gas station, with absolutely no signage to offer a clue to the random passerby that this was a restaurant, let alone what kind. At 11:45 on a Wednesday, the parking lot was full. I circled the block and parked a ways back on Spring.

Picnic tables sat under the canopy once used to shield customers from the elements while they filled up their tank. A slatted screen offered diners privacy from the street, and large planters helped separate the area from the parking lot.

"According to the website, you pronounce that 'See Ou!/Baow/Biskit,'" said Nate.

"That's how Flannery said it. This was Murray Hamilton and Pierce Fishburne's Thursday lunch spot. I've never eaten here. Didn't think you had either."

"I haven't," said Nate. "Their Thursday lunch spot? Did they have one for every day?"

"Just weekdays."

The interior wasn't fancy, about what you'd expect in a former gas station—stained concrete floors and exposed rafters—but the ambiance was fun. The dining room was L-shaped, with a long bar and a row of tables across the aisle. We lucked out and got the last table in the row by the front window.

The menu helpfully suggested we order four to five things to share, which was my favorite way to eat—the sampler's approach. I perused the various lunch options. "There's no sign of a biscuit on this menu. I'm just saying."

We ordered a Japanese cabbage pancake topped with an egg and pork candy, Som Tum with chicken (black bean fried chicken with peanuts and herbs over rice with a papaya salad), Pad Ka Pow (Thai-style minced beef, green beans, chili and basil over rice with an egg), the pad Thai, and the XBB fried rice. Because we had a lot of work to do yet that day, we both stuck with water to drink.

"This place seems a bit bohemian for a couple college professors pushing retirement age," said Nate as our server walked away with our order. "I would've pegged them as the meat and three type, maybe a burger on occasion."

"It definitely has a bit of a grunge/hip vibe," I said. "I don't think Murray was your average college professor."

"So tell me about Flannery," said Nate.

I gave him the high points.

"Your overall impression?" he asked.

"I doubt she's our killer. Her husband could easily be. And she's a bit sensitive on the topic of her husband."

"You think she suspects him?" he asked.

"Hard to say. Maybe. But she's smart enough to not give us anything voluntarily that we could use against him."

"They don't have a garage," said Nate. "But there's a building out back, not connected to the house."

"How do you know that?" I asked.

"I took the opportunity to check out the perimeter while you had Flannery occupied indoors," said Nate. "Anyway, in the building, among other things, is a jug of antifreeze. Doesn't prove anything, but..."

"But it gives either of them means as well as ample opportunity," I said.

"Right."

"You didn't get a chance to dig into John Porcher and Dean Johnson then," I said.

"Not much," said Nate. "But enough."

"What do you mean?"

"As you noted in their profiles, they both have South Carolina drivers' licenses, but the DMV addresses are their home addresses—Porcher's in Aiken, Johnson's in Ware Shoals. I figured maybe they lived in a dorm. But with the help of our friends at Facebook, which led me to their favorite food delivery service, and a little creative hacking, I was able to get their address and phone numbers. Those two are living way above the means of your typical college students. They share a condo above a restaurant on King Street. Korean place—Mama Kim's. Rent is nearly three grand a month. Johnson drives a typical college car—an older Honda. But Porcher drives a year-old Lexus. And his parents are far from wealthy."

"That's interesting," I said. "Especially given that Dean is apparently going to school on a scholarship."

"My thoughts exactly," said Nate. "Want to divide and conquer after lunch?"

"What are you thinking?" I asked.

"I'll call John Porcher, employ a bit of trickery. From what you overheard, he seems to be the alpha. I'll tell him I'm investigating Murray's death and I need to discuss something with the two of them urgently. Naturally, I very specifically will *not* say I'm affiliated with the Charleston Police, but again, quite naturally, he will nevertheless infer that I am. I'll tell them I'm coming to their condo. But as soon as we hang up, I'll text him and ask that they meet me outside Maybank Hall instead. My pretext will be that I've just searched Murray's office and am short on time. The text will have a link to the Charleston Police Department's Facebook page. Embedded in that link will be that handy piece of code that will give us access to Porcher's cell phone and allow us to track him."

I pondered that plan for a minute. While I was thinking, our server returned with a huge pile of food that would barely fit on our table. It looked and smelled delicious.

As we piled samples of each dish on our plates, I said, "John and Dean will be plenty curious what you've found in Murray's office. They were both wound tight yesterday. I can't imagine they wouldn't show."

"That's what I'm counting on," said Nate.

"Now whether he clicks the link or not, I guess we'll see. It's worth a shot. Either way, while you're inquiring about the entries on Murray's calendar, I'll check out the condo."

"Precisely my plan. And he'll click on that link, you wait. He'll be curious what I've sent him. When he gets to the department Facebook page, he'll respond with millennial scorn. But his phone will be ours."

I gave him a look that said, *Maybe so.*

We dug into our lunch. Everything was delicious, but my favorite was the Pad Ka Pow, the minced beef with green beans over rice. I had to speak sternly to myself not to eat too much. We were going to Mamma and Daddy's house for dinner.

Daddy.

There was no sense worrying about his Halloween decorations. We'd all see them soon enough.

FOURTEEN

I made quick work of the lock on John Porcher's and Dean Johnson's condo. The door opened onto a hallway. I did a quick walk-thru to get my bearings. The whole place smelled like dirty socks. The two-bedroom loft wasn't huge, but it wasn't cramped, either, maybe 1,200 square feet. With high exposed-rafter ceilings, brick walls in the kitchen, great room, and hall, and hardwood floors, it was a thousand times nicer than what most college kids lived in. And the living room overlooked King Street in Charleston.

There was one big open living area, with the kitchen occupying the section closest to the hall. It sported dark-stained cabinets, complete with quartz counter tops and stainless-steel appliances. A small dining table stood across from the island. The housekeeping was about what you'd expect from two college-age guys: dirty dishes piled in the sink and on the counter, overflowing trash can, empty pizza box on the table, and various garments draped across furniture in the living room.

Down the hall lay two bedrooms, each with a private modern bath done in white subway tile. Who knew what manner of guy paraphernalia lurked there. I said a silent prayer to find what I was looking for without having to dig through the piles of guy laundry. Thank goodness I had on gloves.

I started in the back bedroom. The furniture had a Danish modern vibe. Whose room was this? Porcher's or Johnson's? I gave the bed with its pile of wadded covers a wide swath. There was a clear spot on the desk, most likely where a laptop normally sat. I fanned through the stack of folders on the corner. Each appeared to hold a term paper. It was early in the semester for either of them to have written even one. Neither of their names appeared on any of the papers.

I sat at the desk and opened the top drawer. A birthday card lay on top of a scatter of pens, paperclips, and index cards. I opened the card. It had a message to John from his mamma, complete with a plea to take good care of himself. This was John Porcher's room. I put the card back and closed the drawer.

Methodically, I worked my way through the dresser, checking the contents of each drawer and also for envelopes taped to the bottom. Then I moved to the nightstand. No surprise, the top drawer had roughly a year's supply of condoms. Well, good, he was practicing safe sex. There was also a gracious plenty of massage oils and flavored syrups. Shouldn't those be refrigerated? I closed the drawer.

The closet was a disappointment. Nothing there but a pile of laundry on the floor—how did he find his shoes?—and a few shirts and pairs of jeans on hangers. On the back wall was another door. Gingerly, I made my way across the room, stepping over still more little piles of laundry, and opened the door. It was a mechanical closet. Inside was a breaker box and the HVAC system.

On the floor beside the unit was a blue jug of Peak full-strength concentrate antifreeze. The contents were green. It said so right on the label. That wouldn't change the color of green juice perceptibly. I took a picture of the bottle where it sat. Then I picked it up and opened it. It was half full. Interesting, but not conclusive. Both gentlemen owned automobiles. I set it back where I found it.

There was nothing half as intriguing in the medicine cabinet or bathroom vanity. The state of John Porcher's bathroom made the rest of the condo look clean. With a shudder, I happily moved on to the front bedroom.

From the doorway, my heart did a little dance. I'd missed it when I glanced in because of the clothes piled on top of it. There was a laptop on the desk. Gently, I moved the clothes to the bed, without disturbing the order they were stacked in.

When I wiggled the mouse, the screensaver gave way to a wallpaper photo of Dean Johnson with a couple who were likely his parents and a girl who might've been his sister. I moved a jacket from the chair to the bed and sat down. The desk was the type with only a single center drawer. Dean's password wasn't there. I fished a small, silver microcomputer out of my crossbody bag, plugged it into the USB port, and launched a sequence to find the password and unlock the computer. While that ran, I explored the contents of the drawer and the surface of the desk.

A stack of folders with what appeared to be term papers sat on Dean's desk as well. Had they bought a bunch in case they needed them? It was common knowledge that it was relatively easy to buy term papers and essays on the internet. But I was somewhat surprised a scholarship student would take such a risk. Professors were using sophisticated tools these days to sniff out this sort of thing.

A soft ding notified me that the password had been found. Dean Johnson's electronic desktop held only one folder named "Outstanding Work." I decided to come back to that and opened his email, scanned for Professor Murray's name. There were many routine emails sent to an entire class. Dean Johnson had been in Murray Hamilton's classes many times over the course of the past three years, and had one class with him this semester. I scanned the subject lines. There. On Tuesday, October 13, Murray had written an email with the subject "The Fork in Your Road."

Mr. Johnson,

I will allow you one week to consider your options and your future.

I have great hope you will do the right thing.

Dr. Murray Hamilton

Had Murray caught Dean using a paper he'd purchased?

I took a photo of the screen, then moved to Dean's internet browser history. Premiumpapers.com was his most frequently visited site. I clicked on a link. *Sweet reason.* You could buy 100 percent plagiarism-free essays, term papers, or a whole list of specialized papers in four easy steps. It was a slick website. Any over-worked coed could type in their requirements, pay, then track their paper's progress, and then download it. There were testimonials. How in this world could this type of service be so bold—so completely available to anyone who cared to look?

My wrist vibrated with a text from Nate. *They're headed to condo on foot. Following.*

Roger that, I replied.

It was less than a five-minute walk to Maybank Hall. I needed to get out of there. I closed the window and exited email. I glanced at the "Outstanding Work" folder on the screen. I'd just have a quick look.

I opened the folder. Inside was a spreadsheet and several documents. The spreadsheet was titled "Papers to be Assigned." I clicked it to open.

Sonavabitch.

It was a list of papers ordered, the names and email addresses of who ordered them, who was assigned to write them, and the due date. Dean Johnson and John Porcher weren't buying term papers. They were selling them. That explained their lifestyle.

I took a picture of the first page, closed the spreadsheet and the folder, and logged off the computer. I put the clothes back the way I found them and was just stepping out of the room when I heard a key in the lock.

Shit!

I darted into Dean's bathroom and closed both doors—the one

connecting the bathroom to Dean's bedroom and the one that gave access from the hall.

No sooner had the door clicked closed than I heard them talking.

"They can't prove a damn thing," said John Porcher. "Not unless Murray told Annalise. We need to find her."

The voices faded a bit. It sounded like they'd stepped into the kitchen. There was only one way out of here for me, and the longer I stayed the more likely I'd be discovered. I eased the bathroom door back open. It opened into the hall and would screen the hallway to some degree from the living room.

"How do you know he didn't tell someone else at the college?" asked Dean.

I stepped into the hallway, hid behind the door.

My wrist vibrated. *U ok?*

"Because he told us we had until Tuesday," said John. "He was as goofy as all hell, but he was a man of his word." Their voices placed them in the living room.

"This whole nightmare could've been avoided. I told you we should never have sold a paper to someone on this campus, let alone someone in one of Dr. Hamilton's classes."

"We've hashed through that enough. It's done. And we're nearly home free."

"I hope you're right," said Dean.

"I know I'm right," said John. "I'm going to stake out Annalise's classes. She could've taken a day or so off, but she's new this semester. So I'm thinking she probably did not."

As quickly as I could move without making a sound, I slipped from behind the bathroom door, eased the door to the stairs open, and slid out.

By the grace of God, they were so engrossed in their evil plot, they didn't hear me leave. Outside, I made my way to Calhoun Street. Nate waited by Sabatino's Pizza.

His face was white. "What happened?"

"I got caught inside. I'm fine. I just had to wait until they were settled to slip out." I wasn't nearly as nonchalant as I sounded. I was rattled.

Nate looked away, then back. "I should never have let you go in there." He ran a hand through his hair. "Why didn't you get out when I texted you?"

"I found something," I said. "I needed just another minute."

He took a deep breath, blew it out. "Slugger, you can't be taking chances like that. It's not worth it."

"Hell's bells, Nate. They're college kids. Maybe they poisoned Professor Hamilton. But people who kill with poison want to avoid confrontation. Even if they'd caught me, they wouldn't've attacked me in their condo in broad daylight."

"We can't know what those two are capable of."

"I'm sorry I worried you," I said. "I'm fine."

He pulled me close, held me tight.

"Let's get away from here," I said. "I think Porcher's headed back out."

We walked half a block down Calhoun and went right on St. Philip Street, making our way to the car in St. Philip Street garage.

"They're running a paper mill," I said.

"What?" He gave me a confused look.

"They run a website that takes requests for all manner of college papers. As far as I can tell, they get other people to write them. Maybe they do some themselves too. Looks like most are downloaded, but they have a couple stacks of hard copies too. Could be those are for input."

"So that's where the money comes from. Murray must've found them out," said Nate.

I nodded. "He did. He emailed Dean Johnson, I'd bet Porcher too, and gave them a week to do the right thing. That was a week before he died."

"It's time to turn this over to Sonny," said Nate.

"What? No—I mean, not just yet. Porcher's going to stake out Annalise's classes—"

"All the more reason," said Nate. "The sooner he locks them up, the sooner she can go home. We can't take chances with her safety."

We'd reached the car. I chewed on that while we settled in. *Damnation.* It wouldn't take them long to tail Annalise back to the Belmond. "I suppose you're right. We need to get them locked up. But...think it through. The only reason to blow up the house was to destroy evidence. Seems like if the evidence they were looking to destroy was something to do with their business, they would've blown up the house with Murray in it, not five days later. Whoever blew up the house must've found out about the cameras after Murray's death. How would the two of them have come by that information?"

Nate shrugged. "Maybe they overheard someone talking about it. Maybe...maybe they were doing a little surveillance of their own. They're tech savvy. Maybe they were eavesdropping on Flannery or Tyler."

"How do we know that they even know who Flannery and Tyler are?" I asked.

"They know who Murray was dating and where she lives. Seems reasonable to me they also know who his next of kin were. They were trying to get into Annalise's last night with malicious intent. Eavesdropping would be a minor crime for the two of them."

I shook my head. "It doesn't feel right. It feels...anticlimactic."

"My little adrenaline junkie," said Nate. "Forgive me if I've lost my appetite for the chase...you in alleys with armed killers."

The clouds parted in my brain, and I realized exactly what was going on with my husband. "*That's* why you insisted on coming with me today."

"Good thing I did," said Nate. "You couldn't have gone into

their condo without me to keep them busy."

"But that's not the point," I said. "You wanted to keep an eye on me. You even hung around Flannery's house while I was inside. *Nate Andrews.* You're babysitting me. *Oooh!* And my daddy is just egging you on. That's what all that was about. He was showing his approval of you watching me like a hawk. The two of you have been conspiring against me."

"That's ridiculous and you know it. Of course I'm not babysitting you. We're doing our job. Just like we've always done."

I shook my head. "No. We divvy things up. We each do our part, and yes, if the job takes two, we work together. But this is different. You don't want to let me out of your sight."

He sighed. "Liz...please be reasonable. You almost died last month in Philadelphia Alley."

"I did no such thing."

"If Sonny had been a half second later getting his shot, we wouldn't be having this conversation."

"You can't know that. I had a vest on—"

"Call me crazy, but I'm weary of my wife going into situations where she needs to wear a bulletproof vest."

"It's not like I just got this job." I was exasperated. "Nate...my job is a big part of who I am."

"I'm not asking you to give up your job. This business is important to me too. I'm just saying, we could do things differently. Stop taking so many risks."

"We've been doing this for years. We're far better at protecting ourselves than we were when we started."

"But you've got to admit, we've both had more close calls recently."

My mind flashed back to Nate being airlifted off Stella Maris after he'd been shot. That stole the breath right out of my lungs. After a minute I said, "How about we compromise?"

"What do you have in mind?" Nate asked.

"We call Fraser. He hired us, even if we're working on Tyler's behalf. If Fraser's satisfied that we have enough to put Tyler in the clear, we turn what we have over to Sonny."

Nate nodded. "Seems reasonable."

I called Fraser on speaker so we could both listen and gave him a full update.

After listening and mulling for a moment, Fraser said, "Well done, Miz Talbot. It seems you have cracked our case in record time."

"You think we have enough to turn this over to Sonny Ravenel?" My words were marinated in skepticism. I might've been hoping he'd want more.

"I do. You have provided him with viable suspects who very likely murdered Professor Hamilton. Far better suspects than Tyler Duval. Detective Ravenel will be forced to thoroughly investigate these two collegiate entrepreneurs. Surely that investigation will uncover the remaining pieces of his case. He will abandon the notion that our young hemp enthusiasts were involved."

"Are you certain?" I asked.

"Miz Talbot, is there something you are not telling me?" asked Fraser.

"No," I said. "I've told you everything we know at this point."

"Then what troubles you?" asked Fraser.

"I just don't feel like we've finished the job," I said.

"Miz Talbot, closing *our* case and closing Detective Ravenel's case are not always the same thing. For the purposes of extricating our client's young friend—and our client's son from possible suspicion—I believe the job is complete. It is not required that you tie up Detective Ravenel's case with a pretty bow for him, only that you relieve him of the notion that Tyler Duval—and by association, Brantley Miller—are the guilty parties. It further is not required that you have a near-death experience to close our case. Perhaps you and Mr. Andrews should take a vacation. You have had quite an eventful year."

"Maybe so." We said our goodbyes and I ended the call, looked at Nate. I drew a deep breath, sighed. "All right. Let's call Sonny."

Nate nodded. "We're running short on time if you're still planning to meet with Annalise."

"I'd better cancel tea with her."

I called Annalise, who insisted we reschedule for the next day. Surely, she thought, the gas company would be finished and we could have tea at her house. She seemed so eager to talk to me. Though as far as we were concerned anyway, the case would soon be closed, something made me agree to go through with the tea. My gut told me there was more to learn. I liked knowing all the pieces to a case, having them put together neatly. It chafed that we were walking away from this one before we had the complete picture.

Nate called Sonny and asked him to meet us at Kudu. We waited in the courtyard. I sipped on a mocha latte while Nate downloaded the video from Annalise's outdoor cameras to a memory card and updated our case file. When Sonny arrived, we all gathered around one of the wrought-iron tables.

We filled Sonny in on the conversation I overheard at the reception, how Annalise had come to be at the Belmond, and what I'd found at the condo. Then we all watched the video of John Porcher and Dean Johnson's aborted B&E at Annalise's house.

"I wonder what's in Porcher's backpack?" I said. "I'd lay money on a quart of antifreeze."

"I wouldn't bet against that," said Nate.

"Can I have a copy of that video?" asked Sonny.

"You can." Nate handed him the memory card.

Sonny cocked his head to the side. "What are y'all not telling me?"

"Nothing." We both spoke at the same time. I looked Sonny straight in the eye.

"So what's your plan?" Sonny asked.

Nate said, "We don't have one."

"You're handing this over to me and walking away?" asked Sonny.

"That's right," I said.

After a moment, Sonny nodded. "I believe that. I just don't understand it. This is very unlike the two of you."

"Tyler Duval may not be exonerated by what we have on Porcher and Johnson," I said. "But you now have way more evidence on them than you do on him."

"That's true," said Sonny. "Murray Hamilton knew about their academic fraud business. One way or another, he was going to shut them down. At a minimum, that would've had a profound negative impact on their lifestyle and their futures. That's plenty of motive to spike his juice. They figured out Professor Hamilton must've told Annalise Mitchell what they were up to. Sure looks like they meant to kill her too. They had motive and means. But did they have access to Professor Hamilton's house? That's the question. If they didn't, they couldn't've killed him."

"I'm betting they somehow got ahold of a key," I said.

"And you're willing to trust me to figure out how all by myself?" Sonny said.

I gave him my best *oh puh-leeze* look. "Sonny Ravenel, you know very well we hold your investigative skills in the highest esteem."

Sonny laughed. "You know I can get a search warrant based on a confidential informant. And once I search their condo and their cars, I'm very likely to find a house key that doesn't fit their condo. Flannery and Tyler still have keys to what used to be Murray's house. If their keys match an odd one in John Porcher's or Dean Johnson's possession, well, there's my case. How they got it really doesn't even matter."

I offered him my brightest smile. "See? It only makes sense. Nate and I can't get search warrants."

"Oh, I agree it makes complete sense for me to do my job," said Sonny.

"Lookit, Sonny," I said. "There are clearly a few things we can do that you're prohibited from doing by your badge. And by the way, did you forget to mention the video cameras in Murray's house Monday at lunch?"

Sonny stretched his lips into a smile that didn't reach his eyes. "I told you everything I could, more than I probably should have. Those cameras were the likely motive for blowing up the house. You can wipe away fingerprints, vacuum up fibers. But whoever rigged that explosion knew Murray well enough to know he was paranoid. They could never be sure they found all the cameras and all the drives where the footage was stored."

"Professor Hamilton had a history with John Porcher and Dean Johnson," said Nate. "They were his students for three years, majored in his field. I'd say they all knew each other pretty well."

"I can't see him telling them he installed those cameras, can you?" Sonny asked.

"Nah, we're thinking they came by that information after his death," said Nate. "Maybe they were in the right place at the right time to overhear Flannery or Tyler mention it, or maybe they were nervous about whether there'd be an autopsy or not, so they were eavesdropping. Somehow, they found out."

Sonny looked mighty skeptical.

I said, "We're handing you most of your case. You could be a little more grateful."

"Oh, I'm grateful," said Sonny. "I just can't for the life of me figure out why the two of you are walking away before someone's trying to kill one of you or both."

Nate shrugged. "Let's just say the customer's satisfied. When the client's happy, the bill gets paid. We can move on to a new case. It's just good business, nothing more."

FIFTEEN

We were early to Mamma and Daddy's house for dinner. As we passed the McKenzie home, I had to say that Raylan and Joetta, Mamma and Daddy's new neighbors, did a lovely job with their fall outdoor decorations. There was an array of pumpkins of various sizes, a couple stacked bales of straw, lovely baskets overflowing with mums, and a whimsical scarecrow. It was charming, looked like something off the October cover of *Southern Living*. I could see what Mamma admired, though it wasn't exactly what I had pictured when Daddy was talking about Halloween decorations. There was a distinct difference between that and outdoor fall home decor.

Then we passed a line of magnolias and Mamma and Daddy's house and yard came into view.

I gaped in shock and dismay. "Oh. My. Stars. *Mamma*...she is going to kill me dead."

"Kill *you*? You didn't do that," said Nate.

He stopped the Navigator at the top of the drive and we both stared.

A giant inflatable black widow spider was on top of the house, its head, with glowing red eyes, right above the front door. Spiderweb covered the visible part of the house and all the azaleas in the bed out front. Skeletons and specters lined the front porch, which was lit with purple goblin lanterns with green faces that flashed on and off.

"That's seizure-inducing," I said.

"But the clown..." said Nate. "That clown looks pure evil."

The inflatable clown was roughly as big around as my car, but about twelve feet tall. He crouched cat-like in the front yard, like he was getting ready to pounce. Unlike any clown I'd ever seen, he had large fangs and wings. He was animated, his head rotating back and forth and his front arms repositioning every few seconds, like he was searching for prey.

Beside the clown was a purple demon that was likely twenty feet tall. Across the sidewalk from the clown and its demon were two animated inflatable zombies and a giant neon green Medusa. The snakes in her hair were moving.

"Oh, sweet reason," I said.

"I've never seen anything quite like this," said Nate.

"He's gone too far," I said. "She's going to kill him. Or leave." Mamma didn't hold with scary Halloween decorations, and Daddy was well aware of that. Our costumes had always been of the Disney variety. She'd let Blake be a pirate once, but that was as scary as Halloween had ever gotten at our house.

"What time was she getting home?" Nate asked.

"I'd've thought she'd've been here by now," I said. "We've got to get him to take this stuff down. Now."

"The only way to get him to do that would be to tell him not to." Nate rolled closer to the house and parked.

"That won't work. He'll never fall for it."

"Give that clown a wide berth," said Nate as he unbuckled his seatbelt.

The front door opened and Daddy came out on the front porch and waved. Chumley, his faithful basset hound, stood by his side. He woofed once, seemed subdued. Daddy must've been watching for us. "Tutti," he hollered. "Did you see my decorations?"

We hopped out of the car. I rushed towards the front porch. "Daddy, where's Mamma?"

"She's not home yet. What d'you think?" He was smiling so big, looked so proud of himself.

"Daddy," I said, "you've gone too far. This...we need to get Ray and Ponder back over here to get this mess out of Mamma's front yard. She's going to have a stroke."

"Have a stroke?" He sounded mildly offended. "What do you mean? It's Halloween. The trick-or-treaters will love it, won't they?"

"I'm serious," I said. "You know very well she hates this kind of thing."

"You haven't heard the sound effects yet." He reached down and plugged something in. Moaning, wailing, and demonic cackling ensued.

"And I thought it couldn't get worse," yelled Nate. I could barely hear him over the racket.

I put my hands over my ears.

Daddy laughed. I could see it, but I couldn't hear it at all.

Chumley threw back his head and let loose the most godawful howl I'd ever heard.

A startled expression stole over Daddy's face. He turned and looked down at his faithful friend. Chumley bolted off the porch. Daddy gave chase. Chumley was fast when he wanted to be. Nate and I moved in to intercept him, but he darted between us and headed across the yard.

"Hound dog!" Daddy stopped, pointed after Chumley, and hollered to us. "Catch 'im." Daddy scrambled up the steps and into the house.

It was hard to tell Chumley's moans of distress from the maniacal soundtrack blaring from the speakers. I was torn between running after him and staying to salvage what I could before Mamma got home. Chumley would come back. Mamma might not.

Nate echoed my thoughts. "He'll be back. As soon as we get rid of all this stuff."

Daddy reappeared on the porch, shotgun in hand.

"Oh no." He was going to expedite deflating the goblins.

Nate nodded, dashed to the Navigator and came back with his

Glock.

"*Nate*," I yelled. "Hell's bells, just unplug the damn things."

"I'm taking that clown out," he yelled. "This'll be faster."

It really was an evil-looking clown.

From the front porch, Daddy aimed at one of the zombies.

"Oh hell no," said Nate. "*Frank!*"

Nate dashed up the front porch steps. He reached down with his left hand and jerked the plug out from the wall. All the racket stopped except for Chumley's tormented howling from a distance. The lights and animation must've been plugged in elsewhere.

"Wait until Liz is out of the front yard." Nate's expression might have been the slightest bit crazed. In the sudden quiet, his voice was very loud.

Daddy lowered his gun, looked slightly sheepish. "You think I can't tell my own daughter from a zombie?"

I drew a deep breath. "I'm thinking I better head over to Phoebe's, intercept Mamma. Maybe I can stall her."

"I'm afraid it's too entirely late for that." Mamma's voice was cold as ice.

Oh dear Lord. She must've parked behind the Navigator. She appeared to be in shock.

I reached for normal. "Mamma, I love your hair." It really did look nice.

Her head swiveled towards me slowly. She gave me a look that inquired after my sanity, but she didn't say a word. Inch by inch, she surveyed the yard, taking it all in.

"Mamma..." I moved to her side, spoke softly. "We're going to get rid of all that lickety-split, you'll see—"

Daddy came down the steps, strode across the front yard. Nate followed. Mere seconds earlier, Daddy had been prepared to expeditiously dispose of his creation with his shotgun. That was when he harbored the notion he could somehow clean this mess up before Mamma got home. Now that she'd seen it, in all its heinous glory, he would bluster through, try to pull off the prank. This was hardwired in his DNA.

Mamma stared at Daddy. "Franklin. What on earth were you thinking? *Why* would you do such a thing to our home?"

Daddy grinned but didn't sound quite as confident as he looked. "You mean you don't like it? You said you wanted some Halloween decorations. Here we worked all afternoon. It was a surprise."

"*Like* it?" Mamma's voice was incredulous and rising. "You've filled our yard with fiends from the depths of hell."

"*Mamma?*" Merry and Joe rushed down the driveway. She tripped and grabbed Joe's arm to keep from falling. They both wore stunned expressions. Normally, Merry would be all in on Daddy's nonsense. But even she could see this was too much. "Mamma. Joe's going to start taking it all down. Right now."

"I'm on it, Mamma C.," said Joe.

"We were just about to take care of that," said Nate.

Mamma's eyes widened as she took in Nate's gun.

"Go inside and get yourself a gun," said Daddy to Joe.

Joe started towards the house.

"Wait." Merry's face scrunched up like mine does sometimes. "Just unplug them. Most of it's inflatable. They've got blowers, right?"

"Yeah," said Nate. "They'll come down pretty fast that way. I'm guessing it's all plugged in inside the garage. But there's nothing to stop them from going right back up."

Mamma looked at Nate. "Give me your gun."

"Hold on now—" Daddy looked profoundly unhappy. "Carolyn..." He made a chopping gesture with his right hand, seemed at a loss for words.

Chumley crept up, stood by Daddy and whimpered. He read the crowd, picked up on the stress level, and went back to howling.

"Hush up, hound dog," said Daddy.

Chumley barked once, then gave a muffled growl and quieted down.

Nate said, "Carolyn, give us thirty minutes. It'll be like it never happened."

Mamma looked at Nate hopefully. "That would be a miracle."

"Hey everybody!" Blake and Poppy came down the driveway hand in hand. He took in the scene, must've figured desperate measures were called for. "Mamma, guess what?"

She looked up at him blankly, didn't say a word.

He pulled Poppy closer to him, put his arm around her.

Realization dawned. Blake must've planned to tell us all at dinner. How did I not figure this out?

"Mamma," said Blake. "Poppy and I got married this weekend."

Mamma looked up at him, her face creased in confusion. "I don't understand. Why would you—"

"What?" Daddy laughed.

"That's fabulous!" cried Merry.

"Oh my stars! Congratulations!" I rushed to hug Poppy.

Nate and Joe both clapped Blake on the back.

"Son..." Hurt and disappointment were all over Mamma's face.

Blake said, "Mamma, I know you wanted to plan a big party. And I promised you could. I hope you'll still want to do that. We'd love a big reception."

"Of course." Mamma was only slightly mollified. "But I still don't understand...I need to sit down."

"Here, let's go inside." Daddy jumped at the chance to do something right. He took her elbow, tried to ease her towards the house.

Mamma jerked her arm back, glared at Daddy like maybe she was trying to set him on fire.

"Carolyn." Daddy was crestfallen, seemed at a complete loss.

Blake took this in. "We haven't even told you the big news yet."

In a synchronized motion, all our heads turned in his direction.

And then my brother said the one thing that could save us all.

"Mamma," said Blake. "Looks like you'll be getting that first grandchild soon."

The sun came out on my Mamma's face. "Oh!"

We all erupted into a flurry of hugs and congratulations.

This explained why Colleen had gone to the airport to meet Blake and Poppy. I was surprised she hadn't gone with them on their trip. Somehow, their child figured into Colleen's future plans for protecting the island. Poppy was very likely carrying a future member of the Stella Maris town council.

"This calls for a toast," said Daddy. "Let me get the champagne. Come on in the house now." We all followed him up the steps. He headed towards the kitchen and the rest of us went into the den.

I gathered the champagne flutes from the cabinet above the wet bar. Daddy came back with a bottle of 2008 Dom Perignon and a bottle of San Pellegrino sparkling water. He popped the cork on the champagne, grinning ear to ear. He kept stealing little glances at Mamma. For her part, Mamma gushed over Poppy, who was literally glowing. The garish Halloween display in the front yard was completely forgotten.

"Oh my goodness." Mamma touched Poppy's arm. "I've forgotten all about dinner. We have to get you fed. Come into the kitchen with me. You can sit on a stool and rest while I get things warmed up. I cooked this morning. I knew I'd be late at the hairdresser." Mamma started in the direction of the kitchen.

"Wait now," said Daddy. "We need to toast my grandson." He handed Mamma a glass.

Nate and I passed around everyone else's. I handed Poppy her glass of San Pellegrino.

Daddy raised a glass and we all followed suit. "To Blake and

Poppy," said Daddy. "May they be as happy as we are..." He put an arm around Mamma.

She looked up at him, must've tried hard not to laugh, but let a little chuckle slip out.

Daddy continued, "...and to our first grandchild. May he be healthy and strong, and always know how much his family loves him...or her."

We all said cheers and drank deeply. It was such a warm, happy moment. Later, I would reflect back on how Daddy somehow knew Poppy was expecting a boy. It wasn't that he especially wanted a grandson over a granddaughter, I knew that. He would adore any grandchild, but if anything, Daddy would dote on a granddaughter just a bit more. He'd tease her just like he teased me, Merry, and his favorite target of all, Mamma.

Later, as we found our places at Mamma's mahogany Duncan Phyfe dining room table—her grandmother's table—I noticed that she'd made the same meal she cooked the first time Poppy came for dinner. It was the night the pygmy goat ended up in the middle of the table, so I wasn't likely to forget it. Neither was Mamma. This had been a subtle message to me when Mamma still thought I could put a stop to whatever nonsense Daddy was up to and a subtle message was in order.

A low vase of blue hydrangeas graced the center of the table—even that was the same. A large serving dish of country-style steak and gravy rested on a trivet right in front of Poppy's place. Scattered around the table were dishes of mashed potatoes, fried squash, green bean casserole, butter peas, and biscuits. Just like before, the sliced tomatoes and fried apples had to go on the sideboard because the table wouldn't hold all the food.

Normally, Nate and I sat on one side of the table, Merry and Joe on the other, with Blake by Joe and Poppy across from him to Nate's left.

Nate said, "Blake, you sit by your wife. I'll sit across the table this evening."

"Thanks, brother." Blake just kept on smiling. He held the chair by me for Poppy, then took a seat to her left.

Mamma offered her hands to Merry on her left and me on her right. As was our custom, we all joined hands and bowed our heads and waited for Mamma to say grace. She hesitated, perhaps gathering her thoughts. "Heavenly Father, thank you for this glorious day. We especially thank you for all of our children's safety and for the blessing of a grandchild. Father, please take good care of our Poppy. Bless this food to our use and us to thy service. And Father, please forgive Frank for that hellish display in our front yard. Please grant me patience, Lord. Some days I need an extra helping. To the glory of thy name, amen."

We all said amen.

Poppy was dabbing her eyes with her napkin, fanning her face.

I put an arm around her. "You okay?"

"I've never been better in my life," she said. "No one's ever prayed over me before. No one's ever called me 'our Poppy.' I haven't belonged to anyone in a long time."

"Best get used to that." I smiled, hugged her.

"Mrs. Talbot—"

"Darlin', for goodness sake. We're family. Please call me Carolyn. Or Mamma, if you prefer."

Poppy's voice cracked. "Carolyn..." She fanned her face some more. "It's like you cooked all my favorites."

Mamma smiled. "I guess the Good Lord guided my hands." She looked at me, daring me to contradict her.

Poppy was still fanning her face.

Mamma stood. "Poppy, I declare, you're never going to get fed at this rate."

Poppy laughed as Mamma stood, walked around the table, and commenced piling food on her plate.

Blake watched and grinned.

"I guess you've been demoted," I said to him. "You're going to have to fix your own plate now."

"I'll manage," he said.

A panicked look crossed Mamma's face. "Where are y'all planning to live? You can't raise a child on a boat."

"Why not?" Blake asked, still grinning.

Practical-joking Daddy had left the building. Serious Daddy looked at Blake like maybe he was going to ground him. "You can't be serious, son."

Blake chuckled. "Relax, Dad. Poppy and I are looking at houses."

"Do y'all have a realtor?" Merry asked.

"Tammy Sue Lyerly across the street's taken up real estate," said Daddy. "Why don'cha give her a call?"

Mamma took her seat. "Now, y'all know I love Tammy Sue. But, Frank, she's just gettin' started. She doesn't even know what she's doin' yet. We need a seasoned *professional*. We can't have someone overlooking lead in the paint and all such as that when our grandchild's health is at stake."

Poppy looked at Blake.

Blake said, "We haven't talked to a realtor yet. We've just been driving around. I've been showing Poppy the different neighborhoods."

Merry said, "I wish something was on the market in my neighborhood. That's a great place for kids."

We all looked at Merry.

Daddy said what we were all thinking. "Are y'all planning to live in that house when you get back from your honeymoon safari?" Daddy's expression telegraphed exactly what he thought of Merry and Joe's upcoming trip. They were only a little more than two weeks away from leaving for a bucket-list expedition/destination wedding to Patagonia, a sore point with both our parents. Thankfully, Blake's good news seemed to have taken all the sharp edges off everything that evening.

Merry and Joe exchanged a glance.

"Part-time," said Merry.

"You're not moving to Charlotte?" Mamma looked at Merry like she knew this couldn't possibly be the case.

"Wellllll," said Merry, "Joe's job is there..."

"Well, I—" Mamma moistened her lips. "—I just assumed he would transfer to Charleston."

Joe looked at Merry. He was way too smart to open his mouth.

"Mamma," said Merry, "that's just not possible."

"Why exactly would that be, Esmerelda?" Daddy's brow furrowed. "You told us he was a banker. There are banks all over Charleston."

Merry said, "Daddy, I told you, Joe's an investment banker. He puts together bond deals for municipalities. There's not—"

"I'll look into it," Joe said amiably.

Daddy grinned, nodded at Joe. "There, you see?" he said to Merry.

Nate said, "I had a cousin once who sold real estate. When he first started, a more experienced agent looked over everything he did. D'you think maybe somebody's working with Tammy Sue?"

Daddy turned to Nate. "I bet you're right. Carolyn, we should look into that, what do you think?"

Mamma tilted her head, considering.

For the next ten minutes, Mamma and Daddy debated various relators, neighborhoods, schools, and everything else related to where Blake and Poppy might live. We all watched the volley of ideas, like one might watch a tennis match. No one else was consulted or allowed to get a word in edgewise.

Finally, Blake started laughing.

Poppy got the giggles.

Mamma and Daddy wore utterly confused expressions. It was clear to me then and there that they were going to micromanage every decision big and small related to Project Grandchild. Daddy was going to have less time to aggravate Mamma, and she would have less time to get riled up. I hoped Blake and Poppy had a dozen children.

Blake just kept on laughing. He was probably thinking the same thing I was. Well, maybe not about having twelve children. After a minute, he said, "Why don't we call Tammy Sue over here and the whole family can interview her after dinner?"

Naturally, this was my brother's idea of a joke. The problem was that on the subject of housing for grandchildren, Mamma purely had no sense of humor.

"That's an excellent idea," said Mamma.

I looked at her. Okay, my mouth might have been just the teensiest bit ajar. I felt a little bad for Poppy, who was brand-new in the family and still adjusting to the general level of crazy. She maybe didn't want her life micromanaged.

"Liz, darlin', you really must stop staring at people with your mouth hanging open like a flounder on the line. It's most unattractive."

"Mamma," I said. "Blake and Poppy are capable of finding their own house—of hiring their own realtor, for goodness sake."

Mamma said, "Yes, and I bet they could've prevented my front yard from being turned into the devil's playground too. If only I'd thought to ask them. But I'm sure they don't mind letting us share in the fun of house hunting." Mamma smiled at Poppy.

"Of course not," said Poppy. "We're happy for all the help we can get."

"There, you see." Mamma smiled at me, gloated a bit, then turned back to Poppy. "We need to find you a house right away. We need to start decorating the nursery. Have you thought at all about color schemes? Do you plan to find out the baby's gender?"

"No," said Poppy. "We want to be surprised."

"That's good," said Daddy. "Some things are better the old-fashioned way."

"But we have settled on names either way," said Poppy. "If it's a boy, he'll be Franklin Blake Talbot Junior."

"And if it's a girl," said Blake, "she'll be Emma Rae Talbot, after Gram."

A giant whirlwind sucked all the air right out of my lungs.

Nate looked at me across the table.

I gasped. The dream. In my nightmare, the little girl who couldn't possibly be mine, the one named Emma Rae. She was Blake's daughter. But she was the younger of the two children in the dream. Colleen had known, she'd always known that Poppy and Blake would have two children.

"Elizabeth?" Mamma said. "Are you all right?"

Colleen appeared on the sideboard, a worried look on her face.

"I'm fine, Mamma," I managed.

"You can't help anyone if you give yourself a nervous breakdown," said Colleen. "When the time comes, you'll know what to do. But you've got to be strong and focus on the things you can control."

Nate.

How was I supposed to stop a giant wave from washing him away? I couldn't, of course. I just had to make damn sure we were all off this island days before a hurricane arrived.

Except my brother was the chief of police. He'd be the last person off the island, I knew that for a stone-cold fact.

"Liz." Colleen snapped her fingers, spraying sparks all over the dining room. "Everybody gets to make their own choices. Focus on your own."

SIXTEEN

I slept poorly that night and got up early, ready to run. I was pent up. Colleen had told me not to take that nightmare literally—it was one of several possible scenarios. But that was easier to do when I had no idea where children—one of them named Emma Rae— might come from. I raced around our normal path in my best time ever, pounding the sand with my running shoes, pushing myself.

"Feel better?" asked Nate as we flopped into the canvas-and-wood chairs on the beach in front of the house.

"Some." I had time. In the dream, the girl looked about three years old, the boy five. If the nightmare was destined to become reality, it was still a long way off. I just had to come up with a foolproof evacuation plan for us in the meantime.

I watched the waves, let my worries slip away on the soft salty breeze. We sat quietly, me digging my toes in the sand and Rhett chasing foam. Nate stared off past the horizon. After half an hour of ocean therapy, we headed to the house.

Inside, I stepped into the mudroom and filled Rhett's water and kibble. He waited politely for me to finish, then enthusiastically attacked his breakfast. I patted him on the head and went into the kitchen.

Nate had coffee already brewing.

I inhaled deeply. "That smells divine."

I put together our usual yogurt, berries, and granola bowls for breakfast. We ate on the deck, lost in our thoughts and the roar of the surf, neither of us saying much. Then we showered and dressed and settled into the sofa in my office with second cups of coffee.

Both our phones alerted. I looked at my screen. There was a text from Sonny: *Got the SW. Going in 9 am.*

Nate texted him back: *Roger that—ty.*

"You never told me," I said. "Did John Porcher click on your link?" The software Nate had embedded in the link he'd texted John Porcher would allow us complete access to his phone—if Porcher clicked.

Nate grinned. "He did, in fact."

"Is he at home?"

Nate opened the app to track him. "Yeah, he'll be there to greet Sonny."

"Sonny will arrest him—Dean Johnson as well if he's there. If not, he'll get to him quick enough. Once Sonny talks to them—tells them what they're charged with—once they realize the cat's out of the bag, Annalise is safe. We should let her know she can go home."

Nate nodded. "As soon as they're in custody."

"Even if they make bail, surely they wouldn't dare hurt her. Knowing that Sonny's on to them," I said.

"The only motive they had to silence her was to keep their enterprise a secret. Once they've been exposed, there's no point."

I stared at the case board, mulled it. Something tickled at my brain, wouldn't let me be. "I know you want to close this case, but I'm just not sold on it."

"Why's that?"

"I'm just not convinced Porcher and Johnson had any way at all to know that the cameras were in Murray's house," I said. "The two of them, skulking around after Murray's body was discovered, trying to find out if foul play was suspected, or if they'd gotten away with it? *Maybe* overhearing something about the cameras by eavesdropping on Flannery or Tyler.... It's too random. The odds of them being that lucky—to be in the right place at the right time— are very long. And as far as listening devices go, they certainly aren't experienced burglars. Why would we think them capable of bugging anybody? Which begs the question, why would they blow up the house on Saturday?"

"Liz, we hashed all this out yesterday. Fraser agreed."

"Maybe so. But it still doesn't feel like a solid case to me. We can't substantiate that John Porcher or Dean Johnson even knew about the autopsy, much less that there were cameras in the house."

Nate mulled that for a few minutes. "I still say it's entirely possible they overheard Flannery or Tyler discussing it. Maybe they didn't plant bugs. I agree, that's a stretch. But they could easily be old-fashioned eavesdroppers."

"That's thin and you know it."

"They were damn sure planning something criminal where Annalise is concerned," said Nate.

"That they were," I said. "What if someone took care of their Murray Hamilton problem, and they planned to exploit the circumstances of his death—make it look like the same person killed Annalise?"

Nate winced. "That's possible, I guess. But I still say John Porcher and Dean Johnson are the strongest suspects. Sonny will build his case. If he can't, well, we're sure to hear about that soon enough. I think Fraser had a fine idea. Why don't you and I take off for St. John for a few days, maybe a week?"

I was not about to be sidetracked. "I think we're right back to Tyler looking guilty. I don't think he *is* guilty, but I think on paper he looks guiltiest. Unless we can prove that John Porcher and Dean Johnson had some way to know that Murray had installed cameras that possibly had footage of them sneaking in to poison him. And we have no idea how they could've gotten in. How did I let you talk me into this?"

Nate opened his mouth, looked like he was going to answer my question, then pressed his lips together. When we'd gotten close to a plausible resolution to our case, Nate had grabbed it with both hands. And I knew why. He wanted to protect me. I'd had one too many close calls.

I walked over to the case board, picked up a dry erase marker and an eraser. "This case is either about the hemp farm—and I think that's likeliest—or it's about selling term papers, or it's about Murray's love life."

Nate looked like he'd taken a bite of a lemon. He did not want to head back down this road. But he knew I was right—he had to see it. "Or it's about Keith Laurens needing money."

I pointed at him with a marker. "Or there's that."

He shook his head. "But the fact remains, Porcher and Johnson...aw, *shit*."

"You don't think they killed Murray Hamilton any more than I do. They were planning to kill Annalise—we have them dead to rights on that. But Murray...that was someone else."

Nate covered his mouth with a hand, stared at the case board like it had betrayed him.

We were back in the game. I felt a little thrill. I knew this case wasn't over. Sometimes a new day brought fresh perspective.

"It's good we handed Porcher and Johnson off to Sonny anyway," I said. "That protects Annalise. But our suspect pool is limited to those who could reasonably have known that Murray's death had been ruled a homicide and knew there were cameras." I turned back to the case board and erased John Porcher and Dean Johnson's names. Then I got rid of the "Unknown Lover," Unknown Student," and "Unknown Subject" lines.

"We can add those back if we eliminate everyone else, but I don't see that happening," I said. "If I'm right, and Murray was murdered because of something to do with the hemp farm, we need to take a closer look at Will Capers. He's the one we know the least about."

My husband did not look happy. "The odds are on family.

Keith Laurens merits a lot more scrutiny before we move on to associates of family members." He let out a long sigh. "I guess we'd better get packed up and head to Charleston."

"I still have tea with Annalise at four. I never did cancel that."

"In the meantime," said Nate, "we need to figure out the best approach to Keith Laurens. He had motive, means, and opportunity. Anything Flannery knew, he knew it too. Which means he knew about the cameras. He also had business with Annalise, remember? Alibis being so problematic in this case, we need a way to eliminate everyone as a suspect, but I say we start with him. Might save us some time."

We both pondered the alibi conundrum for a few minutes. There was nearly a twenty-four-hour window during when the juice could've been poisoned. The explosion could've been set hours before it happened. No one had an alibi for all that time.

Finally, I said, "Remember how paranoid Flannery said Murray was?"

"You mentioned that, yeah."

"It wouldn't've been out of character one bit for him to have had a backup hard drive for his security system. Somewhere offsite. Professor Fishburne's house is right across the street—within Wi-Fi range—and he was his trusted friend for decades. It could've been at his house. Or Annalise's. We don't have to say where it was at all. But whatever was on Murray Hamilton's hard drive that incriminated whoever blew up that house, we could bluff and say we had a backup. Like Murray's substitute cloud. He distrusted the government and big corporations, but he trusted his friends."

"That would be quite convenient." Nate studied the ceiling thoughtfully. "We could use that with every one of them. Pretend we've got the video and are looking for a big payday in exchange for not turning it over to the police."

"Precisely."

"That'll work," said Nate. "But we need to make it clear that the hard drive has been removed from wherever it was. We don't want to unintentionally make Pierce or Annalise a target."

"Good idea. Murray could've stashed that in a neighbor's garage. Could've been anywhere. But now we have it in a safe place." I pondered the plan a bit more. "Yeah, but..."

"Problem?" asked Nate.

"Only that most of these people are suffering from fresh grief. I feel really bad subjecting the innocent ones to this. Seems cruel."

Nate winced. "If we knew who the innocent ones were, we wouldn't need to do this. Like I said, let's start with Keith Laurens. He's the least broken up of the bunch. If he takes the bait, we're done. No need to upset the innocent grieving folks. If he didn't kill Murray, he won't care what we have on video. Then we'll have to decide who's next."

"That works," I said. "But we haven't even spoken to some of these folks yet. No telling what we'll find out. It's still early. I say we use the blackmail option only as a last resort."

"Fair enough," said Nate. "But Keith Laurens is a jackass. I'm not worried about his feelings."

"Eh, me either. We can open with blackmail where he's concerned. I'd like to get through a couple more interviews today. How about we spend some quality time with Pierce Fishburne? He was Murray's best friend. He could know something he doesn't realize is important. I've been putting off talking to him. He was so broken up at the funeral..."

"Provided we don't get a de facto confession from Keith Laurens, then we need to circle back to our young hemp farmers. I fear perhaps you're right and we've been neglecting them," said Nate.

"I'd say we have our day cut out for us."

Nate nodded. "Laurens...best to do that incognito."

"Agreed," I said. "We may need to be somewhere with Flannery and Keith together. Flannery knows me."

"One of us talks to Laurens, the other stays close by and listens." Nate's voice had an edge.

"I'll—"

"I talk to him," said Nate. "And you can talk to Professor Fishburne. We'll take turns. Ladies first. And you're having tea with Annalise, remember?"

"Fine." I sighed, set down the marker, and returned to the sofa. "Look, I get that we've had our share of close calls. We need to be as careful as we possibly can. But I love our life. I love what we do. I don't want things to change."

Nate reached out, touched my face, brushed a stray lock of hair behind my ear. "Neither do I. But the one change I couldn't survive is losing you. We've got to learn to step back before things get out of hand."

I nodded. "I know. I couldn't bear it if anything happened to you." All I could think about was that wave washing Nate out of the boat. I hugged him close.

SEVENTEEN

Professor Pierce Fishburne lived to the left of Annalise Mitchell if you were facing the house. I climbed the steps to the porch, trying to decide if it was a Victorian or a single house. It seemed to have elements of both, with a front porch and an upper piazza along the side with a partial porch beneath it. The white-and-green-striped awning seemed out of place on either architectural style.

I wasn't in disguise. My strategy with Professor Fishburne was simple: gently probe his memory to see if he knew anything helpful. I knew Sonny was tied up elsewhere and wouldn't be across the street at Murray's former house. The activity level seemed to have waned, with only one technician poking around and making notes.

The professor opened the stained-wood door almost immediately after I knocked.

"Good morning, Professor Fishburne. I'm Liz Talbot. We spoke on the phone?" I showed him my credentials wallet, with my driver's license and my PI license.

"Yes. Come in. You caught me at a good time. I don't have classes on Thursdays this semester." He opened the door wider, stepped back to invite me in.

He wore a pressed plaid shirt and khaki pants. His hair had gone completely grey, and he wore a full mustache and beard. I remembered from the profile I'd done on him that he was sixty-one—two years older than Murray.

"Let's talk in the living room," he said. "Can I get you anything?"

"Thank you, I'm fine."

He nodded and led the way to the room on the right overlooking the front porch. A brown leather sofa sat along the far wall. To the right, by the windows, were a pair of matching leather club chairs. The remaining furniture was scattered around the rectangle-shaped room as if he wasn't quite sure what to do with it. On the wall next to the doorway stood a large entertainment armoire, its doors open. A recliner sat directly across the room from it. The furniture arrangement gave the impression that Pierce Fishburne spent a great deal of time alone in front of the television.

He gestured to one of the chairs and took a seat on the sofa.

"You have a lovely home." The hardwood floors were stained a rich chestnut color, and the foyer and living room featured nice woodwork. The living room opened to the dining room, and beyond that lay the kitchen.

You could tell no woman had a hand in the decorating. It was uncluttered to the point of being stark. A seascape hung on the wall above the fireplace. The remaining walls were bare of artwork. A single framed photograph in a distinctive carved wood frame sat on an end table near the recliner. Professors Hamilton and Fishburne smiled widely with Flannery and Tyler at the South Carolina aquarium. It looked recent—like it'd been taken no more than two years ago. A folded newspaper and a pair of reading glasses lay in front of the picture.

"Thanks." He seemed to have exhausted his supply of pleasantries. "How can I help you?"

"As I mentioned on the phone, I'm looking into the matter of your neighbor's death. Murray Hamilton?"

An oppressive weight seemed to bear down on Professor Fishburne. He looked at the floor. "He was my best friend. I've already told the police detectives. I don't know anything that could help you."

"I'm terribly sorry for your loss," I said.

He nodded, waited for me to speak.

"I'm trying to establish a timeline," I said. "When is the last time you saw your friend?"

He took a long deep breath, huffed it out. "Lunch the day before he died. We went to Miller's All Day on Mondays."

"Every Monday?" I asked.

"For a while. We used to go to Hominy Grill on Mondays before it closed. Murray loved those 'nasty biscuits.' Damn heart attack on a plate, you ask me." Professor Fishburne sounded a bit like a curmudgeon.

My mouth watered in memory of the flaky biscuit with fried chicken and cheese covered in sausage gravy. I nodded. "I loved those too."

"I used to give Murray hell for eating that junk. He ate all kinds of fried food. Told him that stuff would kill 'im." Grief seemed to gnaw at him. He looked away. "Should've kept my mouth shut. Let him enjoy what he liked."

"Did he mention any recent stomach issues at all?" I asked.

Professor Fishburne was quiet for a moment. "He did. He canceled lunch on Friday. Said he wasn't feeling well, was going to see the doctor. Murray wasn't one to run to the doctor."

"But he was well on Monday?" I asked.

"Seemed to be fine. Complained he was gaining weight."

"How long did you know Murray Hamilton?" I asked.

Professor Fishburne studied something out the window. "He's the first person I met when I moved here thirty years ago. I'm originally from Marietta, Ohio."

"Do you know his family well? Tyler and Flannery?" Flannery had called him Professor Fish. A nickname indicated a certain familiarity. The photo of the aquarium outing looked like a family shot.

"Sure. Good kids. Murray raised them after his sister died."

"Did you spend time with the three of them?"

He shrugged. "Yeah. I mean, before the kids left home I saw more of them. I'd go over for dinner pretty often, birthdays. Sometimes we'd all go to the beach, one of the plantations, Fort Sumter. But they're older now. Murray saw less of them, so I did too."

"But you know Keith Laurens, Flannery's husband?" I asked.

He raised his eyebrows. "Sure."

"Professor, can you think of anything that happened recently that worried your friend?" I asked.

"Worried? No. Not at all. Murray was a happy guy."

"Any student issues?" I asked. "Maybe someone who felt like they were entitled to a higher grade? Anyone caught cheating? Anything like that?"

"No," said Professor Fishburne. "Not that he discussed with me. Murray wouldn't have put up with crap from students. And he definitely wouldn't have let anyone get away with cheating."

"Were you aware that he was installing a security system?" I asked.

"No, he didn't mention it to me."

"Does that surprise you?"

"Not really," said Professor Fishburne. "Murray was a cautious man. He protected what was his."

"Do you have any thoughts on who might've wanted to kill him?" I asked.

"No. It's...unimaginable."

"How well do you know Annalise Mitchell?" I asked.

He sniffed. "Not very well."

"How would you describe their relationship?" I asked.

"They were dating. Since right before the semester started."

"Did you have the impression Murray was serious about her?"

"He didn't tell me if he was," he said.

"So you couldn't think of any possible motive she might have to kill him?" I asked.

His face took on a hard expression. He seemed to mull that over. "Women. Who knows what they're thinking? Now that you mention it, she could've been the jealous type." Here was a flicker of the anger I'd sensed in him at the funeral home. On some level, he seemed to want to hold Annalise responsible for Murray's death.

"You mean perhaps she was jealous of the other women he dated?" I asked.

"Sure. Why not?"

"He wasn't serious about any of them, was he?"

"Of course not. He had the occasional date. I can't imagine where any of them would've gotten the idea things were serious. Wishful thinking, I guess. Anyway, all that eharmony stuff stopped when he met *her*. But—" He wagged a finger at me. "*She* didn't know that, did she?"

"Would you say he was more serious about Annalise?" I asked.

"I suppose," he said. "He certainly saw more of her anyway."

"Did you ever spend time with the two of them?"

He cleared his throat. "Yes. I had tea with them once or twice."

"Murray loved his tea, didn't he? Tyler told me that."

"He did." Professor Fishburne nodded. "Had tea every single day since I met him. At four o'clock. Of course, that got way fancier when he started dating Annalise. Murray, he'd just make a pot of tea and have a couple cookies. But it was the ritual he loved."

"Professor, we're just trying to get a feel for how free Professor Murray was with his house keys. I'm sure you had one, right?"

"Of course. For close to three decades. He had a key to my house as well. For emergencies."

"Do you happen to know who all else had a key to Murray Hamilton's house?" I asked.

"He wouldn't have handed them out freely. Flannery and Tyler had them, I know. Aside from them...possibly Annalise. I can't imagine anyone else had one."

"Can you think of any way a student might've gotten ahold of one?" I asked.

He thought for a minute. "Not unless they were skilled pickpockets. Murray wasn't the type to leave his keys lying around."

My wrist vibrated. I glanced at the message from Sonny: *Both in custody.*

Professor Fishburne didn't appreciate my divided attention. He gave me a look that said, *I've got better things to do too.*

I tilted my head, smiled. "If I said to you that someone suspected Tyler had killed his uncle, what would you think of that?"

"I'd say that's damn ridiculous. Tyler and Flannery both adored Murray. Like I said. He raised them."

"What about Keith Laurens?" I asked.

Professor Fishburne grimaced. "Flannery deserves much better, but I don't think the kid's a murderer."

"But he'd be a more likely suspect than Tyler?"

"Hell yes," said Professor Fishburne.

"Can you think of anything else you think I should know?"

"Anything else?" He squinted at me. "I haven't told you anything to begin with."

"You've been more helpful than you realize. Thank you."

"No problem," he said. "Is that all?"

"Yes, that's all for now. Thank you for your time."

He stood, an expression on his face like maybe he had a bad taste in his mouth. "Then I'll see you out."

Pierce Fishburne might've been willing to help with our investigation, but he didn't seem happy about it. Perhaps he felt protective of Flannery and Tyler.

EIGHTEEN

We'd taken the Navigator to Charleston because it had more in the way of equipment in the back. Nate had parked in a small lot that belonged to a dental office a block away, near Rutledge and Montagu. When I opened the door on the passenger side to climb back in, Colleen was in my seat.

"Well, well," I said. "Look who's decided to grace us with her presence. Would you get in the back, please?" I might've been the teensiest bit aggravated at her. She could've told me a long time ago those children in my nightmare were Blake's.

"I didn't know that either," she said.

I gave her my best "Oh puh-*leeze*" look.

"Spirit's honor." She raised her right hand.

"If you don't mind, I'd like to get in the car."

"I'm moving already." She did this smoky-flowy transition move into the backseat.

Nate had completed his disguise. Black gel transformed his dark blond hair. He wore it combed back, which heightened the change. He'd added a dark mustache and a pair of wire-rimmed glasses.

I checked him over. "It's not as dramatically different as the Manfred Wright disguise, but it's still effective. You feelin' like Tommy today?"

"Nah. Think I'll be Steve. Colleen thinks I look like a Steve in this getup. That's who I told Keith Laurens to expect."

"Whatever." I smiled at him. "Did you call Annalise?"

"I did," he said. "She's on her way home now. I expect you'll hear from her soon confirming tea at her house."

"What's up?" I asked Colleen. "You've been pretty scarce lately. You must have a reason for being here."

"It's not like you're the only person I need to protect," she said. "Darius is still getting settled. I need to keep an eye on things there. Did you know he and Calista are still dating?"

"Yes," I said. "I had lunch with Calista Saturday. I'm surprised you're not spending all your time with Blake and Poppy."

She lifted a shoulder. "Newlyweds need a lot of alone time. I'm there plenty."

"What I thought," I said. "You could've told me they'd gotten married."

"And take the joy out of him sharing that with your family?"

I might've been the slightest bit miffed at her. "What brings you here?"

"Do I need a specific reason to check on you?"

"So it seems, lately." I tried to look all hurt.

"I missed you guys," she said. "I had a few minutes. Thought I'd check in."

If she had business, I'd have to get it out of her another way.

I turned to Nate. "You said you called Keith, let him know you were coming?"

"Yeah, I told him I was a friend of Professor Hamilton's and I needed a word. I'm supposed to meet him at a picnic table in front of the building."

I pulled up Google Maps and looked at the street view. Keith Laurens's pedicab company, Fun Buggy, was in a painted yellow block building on Pinckney, behind Charleston Carriage Works. "That's almost exactly across from Cru Café. It's early yet. I wonder if I can get a reservation on the porch. That end table would give me a sightline view."

Nate raised an eyebrow, started the car. "Now who doesn't

want to let who out of her sight?"

I ignored the comment. "What do you want? I'll get lunch to go."

"You might get a to-go order, but you'll never get a reservation on this short a notice," said Nate.

Colleen disappeared with a flash.

"Wonder what that was all about," said Nate. "She has been awfully scarce as of late."

"Who knows?" I said. "Lunch?"

"Sure," said Nate. "Hmm...one of their shrimp BLTs sounds good. With Parmesan truffle fries."

"Yummy," I said. "That does sound good. I'm going to call just in case. See if we can get a table."

Colleen popped back in. "No need. They open in ten minutes. The reservation on the last table on the front porch is in your name."

I stared at her. She had never used her abilities for such a mundane favor. "Thanks." I must've been looking at her oddly.

"What?"

"I thought you weren't allowed to do that sort of thing."

"I don't make a habit of it."

"Thank you."

"You're welcome." She wore a wistful look.

"Colleen?" I said. "Is everything all right?"

"Sure. Why wouldn't it be?"

Colleen was a horrible liar while she was alive. She'd gotten no better at it as a spirit. I had no idea why she would lie to me. And that scared me.

Cru Café was in a Charleston Single house on the corner of Pinckney Street and Motley Lane. As requested, I was seated at the last table on the porch overlooking Pinckney. A porch-rail-mounted planter filled with fall flowers helped screen the view of the porch from the street. Ceiling fans stirred the air, creating a nice breeze. No one raised a ruckus over not getting that table as far as I could tell.

I told the waitress my husband would be joining me and ordered iced tea with mint for both of us. Cru's macaroni and cheese was legendary and it called to me. I gave into temptation, but ordered an appetizer portion of the butter lettuce salad with poached pears, another favorite, so I could get my veggies.

The waitress had just stepped away when Nate opened the gate in the white picket fence across the street. The teal-painted picnic table sat under a live oak tree in front of Fun Buggy. Perhaps customers sat there awaiting their pedicabs on busy days. Today didn't appear to be one. A moment later, Keith Laurens walked out the front door and crossed the yard. In khaki shorts, a tucked-in pale yellow golf shirt, and tennis shoes, he looked ready to hop on a pedicab at any moment.

Nate's chin lifted. "Mr. Laurens." This close, with the Bluetooth earbuds, our private two-way channel, and no buildings between us, I could hear him as clearly as if he was beside me.

"You must be Steve." Keith scanned the area, as if checking to see that Nate was alone. "You said you were a friend of Murray Hamilton's?"

"Right now I'd say I'm one of his closest friends," said Nate. "You drive the rickshaws yourself?"

"Yeah." Keith nodded. "When we're busy."

"How many of those things you have?" asked Nate.

"Six. How can I help you, Mr.—I didn't catch your last name?"

"I'm a first-name basis kind of guy. The thing is, Mr. Laurens, as you're probably aware, Professor Hamilton was a bit eccentric. Paranoid, some might say."

Keith flashed a slight grin. "I guess he was."

"What you might not know is that this led him to install a

backup hard drive for his security system. It was close by, but offsite."

"What does that have to do with me?" asked Keith.

"The explosion, thankfully, did not destroy it."

Nate paused. Keith waited.

"Did you know he had cameras installed inside and out?" Nate asked.

"No, I didn't." That had to be a lie. Surely either Murray had mentioned his project in front of Keith or Flannery had told him in passing.

"Yeah, the cameras were all motion activated. The thing is, all kinds of things activated the outdoor cameras. Cats, neighbors, cars...people walking down the street..."

Keith's body language said that Nate had his attention.

"Murray's system keeps thirty days' worth of video," said Nate. "You know what's on there from Tuesday afternoon around 5:30?"

Keith didn't offer a guess.

"It's you," said Nate. "Climbing Annalise Mitchell's steps, banging on the door, looking awfully upset when she wasn't home." Of course, this was the footage we'd gotten on our camera in her front yard, but this was how Nate would convince him his next claim was real.

I couldn't read Keith's expression, but his tone was full of scorn. "So what? I went to check on her. I was worried."

"Were you now?" asked Nate. "Is that the nature of your relationship with her? To check on her, that sort of thing?"

"Not normally, no. But with Murray's death...it just seemed like the right thing to do. What business is it of yours?"

"I'm just a curious sort," said Nate. "But I'm even more curious about the two other clips I saw. One where you entered Murray Hamilton's house on the sly hours before his death. And the other where you were leaving in a hurry the morning the house blew up."

Keith shook his head. "That never happened. Neither of those things happened. I haven't been inside Murray's house in weeks. I don't know who's in your video, pal, but it's not me. I worked late the Monday before Murray died. I clocked out after 1:00 a.m. Went straight home to my wife. Ask her. And his house blew up on a Saturday. I was pedaling people all over town. Didn't even have time for lunch. I was down near White Point Garden with a couple from Michigan when Flannery called me to tell me what happened. Lesa and Dave Dion. Nice folks. They're staying at 21 East Battery. Ask them."

"Wouldn't have taken long to detour by Murray's house, either time," said Nate. "The thing about gas explosions is that you set them in motion long before they happen. Being somewhere else at the time is the whole point."

Keith shook his head. "It's not me. What—are you trying to blackmail me? It's not going to work. Because I didn't do it. I did go by to check on Annalise. Sue me."

Keith stalked across the yard without a backwards glance.

Sonavabitch. It wasn't Keith Laurens. Not that it would be a cause for celebration if he'd killed his wife's uncle, but I really didn't want our culprit to turn out to be someone Murray loved dearly. Somehow that made his death even more tragic.

Nate walked right on Pinckney towards East Bay. He must've circled around. A few minutes later he walked across the porch and joined me. Thankfully, he'd taken the mustache off. "You know what strikes me?"

"What's that?" I asked.

"He didn't mention the police. Someone tries to blackmail you and you're completely innocent, you bring up the law, even if you don't actually call them."

"Maybe," I said. "You read him as guilty? That's not my take at all."

"Nah. I don't think he's guilty of killing Murray," said Nate. "He would never have blown me completely off if he had. He'd have to get his hands on whatever video I had, one way or another."

"Then what?"

"I don't think he's eager to discuss his visit to Annalise's house with the police."

"Interesting," I said. "He could be hiding something unrelated to Murray's death."

The waitress brought our lunch and refilled my tea glass.

We munched, trading bites of macaroni and cheese for the occasional Parmesan truffle fry, setting the mystery of Keith Laurens aside for a few moments. Lunch was delectable, as always. It wasn't until Annalise called that I remembered I needed to save room for whatever she served with tea at four.

As I finished my conversation with her and ended the call, I noticed Nate studying me. "Something wrong?" I asked.

"I'm thinking it would've been a better idea to have tea with her at Twenty-Six Divine. She had tea with Murray the day before he died and sent him home with that pitcher of juice."

NINETEEN

Annalise Mitchell smiled and welcomed me into her home. If I hadn't known she was fifty-three, her age would've been hard to guess. Her ivory skin was unlined, her shimmering red hair shoulder-length. There wasn't a speck of grey in her hair, but the color appeared natural. Untroubled by the white after Labor Day rule, she wore a wispy multi-colored tunic and white skinny jeans with sandals. I liked her immediately.

"Come into the parlor." She led me into the room to the right off the foyer. Her floorplan looked identical to Pierce Fishburne's, but the similarities in their homes stopped there. A white slip-covered sofa, scattered with cream, weathered blue, and soft sand-colored pillows of various shapes and sizes sat in front of the bay window. A pair of chairs, one matching the sofa and one wicker, sat to each side and in front of the sofa, with a sisal rug underneath anchoring the conversation area. Annalise's home could've been the subject of a feature article in *Southern Living* called "Coastal Home Decor."

"Have a seat." Annalise moved to the laden tea cart waiting near one end of the sofa. "I have Darjeeling and Mint. Which would you prefer?"

"Darjeeling, please." I smiled and took a seat in the white chair to the left of the sofa.

She reached for the green-and-white polka-dot teapot. "Darjeeling was Murray's favorite. I'm watching my caffeine.

There's milk, sugar, and lemon on the coffee table." She handed me my cup.

Also on the coffee table was a three-tiered cake plate piled with tea sandwiches, mini quiches, scones, and fruit tarts. Small dishes of clotted cream and strawberry preserves sat to the side. "This is amazing." I hadn't seen a tea spread like this since Mamma, Merry, and I had afternoon tea onboard The Queen Mary while visiting California years ago.

"Thank you. Please help yourself." Annalise took a seat to my right, on the end of the sofa, and began fixing herself a plate. "I think tea is what made Murray and me such fast friends. We both love the tradition and the drink."

I was hit again with how sad it was that Murray, who smelled the roses every day, had been yanked out of a life lived so fully. He'd reveled in life's simpler pleasures—lunch with a friend, tea with a loved one, burgers and mentoring young men. One didn't need to climb every mountain, cross every ocean, or have their face on the cover of *Rolling Stone* to be a light in this world. Whoever had blown out Murray Hamilton's candle, I was determined to see to it they paid for that.

Annalise looked at me, a question on her face. I pulled myself back into the moment, smiled. I selected cucumber, chicken salad, and egg salad sandwiches, thankful that Nate and I had taken a long walk down to Waterfront Park, along the Cooper River, and down to The Battery after lunch. "You have tea every day?"

"Yes," she said. "There's something calming about stopping at four each day for a nice cup of tea. This is my main meal of the day. I have a good breakfast, skip lunch—that's when I have my office hours—and then tea. If I want something else at night, I grab a leftover sandwich."

"I think I'd enjoy that schedule." I sampled the cucumber sandwich. The cucumbers were thinly sliced, with just the right amount of herbs in the cream cheese. If she was attempting to disarm me with food, she was off to an excellent start. No wonder Murray loved this woman. If she made me a spread like this every day, I'd be in love with her too. I had to speak very sternly to myself to get back to the business at hand.

"Do you mind if we talk while we eat?" Although I had asked to speak with her, the question somehow felt rude.

She smiled. "Of course not. Good conversation is part of the tradition."

"Well, yes, but—"

"I know what you meant, dear. Please. Ask me anything you like. There's nothing I'd like better than to get to the bottom of what happened to Murray."

"I'm so very sorry for your loss," I said. "I never met him, of course, but from what I've learned, he was quite a gentleman."

"He was indeed." Annalise sipped her tea. "He was an original. I miss him terribly."

"You said you and Murray were fast friends. Was that how you saw your relationship? You were friends?"

"We were very *good* friends," she said. "We were also romantically involved, if that's what you're asking. But friendship was the foundation of our relationship. I think that's true of the best romantic relationships, don't you?"

"As a matter of fact, I would wholeheartedly agree with that." Nate and I had been best friends, then also partners, before we were romantically involved. "Tell me how the two of you met."

"I was moving into my office over on Glebe Street," she said. "I had way more than I could carry—stacks of boxes. Murray happened by at just the right moment. He offered to help, and I repaid his kindness with tea."

"I understand that you had Murray broadening his horizons a bit." I took a bite of an egg salad sandwich. It was every bit as good as Mamma's.

Annalise laughed. "I suppose I did. The Jet Ski adventure may have been a bit beyond my horizons as well. But I'd never been. I wanted to try it. Murray went along. He was such a good sport." Her eyes watered. She looked down at her teacup.

I sipped my tea, gave her a moment. "Did you get along well with Flannery and Tyler?"

"Oh, they're great kids. I just love them both. They adored their Uncle Murray."

"So you wouldn't think of Tyler as someone who might've been behind Murray's death?" I asked.

"Oh, for goodness sake. Is that what the police think? I talked to Detective Ravenel. He asked me a similar question, and I'll tell you what I told him, though he seems to have ignored me. Tyler Duval did not kill Murray. Neither did Flannery. It's just that simple."

"Do you have any idea who might have done such a thing?" I asked.

She winced. "I honestly don't."

"That's the problem," I said. "There aren't any good suspects. Only those you really can't imagine doing such a thing."

"Ahh." She tipped her head from side to side. "Well, regardless, it wasn't one of those kids."

"Do you know Flannery's husband, Keith Laurens?"

She pursed her lips. Her shoulders rose and fell. "Yes, I know Keith."

"Do you think he and Murray got along well?" I asked.

"They did. Murray tried very hard to develop a relationship with Keith, for Flannery's sake."

"Was that difficult, you think? Developing a relationship with Keith?"

She grimaced. "I wouldn't say that exactly. They just had different interests. Keith is a fitness and health enthusiast. Of course, he pedals those rickshaws, but he also lifts weights, boxes, that sort of thing. It was hard for Murray to find common ground with Keith, and to be honest, I don't think Keith made much of an effort. He had other things on his mind."

"For instance?"

Annalise set her teacup in its saucer. "I probably shouldn't tell you this. The last thing I want to do is make trouble for Flannery, and this likely has nothing whatsoever to do with Murray's death. But I can't be sure. I didn't mention this to Detective Ravenel. Somehow that felt like a betrayal of family trust, but perhaps you can explore this discreetly, see if it's important or not."

"I'll do my best." I waited for her to get her thoughts together.

"Murray saw Keith with another woman a week or so before he died."

"In a compromising situation?"

"They were together at the Thoroughbred Club. It's the bar inside the Belmond. It's very nice. I had a drink there myself recently. Anyway, Keith was cuddled up with what Murray called a floozy, more because of what she was doing in public with a married man than anything else."

"What exactly was she doing?" I asked.

"They were very familiar with one another, from what I understand. Snuggled up on a sofa in a corner. Several kisses were exchanged. In public. One can only imagine what they did behind closed doors."

"I see. Did Murray confront Keith?"

"He did. He walked right over and told him, in front of his...girlfriend...that he should be ashamed of himself. He had a wife at home who was far better than he deserved. Murray told Keith he had one week to tell Flannery himself what he'd been up to, or he would tell her himself."

Another one-week ultimatum? That was starting to sound like a theme with Murray. It seemed he was a fan of giving folks the opportunity to make things right themselves. I'd lay odds that Keith had not told Flannery, and he was now trying to see if Annalise knew his secret. Hence, his arrival on her front porch Monday evening. "Did Keith come clean with Flannery?"

"I have no idea. Murray was trying to figure out the best way to approach her to see. He didn't want her to think he was prying. And especially if Keith *had* told her, Murray was afraid she'd be embarrassed."

"Have you spoken with Keith since Murray's death?" I asked.

"Me? No. Well, only at the funeral home and the church."

"I wouldn't be surprised if you heard from him," I said.

"You're thinking he'd want to see if Murray told me? That would mean he hadn't said anything to Flannery. Otherwise, it wouldn't make any difference what I knew."

"That would be my guess," I said. "Annalise, would you walk me through the timeline? From the day before Murray died—Monday the nineteenth—until you got the news?"

"Certainly," she said. "Murray and I both had morning classes. I had student appointments at lunch. Murray had lunch with Pierce Fishburne. I have an early afternoon class. I usually get home around three on Mondays, and I did that day. Murray and I had tea together at four. Right here. He sat where you're sitting right now. He left at 5:30. Tyler and his friends were coming over for burgers, although I can't imagine how Murray could've eaten again so soon. He really enjoyed his Monday evenings with the guys."

"Did you speak with him or see him again that evening? After Tyler and his friends left?" I asked.

"Yes. He called me. I guess it was about 10:30."

"Was he all right then?"

"As far as I know. He didn't mention feeling bad. We talked about the boys. He told me Tyler had asked him to invest in the hemp farm. I think the boys really needed the money, but Murray felt like that was a risky investment."

"Do you know if they argued?"

"They did not. I'm sure Tyler was disappointed, but he and

Murray loved each other. They didn't argue about that or anything else," she said.

"Murray told you Tyler came back to see him—after he'd left with his friends?" I asked.

"That's right. Tyler's such a sweet kid. He was worried Murray might think he was upset. He just wanted to make sure Murray knew that he understood his decision. He was only there about ten minutes."

"You're certain Murray would've told you if they had argued?"

"Yes, I am. Murray and I shared everything that was important to us. Family was the most important thing to Murray. Period. He would've been upset if they'd argued, and we would've talked about it. I'm certain."

"So you hung up the phone at about what time?" I asked.

"We talked maybe fifteen minutes, so 10:45? I can't be certain, but about that. I was in bed by 11:00. Then I had classes the next morning. Flannery called me a little before 10:00 to tell me he was gone." A tear slipped down her cheek. She reached for the box of tissues on the end table.

"I'm so sorry," I said.

She waved a hand. "No, no. It's not your fault. You're here to help."

"What did Flannery tell you had happened?" I asked.

"She said she didn't know what had happened to him. Later, she was very upset because the doctor was calling it a heart thing, and she didn't think that was right."

"Did Murray mention his recent stomach problems to you?" I asked.

"He did." She nodded. "He started feeling ill on a Thursday evening, a little more than a week before he died. At first, he thought it was a virus, but then he said he had a fluttering in his chest. He did see the doctor on Friday. I know the doctor ordered some tests just to be on the safe side, but I think the doctor thought it was a virus too."

"He never mentioned feeling ill to you again?"

"No."

"I hate to ask you this, but could you tell me about the juice?" I asked.

She closed her eyes, shook her head. "It's beyond ironic. I've been a juicer for years. It's done wonders for my health. I have green juice with my breakfast every morning. I'd been trying to convince Murray of all the health benefits, but he was not interested. At all.

"The Sunday before he died, he gave in. Said he'd give it a try since I seemed to be in such good health. He'd started to fret about his weight. He'd put on a few pounds. Anyway, I press my juice fresh every morning, but Murray has breakfast at home most days. So on Monday, when I made my juice for the morning, I made Murray a pitcher. Enough to last a few days. He took it home with him after tea Monday afternoon." She spread out her hands, palms up. "I have no idea how the poison got in the juice. He must've had a glass Tuesday morning and it killed him."

"And the only people you know of who were at Murray's house Monday evening were Tyler, Brantley, and Will?" I asked.

"That's right. But that certainly doesn't mean someone else wasn't there."

"Did you know Murray was installing a security system?"

"I did, yes."

"Did you mention that to anyone else?" I asked.

"Why, no. Is that important?"

"I'm just gathering all the information at this point. Did you have a key to Murray's house?"

"Yes, we exchanged keys around the first of the month," she said.

"Okay, so, back to this hemp business. Did Murray share his concerns with you beyond the fact that he thought it was risky?"

Annalise averted her gaze. "More tea?" She rose and moved to the tea cart, refilled both our cups. When she was seated again, she took a sip of tea, set down her cup and saucer, and looked me in the eye. "This may be another situation that requires discretion."

"I see." There was something else she hadn't told Sonny. I'd bet she'd invited him to tea and he'd turned her down, which was clearly a mistake. I took a bite of a chicken salad sandwich.

"The reason Murray was at the Thoroughbred Club to begin with, when he saw Keith?"

I nodded, took another bite of sandwich, as if we were two friends sharing confidences over tea. Had she known Murray met with Will alone?

"Murray didn't trust Will Capers." She picked up her cup and saucer, sipped her tea.

"He followed Will there?" Maybe those notes on Murray's calendar weren't meetings between him and Will after all.

"Not that same night. A couple weeks before that. Tyler mentioned that Will was meeting with more potential investors at the Thoroughbred Club, and that he and Brantley preferred not to get more strangers involved. It was their venture. They wanted to keep it close. Murray went to the Thoroughbred Club and waited to see who Will would meet with, what kind of people they seemed to be."

"How interesting," I said. "What did he find out?"

"Well, I really don't know. He did go back at least once more, because that's when he saw Keith out fooling around. Murray was so upset by that. That's what we talked about, and then I changed the subject to something less upsetting. We never did get back to Will. But I know Murray had concerns that he was too aggressive with pursuing investors. Tyler and Brantley just weren't on board with that. Murray felt Will wasn't honoring their wishes."

"When I talked with Tyler, he mentioned Will finding more investors," I said. "I had the impression he was aware of it at least."

"After Murray turned them down, Tyler and Brantley had accepted that's what they'd have to do. But before that, they really hadn't agreed to it. Murray felt like Will just kept pushing the idea, trying to sell Tyler and Brantley on it."

I needed to spend some quality time on Will Capers, no doubt. Nate was apparently right. We'd been neglecting the hemp farmers. "Have you spoken to Tyler about this?"

She winced. "No. I was afraid he'd think I was meddling, and I didn't want him to feel that Murray had violated his confidence by discussing his business with me. Do you think I should?"

"Not just yet. Surely Murray must've shared his concerns with Tyler."

"I think he did at first, but Tyler was a bit defensive of Will. Murray was just doing due diligence—that's what he called it—to make sure Tyler wasn't being taken advantage of. I'm sure he would've discussed it at length when he felt that he had all the facts."

"That makes perfect sense." I waited to see if she had anything else to add.

She seemed focused on a cucumber sandwich.

"Annalise, is there anything else that you think might need to be looked into discreetly? Anything else you haven't mentioned to Detective Ravenel?"

"No, I think that's everything."

I nodded, sipped my tea. "Did Murray mention any problems at work to you?"

"Oh no, Murray loved teaching. It was his calling. And of course he loved history."

"No student problems?" I asked.

Her eyes widened a bit. "Now that you mention it, there was something going on with two of his seniors, but I don't know the details. Murray seemed to think he had it handled, whatever it was."

"There is one delicate issue I'd like to ask you about. If you don't mind, of course." I smiled warmly.

"Of course. Ask me anything."

"The other women Murray dated...Rose Kendrick, Clairee Pringle, Alice Vaughn, and Unity Sinclair...did you know about them?"

She threw back her head and laughed. "Of course I did. Murray said that's what I saved him from—a future with one of them. He joked about his internet dating days. Said they made him appreciate me more."

"I didn't think you'd have any reason to be jealous of any of them."

She stopped, her cup and saucer lifted just below her face. She'd been just about to take a sip. She smiled. "Oh no, dear. I had no motive in this world to hurt Murray, if that's what you're thinking."

TWENTY

We snagged seats at the bar at Minero, the quirky, casual Mexican cantina on East Bay where Tyler worked when he wasn't on the hemp farm. Ordinarily, I'd've preferred a booth along the brick wall. But since I wouldn't be able to hold another bite for a week and we needed to talk to our client, the bar worked out. I introduced Tyler and Nate as we climbed onto our stools.

"Nice to meet you." Tyler gave Nate a measuring look, then a nod. He seemed a little less relaxed than when I'd talked to him at his place on Monday. Tyler was young and might've had an abundance of testosterone he didn't know what to do with.

"Likewise." Nate smothered a grin and ordered the fresh guacamole, the Queso Fundido app, and two Al Pastor tacos. "Just bring it all together."

I gave him a questioning look. "That seems like a lot of food."

"Usually when you say you're not hungry you end up wanting just a bite or two."

"Trust me. This won't be one of those nights."

Nate shrugged. "We'll see."

The bar business was steady, but we had time to chat with Tyler while he mixed and poured. Nate had a Cadillac Margarita and I had a Mango con Chile to be supportive.

"Y'all getting anywhere?" Tyler set our drinks in front of us.

"We know more now than we did Monday morning," Nate said easily.

I sipped my drink. "This is good. Is there a good reason why you didn't tell me you went back to your uncle's house the Monday night before he died? After the three of you left?"

Tyler winced. "I forgot about that. Didn't see it was important, I guess. If I'd wanted to poison Uncle Murray, I could've done it before I left. I didn't need to go back to do it."

I shrugged. "Could be you wanted to be sure Will and Brantley didn't see you do it."

"If you think that, why are you trying to help me?" Tension crept into his voice.

"Easy, sport," said Nate. "The lady is making a point. She's on your side."

"Sorry," said Tyler. "This is stressful as hell."

"Did Brantley ask you for the combination to your uncle's office on campus Monday afternoon?"

"Yeah. He left something there. Why?"

"Brantley didn't tell you?" He'd surely had ample opportunity.

"Tell me what?"

"That he took your uncle's desk calendar. He would've taken his computer if it'd been there."

"Why would he do that?" Tyler's face contorted.

"He said it was to protect you," I said. "According to Brantley, Will was the lookout. He and Will thought it might look bad that y'all were on Murray's calendar."

"That's ridiculous," said Tyler. "The three of us spent a lot of time with Uncle Murray. That wasn't a secret."

A server set Nate's food in front of him and he dug in. Even though I had no appetite, my mouth watered. The mingle of savory aromas was enticing.

"Which one of them does that surprise you the most about?" Nate picked up a chip and scooped some guacamole.

Tyler thought for a minute. "Brantley. I can see Will coming up with something like that. Probably his idea."

"Which begs the question," I said, "what did Will have to hide?

Do you trust him?"

"Of course I trust him. He's my friend. And my business partner."

"Did you know that your Uncle Murray had concerns about him? Did he tell you that?" I asked.

A look of exasperation passed across Tyler's face. Someone down the bar signaled him for a drink. "Be right back."

"You should taste this Queso Fundido," said Nate.

I studied the appetizer. "Hmm...maybe just a taste. Murray Hamilton must've had a miraculous metabolism. On an average Monday, he ate lunch out with his buddy, had tea with Annalise, and then cooked for Tyler and his friends. Murray was a trim man—I don't know where he put it all. Though both Professor Fishburne and Annalise mentioned he was concerned he'd been gaining weight."

Nate put a bite of cheese, poblano, and chorizo together for me.

The flavor medley was smoky, spicy, and creamy—out of this world. "I wish I could hold more of that."

Tyler walked back to our section of the bar. He seemed to've settled down a bit, more like the easy-going guy I'd spoken with before. "Uncle Murray did ask me about Will. You'd have to know Uncle Murray. He was just excessively worried about things. We got into farming, all of us, because we didn't want these big corporate jobs with everyone climbing over the top of each other to get ahead. I trust my partners."

"What about the calendar?" asked Nate.

Tyler shrugged. "I guess it was just like Will said. He thought it might look bad for me."

"You know what looks bad?" I asked. "Brantley stealing and burning your uncle's calendar. *That* looks bad. It's destroying evidence."

"Yeah, I get that," said Tyler. "Will shouldn't've asked Brantley to do that. It puts him in a bad spot, and it was completely unnecessary. I'll talk to him."

"Let's wait on that," said Nate. "We'll get back to you."

"For now," I said, "don't talk to anyone about your uncle or anything to do with this case."

"All right," said Tyler.

"Did your uncle mention anything going on at work that concerned him?" I asked.

"No." Tyler shook his head. "That would've been unusual."

"It seems he caught a couple of his students in a paper-selling operation." I filled him in on John Porcher and Dean Johnson. "I think Detective Ravenel is more interested in them at the moment than he is you."

"Well, that's good news," said Tyler.

"It's encouraging," said Nate. "But we aren't finished."

"Understood," said Tyler.

"Murray get along well with your brother-in-law?" Nate asked.

"Keith? Sure."

"Do you get along well with Keith?" I asked.

He shrugged. "Yeah, I guess. If you're asking me if I think he's worthy of my sister, not really. But I guess most brothers feel that way."

I thought about Blake, and how he and Nate were like brothers.

"No," said Nate. "Trust your instincts."

"Do you know something about Keith I don't?" asked Tyler.

"Your Uncle Murray caught him with someone else," said Nate.

I turned to him, squinted. We hadn't discussed telling Tyler that. He could fly off the handle, which wouldn't be helpful.

Tyler's face hardened. "Is that a fact?"

"It is," said Nate. "He gave him a week to tell Flannery. I figure he'd want you to know. In case Keith forgets to have the conversation with his wife."

"Thank you," said Tyler. "I 'preciate it."

Someone waved at him and he walked to the other end of the bar.

I turned to Nate. "The other day in Fraser's office, when Will and Gideon Capers met with Sonny, you stayed in Fraser's office and listened while they were in the conference room, right?"

"That's right."

"You haven't met either of them?" I asked. "As you, I mean."

"Not yet."

"And Brantley, you've never met him, have you?"

"No, why?"

"Have you ever thought about investing in a hemp farm?"

"I can't say I have. Should I reflect on that?"

"I think you should have Darius tell the boys he has a friend who might be interested in getting in on the ground floor. Have him set up a meeting with Will."

Nate nodded. "I'd say young Will has moved to the top of the case board. That's a good idea. I'll make the call."

"Or..." I said, "...we could head over to the Thoroughbred Club. It's Thursday night. According to Murray's calendar, Will went there on Thursday evenings. Maybe we'll find an opportunity to introduce ourselves."

"You mean Tommy and Suzanne?"

"Probably best," I said. "No doubt Will has heard our names from Brantley."

Nate opened the tracking app on his phone. "His truck's in the Cumberland Street garage. Only a block and a half away. There's a good chance he's there tonight."

"It's been a really long day," I said. "I'd love to shower and change first."

"I'd be willing to bet the Belmond can accommodate your request."

TWENTY-ONE

We walked up the two steps from the lobby of the Belmond and into the Thoroughbred Club. I scanned the room. We'd eaten at Charleston Grill next door but hadn't spent time here. It was what you'd expect: rich wood-paneled walls, comfortable-looking leather sofas, scattered tables for two or three, and oil paintings featuring horses. Piano music drifted softly through the bar. It reeked of money trying to look like old money.

"There." Nate nodded towards a table in the corner by the fireplace. The two chairs sat at an angle, backs to the corner walls.

Will sat back in one of the wine-colored upholstered chairs, explaining something with an earnest expression to the balding businessman across the table. Tonight's button-down shirt was white. It was a nice contrast against his milk chocolate skin. Both the shirt and Will's khakis were starched within an inch of their lives. He looked the part of an enterprising young man.

The businessman in the tweed sport coat wore an expression that said he wasn't buying what Will was selling. Perhaps hemp wasn't all that hot after all. Will pressed on.

A pair of sofas sat back to back near Will and his companion. The couple on the sofa facing us stood. She gathered her wrap and purse. "How about there?" I murmured.

"That'll work." Nate started in that direction.

"Wait." I stopped, took a step away from him.

He gave me a questioning look.

"Let's split up," I said. "Maybe after his friend leaves, he'll try to chat one of us up. He's less likely to approach a couple."

Nate nodded. "I'll take the bar."

I sashayed over and settled in on the sofa, my back to Will. A waitress appeared to take my drink order. I watched as Nate slid onto a barstool and ordered, no doubt Woodford Reserve.

"I'd like club soda with a twist," I said. My tolerance wasn't quite as high as Nate's, and I'd had the mango concoction at Minero less than two hours ago.

Discreetly, I slipped my earpiece out of my purse, popped it in my left ear, and covered it with my hair. While if the occasion came to give our names, we'd be Tommy and Suzanne, we weren't in costume.

"...I'd love to get you a copy of our business plan to review." That had to be Will talking.

"I'll take a look at it." The sound of ice in an empty glass. "No promises."

"I understand," said Will. "I think you'll like what you see."

"It's clear you're under-capitalized."

"We'd love to hear your perspective," said Will. "Should I drop it off at the front desk?"

"That'll be fine. I'll be in touch."

"Thanks for your time," said Will.

The waitress brought my drink. Will's companion crossed behind her and headed for the hotel lobby. Now I wished I'd taken a spot where I could see Will. Did he make more than one appointment with potential investors on the same night? That might be tricky. Could put him in the position of having to rush a good prospect. On the other hand, that might create the illusion of high demand. Was that an illusion?

Across the room, Nate raised his glass. I took a moment to admire my husband. His dark blond hair was just getting long enough that a lock was starting to curl on his forehead. He'd have that cut soon, no doubt. His smoky blue eyes met mine, delivered a challenge, or perhaps a promise. How did he keep that golden tan year-round? He was a handsome piece of work, and I was a lucky girl.

A lanky brunette in a cocktail dress took the barstool beside him. Of all the nerve. He was wearing his wedding band. She leaned in, said something to him. I couldn't see his response. She was blocking my view.

Well. It was time to make something happen.

I picked up my glass, stood, and surveyed the room. Will was sipping his drink. I let my gaze settle, meet his. I offered him a hint of a smile. He nodded.

I perambulated over to his table. "Do I know you from somewhere?"

"I feel sure I'd remember that. Join me?"

"Why not? This looks like a comfortable corner." This was new territory for me. I'd never picked up a stranger in a bar, let alone one so much younger than me. But I wasn't leaving the bar with him under any circumstances, so I supposed it didn't count.

"Things not work out?" He raised an eyebrow, looked in Nate's direction.

Will must've been watching us making eyes at each other. Or maybe he saw us walk in together. I shrugged. "Not his lucky night."

He signaled the waitress. "What are you drinking?"

"Grey Goose and soda with a twist." I'd have to nurse that.

He ordered my drink plus a beer for himself. "Are you staying at the hotel?"

"I am," I said.

"I'm Will Capers," he said. "I live not far from here."

"Suzanne Moore. I'm from Greenville."

"I know Greenville," said Will. "I went to Clemson."

"Go Tigers." I smiled. "What was your major?"

"Agriculture."

"You're a farmer? What do you grow?"

"Hemp."

"*Reeeally*?" I said it like that was the most amazing thing I'd heard in my whole life. "Is that legal now?"

"Hemp is, but you can't smoke it."

I flashed him my ditzy blonde look, tilted my head, all confused like. "What good is it then?"

He launched into a monologue on the miracles of hemp. I reached for an enthralled look and hoped to appear way more interested than I was. Partway through, our waitress saved me by arriving with our drinks. I took a sip.

Then Will got off on supercapacitors. A few sentences in, he looked up. "Now I wonder what he wants?"

I glanced over my shoulder. Nate approached our table. A flicker of a smile played around his lips. What had happened to the tart from the bar?

I gave him a bored look, turned back to Will. "You were saying?"

Will glanced from Nate to me and back.

Nate said, "Suzanne Moore. I didn't know you were in town."

"Of course you did." I rolled my eyes to Will. "I'm sure my mamma mentioned it to yours."

"Hello." Nate offered Will a hand. "Tommy Wright."

"Will Capers."

"Nice to meet you, Will," said Nate. "Have you known Suzanne long?"

"We just met," said Will.

"Is that a fact?" asked Nate. "She and I go way back."

Will looked at me, uncertain, likely wondering if he should invite Nate to sit down.

I gave a dismissive wave. "Don't pay him a bit of attention. Our mammas were sorority sisters. They've been trying to marry us off since we were in the cradle. My mamma is particularly impressed with his trust fund."

Interest flickered in Will's eyes. "Well, if he's an old friend...would you care to join us?"

"That's awfully kind of you." He set his drink on the table and pulled up a chair. "No sense in drinking alone."

"I thought you were with a friend," I said.

"She mistook me for someone else." Nate's eyes layered meaning onto the simple statement.

"Do you live around here?" asked Will.

"Sullivan's Island," said Nate. "How about you?"

"I'm from Johns Island. That's where my farm is."

"Ah, a farmer," said Nate. "Tomatoes? I love a Johns Island tomato as good as the next person."

"Will's a hemp farmer," I said. "He's on the cutting edge of the most promising new green energy technology." I parroted some of what Will had said to the best of my ability.

Will grinned. "That's right." He turned to Nate. "What field are you in?"

"Investments, mostly." Nate took a drink of bourbon.

Will leaned in, eager. "We should talk. I have a ground-floor opportunity for a select few investors."

"Is that a fact?" Nate wore a bored expression.

Will was up for the challenge. "Hemp is one of the oldest domestic crops in the world. Its use in a wide variety of renewable products makes it a super crop. In addition to its many commercial uses, hemp slows down soil erosion and detoxifies the soil. In fact, hemp—"

"That's all fascinating, Will," said Nate. "But perhaps a topic for another time. I'm afraid I've had a rather long day. I'm about ready to turn in."

Why would he cut this short? What was he up to?

"Sure, sure." Will reached for his pocket. "Let me get you my card. Is there a way I can get ahold of you?" He handed Nate his card.

Nate took the card and slipped it into his pocket. "I'll be in touch." He stood, offered me his hand. "Suzanne?"

I stared at his hand, raised an eyebrow, then smiled and placed my hand in his and stood. "It was nice meeting you, Will."

Will stood. "My pleasure." His eyes lit with a grin.

Who knows what he thought about us?

"Let's have a night cap, why don't we?" Nate's eyes were locked on mine, the invitation clearly to me alone.

"I'll look forward to hearing from you," said Will.

I lifted my chin, walked towards the door.

Nate followed.

In the lobby, I said, "Why'd you pull the plug?"

"Two reasons," said Nate. "One, we want him to work for it. Otherwise, he might get suspicious."

"And two?"

"I have the key to a club level suite and a hot wife."

TWENTY-TWO

I stretched and snuggled deeper into the decadent covers on a mattress that must've been made from clouds. The room brightened. I peeped out from under my eyelids. Nate stood by the window, looking out.

"Did you sleep well?" he asked.

"Like a baby," I said. "This bed is downright sinful. Also, I was tucked in quite well." I probably sounded like the cat who'd had all the cream. I surely felt like I might purr.

He was dressed, looked like he'd been up for a while, and had a cup of coffee in his hand. "Your emergency coffee's on the bedside table."

"You are a gentleman and a scholar, as I often maintain." I sat up, plumped my pillows, and reached for the mug. I inhaled deeply, the smoky, toasty aroma chasing the last vestiges of sleep away.

"I thought we'd stay in town today," said Nate. "Do you have everything you need?"

I glanced around the spacious room, through the doorway to the spacious living room with two couches and a balcony overlooking the city. Beyond that was a dining area that accommodated eight. The suite had two bathrooms. "I'm reasonably certain we could live here in comfort. I don't even want to know what this cost."

"No need to worry yourself."

"Seriously, we can't bill Darius for this suite. We could've stayed at The Hampton Inn."

He raised an eyebrow. "Would you have preferred that?"

I blushed. "Of course not."

"I can afford to occasionally treat my wife." His voice was neutral.

I felt like a shrew. "Of course. I'm so sorry. This place is spectacular. Thank you." It was an adjustment for me, this dealing with our money and what *we* could afford versus *his* money, which I really didn't have a grasp on at all. I had no separate money of my own, none to speak of anyway.

He smiled an easy smile, looked relaxed. "My pleasure. What I meant was, do you have all the clothes and things you need to stay another night in Charleston."

"I think so." I did a mental inventory. The overnight bag I kept in the car had a couple changes of clothes, a toothbrush, and duplicates of my essential cosmetics. The hotel had nice shampoo, body wash, and all like that. "I'm good. I'll call Merry and ask her to pick up Rhett."

He nodded, seemed to be lost in thought.

"What are you thinking about?" I asked.

His expression changed. He seemed to come back to the present moment from elsewhere. "Ah. Will Capers. My sense is that he's somewhat of a chameleon. To Brantley and Tyler, he's one of the guys. But he strikes me as a hustler. I don't know if he sets appointments with people and just chooses to meet at the Thoroughbred Club, or if he hangs out there looking for opportunities. Either way, he's a different breed from these other two boys."

"We need to get inside Will's apartment," I said.

"Agreed," he said. "But first, we need to get inside his phone. I know you're going to want to do the snooping. Before you do that, I need eyes and ears on him. I need to create some online background for Tommy Wright on Sullivan's Island. Then I can text Will, include a link. That will be catnip for him because he's hoping to verify that Tommy's loaded. He'll take the bait. But all that's going to take me a while to set up. Do you have something to work on?"

"I've been trying to get to scanning social media for the day Murray died and the day the house exploded. Maybe someone caught something in a photo they don't know they have. We just need to know who was in that immediate area. That's a time-consuming project."

He nodded. "We can work in the club lounge. You ready for breakfast?"

"Sure, just let me get dressed."

His expression changed, his eyes sliding from mine slowly down the rumpled pile of covers I was under and back. "Mrs. Andrews, I am sorely conflicted."

I threw a pillow at him. "You're a rascal of the first order."

"Don't you ever forget it."

After gorging on a sumptuous breakfast buffet that featured a veggie frittata, French toast, bacon, grits, biscuits and gravy, and a dizzying array of pastries and fruit, we settled into a corner table in the club lounge with our laptops. As places to work go, you'd have a hard time beating the creature comforts. The two-story space was bright and airy, with a spiral staircase rising from the seventh floor to the eighth. A full bar occupied one wall, and a bartender seemed always available to tend to any alcohol-related needs that might arise. If we'd wanted more breakfast, it was nearby, as was an endless supply of great coffee and a variety of juices. The furniture was cushy, and we had room to spread out. After the morning rush, aside from the bartender, attentive but discreet buffet attendants, and an occasional couple across the room, we had the place to ourselves.

I started with Facebook. I typed in "Montagu Street,

Charleston SC" in the search bar, then scrolled past a few pages I'd liked and posts by friends. The videos all seemed to be related to real estate listings. I skipped to photos, clicked "All," and commenced to scan. I was looking for photos taken on the morning of Tuesday, October 20, the day Murray died, or, and this seemed more promising, Saturday, October 24, the morning Murray's house exploded. It wasn't quite like looking for a needle in a haystack, but after three hours of scrolling past real estate listings, lost dog notices, community announcements, and the like, my eyes watered.

I clicked on everything that looked like a vacation photo, weeding through those taken outside my target time windows. My stomach was starting to bring up lunch when I found what I'd been hoping for: a photo of three women in front of 60 Montagu, the Galliard-Bennet House, taken at 11:45 in the morning on Saturday, October 24. About two hours before the explosion.

The photo had been posted by Rachael Palasti from Tampa, Florida. *Damnation.* I couldn't see much about her. Her privacy settings were better than most. Good for you, Rachael. She was beautiful, thirty-ish, with a warm smile. She looked like she had some Spanish or perhaps Latin American heritage. She'd tagged the two women with her: Misty Partin, a tall, gorgeous, reddish-blonde thirty-something from Lowell, NC, and Tracie Crane, a lovely woman with short salt-and-pepper hair from Myrtle Beach. Her age was hard to place, maybe late forties?

Something about the photo screamed "Girls' Trip." They leaned into each other, posing, all with bright smiles. I could see a couple shots from each of their timelines from the same day, a couple of them in a red BMW convertible. They looked like they were having a ball. They'd been to Poogan's Porch and 82 Queen, and all over the peninsula to homes, gardens, fountains, and graveyards.

I messaged each of them: Hi, my name is Liz Talbot. I'm a

private investigator from the Charleston area. I hope you can help me. I just want to ask you a few questions. It's important to a case I'm working. I promise not to take much of your time. Thank you so much! I gave them each my phone number.

Nate said, "Are you at a good stopping point for lunch?"

"Perfect timing."

"I just sent Will a text inviting him to dinner this evening," said Nate.

"Did he take the bait?"

"All of it. I have full access to his phone. And he's going to meet us at 7:00 p.m. at Grill 225."

"I'm going to need a dress," I said.

"Let's grab some lunch and pick one up," said Nate. "Will's at the farm. So are Brantley and Tyler. If we work together, we can give Will's apartment a thorough going-over before he comes home to shower and change."

TWENTY-THREE

After a quick lunch at Brown Dog Deli, we stopped at Berlin's for Women on King Street for a dress. In less than five minutes I was in a dressing room with a silk crepe de chine belted midi dress with a deep V-neck, t-shirt sleeves and a flared skirt. The print was an amalgamation of prowling leopards, blooms, and golden medallions that I might otherwise not have chosen, but in the end was quite happy with. It was elegant, it fit, and it was appropriate for dinner out in a nice restaurant. Still, the price tag was way higher than what I normally would have paid for a dress, and I balked.

"Slugger, we don't have time to hunt for bargains today." Nate took the dress to the register and handed the clerk his credit card.

I had my head in our case and decided to save the budget discussion for later.

That may be the fastest I've ever picked out a dress.

We headed south on Highway 17, crossed the Ashley River, and went left on Folly Road Boulevard, then took Maybank Highway. Once you cross the Stono River, you're on Johns Island. Along the way, Nate popped in Bluetooth earbuds to his phone and brought up the sound for Will's phone. The malware Nate had installed allowed him to eavesdrop using the microphone to Will's phone even if he wasn't on a call. Since Will was fiddling with plants and dirt, most of this was just background noise. But you never knew. Nate set an alert in case his location changed.

Will lived in a newer apartment complex on Johns Island, just off Maybank Highway. The Apartments at Shade Tree tried hard to look like a resort for young professionals. I was betting the rent wasn't budget friendly.

"According to Tyler," I said, "the farm is Will's only source of income. But he didn't start drawing checks until last month, and those are about to come to a screeching halt. But interestingly, Will did not try to talk Murray into investing the night Tyler asked."

"No way he could afford rent here on fifteen dollars an hour," said Nate.

Will's apartment was on the second floor in a pale green building overlooking the pool. Breaking and entering was easier when you had a lookout. I took my pick set out of my crossbody bag and let us in while Nate kept an eye out for company.

It was a one-bedroom apartment of maybe seven hundred square feet. We did a quick walk around to make sure there were no surprises, like an unfriendly dog or a leftover friend from the night before. Sparsely furnished in what looked like hand-me-downs and Goodwill Store finds, the apartment screamed "Bachelor Pad."

"Looks clear," said Nate. "What's your pleasure?"

I spied the desk in the corner of the living room. "I'll start in here."

"I'll be in the bedroom."

Sadly, Will had not left a laptop behind, and he had no desk calendar. Probably kept an electronic one. A stack of bills caught my eye. Nothing unusual there, typical utilities. None of them were past due. I moved on to a stack of bank statements.

Will had two accounts: a personal one and one for BTW. The most recent statement was on top, from the end of September. The BTW account had less than $10,000. Tyler had known they were low on funds, but this was all that was left of Darius's investment? When had Darius given them the $100,000? I scanned for the deposit. There, on September 21. They'd blown through ninety percent of that in around a week.

Will's personal account, on the other hand, had $375,000 dollars in it. Where did a recent college graduate come by that kind of cash? In September, there were the payroll deposits from BTW, but also two large deposits, one for $25,000 and another for $50,000. The statements listed both as simply a "check deposit."

There were withdrawals for rent and utilities, gas and groceries, and a string of restaurants. He'd been a regular at the Thoroughbred Club. I snapped pictures of each page and moved to the August statement.

Shit. In August, there were four deposits of $25,000 each. He must be finding investors and depositing the money straight into his account. He'd been smart enough not to do that with Darius's money. But how many other investors were there and what kind of deals had they signed?

I looked around for a filing cabinet. There wasn't one in the living room. I stuck my head in the bedroom door. "You see a filing cabinet anywhere?"

"No," said Nate. "There's not one in the closet either. Could be they use electronic documents. DocuSign, something like that."

"I think I figured out why Will wants to bring in so many investors," I said.

"Yeah? Why's that?"

"Because he's depositing the money into his account, not the company's. No telling how many people have a piece, or how big a piece they think they have."

"Any evidence he's paid any of the money back to investors? Like a Ponzi scheme?"

"Not so far. I'm going to check for another closet somewhere."

I wandered into the kitchen and pushed open the door on the back wall. Laundry room. There, across from the washer and dryer, next to the water heater, was a two-drawer file cabinet. I opened the top drawer. There were fourteen folders, loosely hanging. I picked up the first one and opened it. The only document was a contract signed by Darius Baker and all three partners. I refiled it and moved to the next folder.

This contract was between BTW and Harold Holder. It was long and convoluted. He'd invested $25,000. Looked like he'd be paid back after the first harvest, plus 10 percent of the harvest profit. There was no mention of what that profit was projected to be. Still, to pay back an investor after the first harvest seemed aggressive, but what did I know? The document was signed by William Fields Capers, President of BTW.

Was Will the president? I'd had the impression the three of them were all making decisions together, with no one in charge. I called Tyler.

"Is Will Capers the president of your company?" I asked when he answered.

"What? No. Nobody is. The three of us are all owners. Why?" he asked.

"I'll fill you in later. Whatever you do, don't tell him I asked."

He was quiet for a few seconds. "You'll need to ask Flannery about that, but I don't think anybody inherits anything except her and me."

"Will's right there, isn't he?" Shit. Of course. Stupid, stupid, stupid.

"That's right."

"Talk soon."

Shit.

I took a picture of the contract, then refiled it and moved to the next folder. Same contract, different name. The contract in the next folder accepted an investment of $50,000, with repayment after first harvest plus 20 percent of the harvest profit. What percentage of that first harvest profit had he signed away? This scheme of Will's was no doubt what had gotten Murray Hamilton killed. He'd been suspicious of Will, reconnoitered the situation, and wound up dead for his trouble.

Nate came to the door. "We need to roll. Will's left the farm. Looks like he's headed here. He's twelve minutes out."

"It's only 3:30," I said.

"Maybe it takes him a while to get pretty." Nate's face was tense.

"Did you find something?" I asked.

"No. I heard the conversation between Tyler, Will, and Brantley after you called," he said.

"I can't believe I was so stupid."

"You didn't hurt anything. Tyler covered it well. Said it was you, asking about the will. Said he was thankful to Darius for hiring us."

"And?"

"Brantley jumped in, tellin' how you're convinced he set the fire that killed his parents, that you're like a dog with a bone. Probably never gonna let that rest 'til somebody's in jail, probably him."

"That's not true. I actually had a nice chat with Brantley Tuesday morning. I'm willing to allow it might've been an accident. Why is that making you look stressed?"

He rubbed his neck with the back of his hand. "I wish now we'd taken the time to get into disguises last night. Makes me nervous two of them knowing you as Liz and the other as Suzanne."

"It's not like they have a picture of me and are comparing notes."

"You ready?"

I closed the file cabinet and followed him out.

We were crossing the Ashley River on the way back into town when I got the call from Rachael Palasti, one of the women I'd messaged through Facebook. She was still in town, spending another week in Charleston with her husband.

"Tracie lives in Myrtle Beach," she said. "And Misty is in Ladson, visiting her aunt. That's only thirty minutes away. Tracie said she didn't mind driving back. We can't imagine how we could help possibly with an investigation, but it sounds fun. We were thinking we'd get to see each other again if we all met in Charleston. We wanted to go to Twenty-Six Divine anyway, and we couldn't get reservations before they left. Could we all meet there at 3:00 tomorrow afternoon for tea? I made a reservation, just in case."

Naturally, I agreed. The symmetry was irresistible. With any luck, one of them caught Will on camera at Murray's house right before the explosion.

TWENTY-FOUR

I'd just gotten out of the shower and wrapped up in the Belmond's waffle weave robe when Colleen popped in. I'd shut the door and the bathroom was steamy, the mirror fogged up. Normally, Colleen would amuse herself writing on the mirror. She seemed subdued that afternoon.

"What's wrong?" I asked her as I reached for my moisturizer.

"I've been thinking a lot lately," she said.

"Clearly not happy thoughts."

"I'm afraid I've given you a false sense of security. That you take chances you shouldn't because you think I'll always save you."

"Have you been talking to Nate, or my dad?"

"Liz, I'm serious."

I put the moisturizer jar down, looked at her. She was as serious as I'd seen her in quite a while. "What are you telling me?"

"I will always protect you if I can. But there are times when someone else might take priority. I don't get to choose."

"I know that. And I can take care of myself, you know. Like the time in Magnolia Cemetery, when you were looking after Daddy. I managed just fine on my own, didn't I?"

"This is exactly what I'm talking about."

"You don't want me to take care of myself?" I asked.

"Of course I want you to take care of yourself. The best way to do that is to avoid situations where you might get shot at or stabbed or hit over the head or whatever."

"I assure you, I do my best to avoid getting killed."

"You could do better."

"Colleen. Right now, I'm not aware of any threat to my safety. Is there something in specific you want me to avoid? Just tell me. I feel like we're playing games here."

"You love Nate, don't you?" she asked.

"You know I do."

"So much that...it would be really, really hard for you if anything happened to him." Tears glimmered in her eyes.

"Colleen, you're scaring me. I don't know what I'd do if anything happened to Nate. I just couldn't bear it."

She swallowed hard. "I know. Just remember that he feels exactly the same way about you. If you're in danger, he's not going to wait to see if I show up or not. He's going to do whatever he has to do to save you."

What was she not telling me?

Colleen drew a deep breath. "Even if it costs him his life, he will save yours. I can't intervene to save Nate. That would be a breach of my hard-and-fast mission rules. I'd be changing the course of human history—the way things are meant to play out. I'm breaking the spirit of the rules by having this conversation."

Something cold and hard clamped down on my heart.

"Promise me," she said, "that you'll be careful to stay safe so it never comes to that."

"I promise." What nightmare was headed our way?

"You know how sometimes you feel like your Gram is watching you?"

I squinted at her, nodded.

"Sometimes she is. People that you love are never really gone. Even the ones most people can't see, like me. Even if you couldn't see me, I'd still be around."

"I'm glad I can see you and talk to you. It's almost like it was when you were..."

"Mortal. I know. But even if it wasn't, I'd still be around. Don't forget that. Promise me."

"I promise, but—"

"I have to go. Bring me a doggy bag. I bet tonight's meal is going to be fabulous."

She disappeared in a pouf of grey smoke and sparkles.

My hands were shaking so badly I could barely put my makeup on.

Grill 225 was one of my very favorite restaurants in Charleston. That particular evening, I wasn't sure if I'd be able to eat a bite. Colleen had scared me badly. I had this deep sense of foreboding, but it made no sense. There were no threats to our safety, at least none that I could see.

A smiling valet escorted us to the hostess stand. Normally, we love to sit in one of the curved-back booths, but for our purposes that evening, Nate had requested the corner table by the window. Our reservation was for 7:00 p.m. We arrived right on time, but Will wasn't there yet. Nate asked the hostess to go ahead and seat us.

In a well-fitting black sheath dress, like her surroundings, she exuded elegance. "Of course." She smiled and led the way, gliding across the gleaming hardwood floors in her four-inch stilettos. I admired her dedication, but was thinking how she would likely wish for different shoes before the evening was over.

Nearly every white-clothed table was taken in the dark-wood-paneled dining room, but somehow, the noise level was subdued. A jazz combo played in the adjacent bar, music drifting through the restaurant at a level that diners could enjoy while still having a conversation. The high tray ceilings bordered by thick moulding added to the opulent ambiance.

Nate held the chair at the seat facing out the window for me, then took the seat with his back to the corner. I'd started my phone recording before we came in. Nate still monitored Will's phone. At ten after seven, Nate raised his chin, looked in the direction of the host stand. "Here he comes." Nate discreetly slipped his Bluetooth earpiece out.

We stood and said hey and all that, then Will sat across from Nate, to my right. If Will had any opinions about seeing Suzanne with Tommy after my somewhat fickle response to him last night, he covered them well.

"Why don't we settle on cocktails?" said Nate. "I know Suzanne is going to want a Nitrotini of some sort." I had planned to pace myself, but perhaps my husband knew I needed something to settle my nerves. I did love the signature cocktails here. The Nitrotinis were a line of martinis chilled to minus 320 degrees by infusing them with liquid nitrogen.

"Maybe the Peach Blossom this evening," I said.

Will perused the cocktail menu.

Our waiter approached and welcomed us.

Nate said, "I'd like a classic vodka martini—the really cold one—with olives. The lady will have the Peach Blossom." He looked at Will.

"I guess I'll try the 225 Rum Punch Nitrotini." He laughed as he said it, like maybe he was uncomfortable.

"I'll be right back with those." The waiter left us to study the menus.

"I'm really glad you called," Will addressed Nate. "I've got several people who want in on BTW. I like you. I hope we can work this out. I'd like to see you make a lot of money off this."

Nate held his gaze. "Is that right?" His tone was low, easy. I was probably the only one who recognized the challenge in his words.

Will cleared his throat. "I've got a limited number of opportunities—"

Nate said, "Let's not get in a rush now, Will. We haven't even decided on dinner yet. There'll be plenty of time for talking business after we've eaten."

Will pursed his lips, nodded. "Of course."

We lingered over our cocktails. After a couple sips of the icy liquid I felt my nerves ease. This would be a long meal, and a delicious one. No sense ruining it worrying about things I had no control over.

For our first course, Nate and I had the Creme d' Crab and Will ordered a shrimp cocktail. Then Nate had the 225 Chopped Caesar, I had the bibb lettuce salad, and Will had the iceberg wedge. I ordered the filet foie gras for my entree, my favorite thing at Grill 225. The flavor combination of the steak, the sliced foie gras, the truffled Béarnaise, the Parmesan, and the fig demi-glace was purely divine. Nate and Will ordered rib eyes, big ones, and Nate ordered sautéed maitake mushrooms, creamed corn with jalapeño and cheddar, and hash browns for the table.

And naturally, Nate ordered wine—pinot grigio for the first course and salad, and Cabernet for the steaks. By the time the waiter was offering us dessert menus, we were all stuffed. Naturally, that didn't stop me from ordering the chocolate mousse cake. I had a role to play. And the dessert was quite good, even if I could only hold a bite. The cloud-like chocolate over a macadamia nut fudge crust, with a rich chocolate ganache and strawberries, was truly remarkable.

"I should take this home," I said. Colleen would love it. *Colleen.* Anxiety coiled itself around my throat and squeezed. I struggled to breath.

I fake-dropped my napkin, slid my phone out of the side pocket of my purse, and laid it on the floor between Nate and me. I didn't want to miss recording any of his conversation with Will. "Would you gentlemen excuse me?"

Nate stood. "Are you all right?"

"I'm fine." I smiled. "I just need to powder my nose."

Will gave me a half nod. He seemed eager for me to leave so he could talk business with Nate. That was fine with me. All we needed tonight was him on tape offering something he couldn't possibly deliver. The longer he was prevented from pitching Nate, the more likely he was to give us that.

When I returned from the ladies' room, Will was in mid spiel. "...return on your investment."

Nate stood as I returned to the table.

Perhaps to impress him, Will did as well.

"Suzanne, honey, what do you think? Our friend here has offered me 25 percent of the profits on their first harvest. I have to say, it sounds promising, this venture."

"Tommy, I'm sure if you think it's a good deal, it must truly be." I smiled that smile I'd seen on my mamma's face a million times—the one that said, "You are the man, and therefore truly brilliant," but actually meant, "I honestly couldn't care less than a tinker's damn."

Nate smothered a laugh. He knew me well. "Will, how many other investors do you currently have?"

"One major one. You might've heard of him. Darius Baker?"

Nate grinned. "Ah—the *Main Street USA* guy. Right. Sure. *He's* one of your investors?"

How many people had Will lured to invest by trading on Darius's name?

"Sure is," said Will.

"Aside from him," said Nate, "how many other investors are there?"

"Two right now," said Will. "But they each only get a 5 percent of the first harvest profit. That's why, like I told you, I only have room for one more significant investor, or several smaller ones."

Nate signaled the waiter for our check. "I guess I'd better get on board then. How fast can you have the paperwork ready?"

TWENTY-FIVE

It took me a few minutes to place the noise. The hotel room was pitch black. I glanced at the clock. One fifteen. I reached for my phone. The alarm at the house had been triggered. I'd installed the system myself, right after I'd moved home. It wasn't monitored by a service. No one would be alerted aside from us. There were wireless cameras tied into the Wi-Fi in trees around the yard and in air vents all through the house. All of them were motion-sensor activated.

I scrolled through the camera displays. Everything was quiet. Had an animal triggered one of the outdoor cameras? I pulled up the notifications. The Wi-Fi was down. The system had switched to the cellular backup I'd installed after an incident involving a snake.

What in this world was going on? I continued scrolling through the live feeds, then tapped the history icon and reviewed the last thing recorded.

Sonavabitch. On the screen, Will Capers came through the front door.

We must've somehow blown our cover.

Rhett.

He was at Merry's house. Thank goodness.

I reached over and shook Nate awake. "*Sweetheart.*"

"Hmm?"

"We have a burglar."

He sat straight up, instantly awake.

I handed him my phone.

"What the hell?" he asked.

"He was so eager to do business with us not four hours ago. I don't understand it."

He rubbed his hands over his face. "This makes no sense." He jumped out of bed and started throwing on clothes.

I followed suit. "Should I call Blake? Wait—no." I didn't want my brother walking into a situation where we didn't know what to expect. He was going to be a father soon.

"It's Will," said Nate. "He's a kid. We can surely handle this. We just need to get home. Fast."

"Well, we can't board the Amelia Ruth until 6:30."

"We need a boat," said Nate. "Something small we can land on the beach."

"If I call Sonny, he'll call Blake, no doubt about it. Blake'll be there before we can possibly get there."

"Don't do that."

"I know." I picked up my phone. "James Huger has a sailboat at Ripley Light Marina. It has a dinghy."

Nate landed the Zodiak on the beach in front of the house. We hopped out and ran for the walkway, then soft-footed it up to the backyard. As soon as we cleared the dunes, we jumped off into the sand and dashed under the deck. It was 2:20, just over an hour since I'd gotten the alarm. Will was still in the house. I'd monitored him on my phone as best I could in a small boat in the pitch dark. The ride was choppy.

"Where is he now?" Nate asked.

I looked at the screen, tapped through the cameras. "I don't see him. But five minutes ago he was outside our bedroom. What the devil is he doing?"

"I'm going in the front and straight up the stairs," said Nate. "Wait here, under the deck."

"Like hell I will," I said. "You're not going in there by yourself." I was truly torn, had no idea the best course to keep my husband safe. I knew deep in my bones that I was living what Colleen had warned me about. She wasn't coming. And I had to avoid putting myself in danger or it might cost Nate his life.

On the other hand, letting him go in alone might also risk his life. I'd debated it with myself all the way from Charleston. There was no easy answer.

Nate sighed, shook his head. "Fine. Put your Bluetooth in." He tapped his phone and opened our two-way channel, then slipped his earpiece in.

I pulled mine out of the backpack I'd brought and put it in. "Test."

"Gotcha. Wait a minute, then climb the stairs to the deck. I'll let you know when I'm going in the front. You come in through the back at the same time. We'll clear the house room by room, starting with our room and working our way down."

I nodded. "Be careful."

His eyes blazed hot and bright. "*You* be careful."

He took off running around the house towards the front. It took everything I had to let him go. I crept towards the bottom of the deck steps. Because the house was raised, sitting on top of the over-sized garage, the deck was sixteen feet off the ground. There were twenty-five steps. To maximize the views, the back of the house had a lot of glass. I crouched as low as I could and tiptoed up the steps, then eased across the deck to the back door. I kept an eye on my phone, trying to catch Will when a camera picked him up.

Nate's voice murmured in my ear. "I'm going in now."

I slid my key in the deadbolt and unlocked the back door, then eased it open and closed it behind me. I slid the key back into my backpack and strained my ears to hear anything.

Creak. The third step. Nate was on his way up.

I put my phone in the backpack and pulled my Sig 9 out of my waistband. Then I headed through the sunroom to the entry hall.

As quietly as possible, I crept up the stairs. My head cleared the landing. No one was in the hall. I moved to the first room on the left, Nate's office. I scanned the room in the darkness. No one was there.

I stepped out into the hall and moved to the next room, a guest room overlooking the back of the house. I cleared it and moved on to the largest of the guest rooms, the one overlooking the front that had once been mine. It was empty too.

A sound I couldn't identify came from the hallway.

"Freeze, you sonavabitch. What the hell are you doing in my house?" Nate's voice.

I flew to the doorway.

Nate stood outside our bedroom, his gun trained on Will at the opposite end of the hall near the top of the stairs. He held a backpack by the top loop with his right hand.

"Your house?" Will's voice was incredulous. "What the hell? I thought you lived on Sullivan's Island."

Then he saw me in the doorway. Disbelief battled with confusion on his face. His expression changed, realization dawning. Then his face hardened. "I guess this means you won't be investing." He hurled the backpack towards Nate and shot down the stairs.

I gave chase.

The backpack landed in my path. My right foot caught in one of the straps and I went sprawling. "*Damnation.*"

"*Liz.*" Nate closed the distance between us, reached out a hand.

I grabbed it.

He pulled me up. "You all right?"

I darted towards the stairs. "Fine, just pissed."

Nate was fast on my heels.

The front door stood open, no sign of Will.

I flew out onto the front porch, scanned the yard. In the darkness, I could only see partway down the driveway. He was nowhere to be found.

Nate pulled up behind me. "No car. Maybe he parked down the road. Or at Darius's place. Could be he's staying with Brantley."

"*Dammit.*" I pulled the backpack off my shoulder, grabbed my phone from the front pocket, and opened the tracking app. "We were focused on monitoring him with his phone and our security system. His car's at Darius's house. I'll call him, give him a heads up."

"Let's make sure Will's left the premises first," said Nate. "I'll check the garage."

"I'll lock this door behind me and bolt it, then clear the house."

"I'll clear the perimeter," said Nate.

I went inside, threw the deadbolt, and put the floor bolt in place. Will might've picked the lock, but the floor bolt was another matter altogether. It could only be secured from inside, and the only way to breach it was to ram the door with something substantial. We'd be more careful about making sure the floor bolts on the front and back doors were engaged when we left from now on. The mudroom door didn't have one—we had to get out somehow. But the walk-through door to the garage did. Was it in place?

I moved through the downstairs checking each room. Empty.

"You okay?" I asked Nate through the headset.

"Fine. Coming up through the garage."

"I'm in the sunroom." I opened the door and stepped out onto the deck, walked over to the stairs, and scanned the yard.

My mind raced, trying to wrap around what Will was doing here and why. He'd been confused to see us at first. He knew us as Tommy and Suzanne. Brantley and Tyler had told him Darius had hired Talbot & Andrews Investigations. Had we not blown our cover after all? Did he not know Tommy and Suzanne were the same people as Liz Talbot and Nate Andrews until he saw us on the landing? If not, what possible motive could he have to break into our home?

I heard running, turned.

Will was three feet away from me, gun pointed straight at my head.

Faster than I could possibly have imagined, Nate flew into him and catapulted both of them over the rail.

I screamed, scrambled for the steps.

It took forever for me to get back down those twenty-five steps. My ears roared. I couldn't hear anything.

Just as I made the bottom step, Nate, whole and unscathed, appeared on the path from the left side of the yard. He walked towards me in a shimmery glowing white puffy cloud.

Oh my sweet Lord. Nate was dead. He must be dead and somehow he could come to me, like Colleen. What had she said?

"Liz? Sweetheart?" He put his arms around me and pulled me close "Shhh. Shhh. Shhh. It's all right. I'm all right."

I only realized I'd still been screaming when I stopped. I pulled back, confused, searched his face.

"It must've been Colleen," he said. "I never hit the ground. I'm fine."

I grabbed him and hugged him tight, gulped in huge lungfuls of air.

"Will?" I asked.

Nate shook his head. "He's gone. Broke his neck in the fall."

And then above us, there were fireworks. Shimmering gold and white fireworks, the prettiest I'd ever seen. Colleen. She'd saved Nate and broken the rules. I knew she was telling us goodbye.

I sat down on the steps and cried.

Nate held me close and I prayed, thanking God he was alive, begging God not to be mad at Colleen. And I began the process of mourning the loss of my best friend for the second time.

TWENTY-SIX

Getting a forensics unit from the sheriff's department to Stella Maris takes a while in the wee small hours of the morning. We sat in Blake's Tahoe while he, Clay Cooper, his second in command, and Doc Harper, the town doctor who served as our medical examiner, did their jobs. By the time the forensics team arrived, we were headed back to Charleston to shower and change.

We met that afternoon at 1:30 in Fraser and Eli's conference room: Tyler and Flannery, Brantley and Darius, Nate and me, and Fraser and Eli. Nate and I took turns talking, explaining what all had happened in the last twenty-four hours. It hadn't taken long to figure out exactly what Will had been up to, and why, once we looked inside his backpack. It took a while to explain it, though.

We'd given Fraser the highlights. He was uncharacteristically quiet while we explained things to the clients, at least at first.

"Brantley," I said, "remember when I asked you if your family in Travelers Rest knew Will and Tyler?"

He nodded, "Sure. I told you we all spent a lot of time there."

"Sorta like you did at Murray Hamilton's house here, right?" asked Nate.

"Yeah, I guess," said Brantley.

Darius said, "Is this gonna be a long story? If it is, I wonder if we can just do the Cliff's Notes version. Just rip the Band-Aid right off. Y'all got me apprehensive already."

I cut Darius a look. This was going to be difficult for Brantley. But we were exhausted, running on fumes. I wasn't even sure how to tell this story gently. I turned back to Brantley. "When you were discussing Professor Hamilton's death, you told Will that Darius had hired Nate and me, right?"

"Right." Brantley still wore a mystified look. "We all talked about it. You helping Tyler."

"You told him our names?" Nate asked. "Not just that investigators had been hired?"

"I know I mentioned your names," said Tyler.

"Yeah, we all talked about y'all," said Brantley. "I told Ty and Will that y'all had worked for Darius before. Why? Was that supposed to be a secret?"

"No, not at all," I said. "When you were at the farm yesterday, you and Tyler and Will, you mentioned to them, didn't you, that one of the other things we looked into for Darius was your adoptive family's deaths? You thought Nate and I were still pursuing, perhaps relentlessly, what caused the fire that killed your family?"

Brantley flushed. "Yeah, I said something like that."

"Did you say that you thought I wouldn't leave that alone until someone was in jail?" I asked. "Probably you?"

Brantley cleared his throat, looked away. "Yeah."

Darius said, "Why are we still talking about those poor folks up in Travelers Rest? I thought we were here to talk about who killed Professor Hamilton. Can you please leave Brantley's—"

"Mr. Baker?" said Fraser.

Darius turned to Fraser, squinted at him.

"I am certain Miz Talbot and Mr. Andrews will get to that momentarily. I beg your indulgence." Fraser nodded at me to continue.

Darius sighed, shook his head. "Fine."

"Brantley," said Nate, "did Will ever visit you at Darius's house?"

"Yeah," said Brantley, "several times. He came over late last night. Was all excited about a new investor. Someone from

Sullivan's Island. He spent the night, but he was gone this morning before I got up."

"Did you ever tell him where we lived?" I asked. Of course, Will could've gotten that information from real property records, but he might not've known that.

Brantley gave a half shrug. "Well yeah, you live right down the beach from Darius."

Tyler said, "We were all there for dinner Wednesday night. The three of us went for a walk on the beach. Brantley pointed out a bunch of different places, The Pirates' Den, the marina. And your house. Nice place."

"Thanks." I gave Tyler a small, sad smile. "I hate to be the one to have to tell y'all this, but Will died this morning."

"*What?*" Brantley and Tyler spoke at the same time. Shock and confusion covered both their faces.

"What the hell happened?" asked Darius.

Nate took them through it, from the time we woke up to the alarm, until Will had a gun to my head. "I knocked him away from Liz, at a run. We both went over the side of the deck. It's a sixteen-foot drop. I was very lucky. Will was not. He broke his neck in the fall."

"I'm just tryin' to think *why* in this world Will Capers would want to *kill* y'all?" Darius's entire face was puckered up like someone had tried to close it with a drawstring.

"We were stumped by that too," I said. "Until we saw the contents of his backpack."

"Well, tell us," said Darius. "Y'all're killin' me. What was in there?"

Nate said, "Two Ziploc bags of dead batteries, some nine volt, some double A. And some fresh double A's loose in the backpack."

"Say what?" asked Darius.

I said, "Most of our smoke alarms had bad batteries. Nate just changed them Tuesday morning. But Will was in the process of swapping them all out for dead batteries. After which, I'm sure his plan was to come back and set fire to the house one night when we were home, asleep in bed."

"You're thinking Will killed my family the same way." Brantley wore a stunned look.

"I'm afraid so," I said. "It appears he wanted to get rid of us because we wouldn't let their deaths go, and if we kept digging long enough, we might figure out it was him, not you. By killing us the same way they died—in a fire, with smoke detectors that failed to function—our theory is that he hoped to cast suspicion on you."

Tyler asked, "But how did he get back in the house? After he ran out the front door?"

"One of two ways," said Nate. "We may never know for sure which. Either he never left the house to begin with, just opened the door to make us think that, then slipped back up the stairs while we were on the front porch, or, he circled around the house and came back in through the garage, the same way I did, but ahead of me. Again, he must've gone back upstairs while we were outside."

"But why would he come back?" asked Brantley.

"When he ran, it was an act of desperation," I said. "Nate had a gun on him. Nate wouldn't have fired at an unarmed man, but Will couldn't have known that. He wasn't going to wait for us to call the police and have him arrested either. Will had to run, but he'd be faster without the backpack, and he needed something to throw as a diversion. But inside the backpack was his gun and the dead batteries."

Nate said, "He figured out we'd put everything together when we saw the dead batteries. He came back for the backpack, but also, it appears, because he decided to kill us more expeditiously, with a gun. When we caught him in the act of switching out the smoke alarm batteries, he had to change plans. And he must've figured we were onto him about some other things once he figured out who we were."

"I told you Brantley didn't have nothing to do with any fire," said Darius. "But, uh...why would Will kill the Millers to begin with? Y'all not saying he was some kind of psychopath, are you? Because I spent time with that boy, and he didn't strike me as a stone-cold killer."

"It was the money." Brantley's voice was bitter.

"What money?" asked Darius. "The insurance money?"

"That's right," said Brantley. "That's the first money any of us had, for the farm. That was our original seed money. I didn't give him all of it. I told you." He looked at Darius, then me.

"Fifty thousand dollars," I said.

Brantley nodded. "That's right."

"*Day*-um." Darius shook his head slowly. "L'il sucker looked like a altar boy or somethin'. All innocent. Goes to show you."

"You think you know somebody," said Tyler. "I would never a dreamed Will was capable of something like that."

Brantley's eyes shown with unshed tears. "Me either. And I have to live with that. I brought him into my family's home. And he killed them all. For fifty thousand dollars."

Darius put a hand on his son's shoulder. "Monsters like that are good at hiding what they are. No way you coulda known." He turned to Nate. "What 'other things' was Will into? What ch'all mean, 'he figured out who you are?'"

Nate and I went through the multiple investors, the percentages promised, the money that went directly into Will's account, and Tommy and Suzanne's sting operation.

Fraser said, "We have a capable forensic accountant who will sort out the financial end of things. We will need to disentangle Mr. Miller and Mr. Duval from Mr. Capers's estate."

Tyler said, "So when he broke into your house to swap out the batteries in your smoke alarms, he knew Liz Talbot and Nate Andrews were investigating both Brantley's family's deaths and Uncle Murray's death, but he'd only ever *met* y'all as Tommy and

Suzanne?"

"That's right," said Nate. "He was shocked when he saw us in the house. Liz and Nate were just names to him."

"Did Will kill Uncle Murray too?" asked Flannery.

"We can't prove that yet," I said. "But it sure looks that way. Your uncle was suspicious of Will. He knew that Tyler and Brantley wanted to keep the company close. But Will seemed forever to be meeting with potential investors. Professor Hamilton went to Will's favorite meeting place, the Thoroughbred Club, a few times. We think it's likely Will saw him there, figured out he was on to him, or at least that he was suspicious and might influence Tyler to extricate himself from the partnership."

"That's why Will wasn't gung-ho about getting Uncle Murray to invest," said Tyler. "It's hard to believe he was cheating us the way he was. And I hate to think what would've eventually happened. I guess he was planning to take the money and run, leave us holding the bag. All of that seems surreal. But that he killed Uncle Murray—and Brantley's family too. That's a real hard pill to swallow."

"So many lives destroyed because of one man's greed." Flannery shook her head.

"I just can't believe it," said Brantley.

"It's like he wiped out a big chunk of our lives," said Tyler. "Uncle Murray...of course he's the most important thing—to Flannery and me—but insult to injury, all the memories in his house. That was our home too, for a lot of years. Our childhood pictures. Things that belonged to our mother."

Flannery nodded. "I was just thinking about that same thing. Mamma's picture albums. Her journals. There were so many things I hadn't gotten around to getting since Keith and I got married—since I moved out. I always thought I had plenty of time, no rush. We make that same mistake all the time, don't we? Thinking we have time?"

I had trouble catching my breath, couldn't help but think of Colleen. I was heartsick and mad as hell at what Will Capers had nearly cost me personally, and what he had cost me. I almost missed what Flannery said next.

"...that picture, you know, the one in the carved frame? From the aquarium—with Professor Fish? I'd love to have that picture. I kept meaning to have it copied."

"I think I saw that," I said.

Flannery looked confused. "I'm afraid it blew up in his house. There was only one. They took it at the aquarium, one of those memento things they do with your group."

TWENTY-SEVEN

I wanted to head straight to Professor Fishburne's house. But I needed time to think, needed to plan. Besides, I would've felt awful canceling on Rachael, Misty, and Tracie at the last minute. Could it possibly have been only twenty-four hours since I'd spoken to Rachael on the phone? Tracie had driven more than two hours from Myrtle Beach. Misty had driven down from nearby Ladson. I barely had time to get to Twenty-Six Divine after we left Rutledge & Radcliffe.

Rachael had arranged for a table near the back, overlooking a small courtyard. We poured our tea—Tracie and I had peach and Misty and Rachael had Charleston Breakfast tea—and added our choice of sweeteners, milk, and lemon.

"How long have y'all known each other?" I asked.

Tracie said, "A couple years. We met online, in a Facebook group, if you can believe it. We all like to read books set in the South Carolina Lowcountry."

"Sounds fun," I said. "So y'all decided to spend time here together?"

"Rachael lives the farthest. She's in Florida," said Misty. "When she decided to come here with her husband for vacation, we added on a few days for a girls' trip. He was a good sport about it."

"Tell us about your case," said Tracie.

"How can *we* help?" asked Rachael.

Our server arrived carrying tiered cake plates overflowing with assorted sandwiches, deviled eggs, scones, biscotti, cake pops, and tarts. She set small dishes of lemon curd and clotted cream to the side. As we fixed our plates, I asked if they'd heard about the explosion on Montagu hours after they'd been there.

Misty's eyes got huge. "Yes! We couldn't believe that. We heard it on the news and we've been trying to follow it, but there hasn't been much said after the initial reports."

"Is that your case?" asked Rachael.

"It is," I said. "I think we have it mostly wrapped up. I can't talk about the particulars, of course, but I was wondering if maybe y'all had seen something in the area. Maybe something that didn't strike you as important at the time?" I pulled out my phone and showed them photos of the mostly empty lot where Professor Hamilton's house had been.

They each took a bite of sandwich, seemed to mull it over.

"Like, what kind of thing might we have seen?" asked Tracie.

"Someone where they shouldn't have been," I said. "Anyone at all in this yard, where the house exploded."

Rachael shook her head. "I really don't even remember the house. We were on our way to tour 60 Montagu."

Misty said, "We were all talking, having a good time. I don't think we were very *aware*."

"Well," I said, "it was worth a try."

"Did you say you'd solved your case?" asked Tracie.

"Yes." I smiled. "So we can just relax and enjoy our tea."

"That was such a fun day," said Rachael.

"I can't wait to do it again," said Misty. "We're hoping to make it a yearly thing."

"I want to rent the exact same convertible," said Tracie. "But maybe we'll let Misty or me drive." She and Misty laughed.

"What do you mean?" asked Rachael. "There's nothing wrong with my driving."

"Tell that to the old guy you practically ran over," said Misty.

"I'd forgotten all about him," said Rachael. "That was scary."

"What happened?" I asked.

"We were driving down Montagu—right before we went to tour 60 Montagu—and this man just ran straight out in front of us. I barely stopped. Like, the car was touching him. He had this crazed look on his face."

"Yeah, and he was holding on to something," said Rachael. "Clutching it to his chest."

"It was a picture," said Misty. "I thought he was having a heart attack or something. But he walked away and into a house on the other side of the street."

Sweet reason, they'd seen Pierce Fishburne right after he set Murray Hamilton's house to explode.

"Would you recognize him, do you think?" I asked.

"Maybe," said Rachael.

I pulled up a picture of Pierce Fishburne from his electronic profile and showed it around.

"Yep, that's him," said Rachael.

Misty and Tracie both nodded.

TWENTY-EIGHT

Pierce Fishburne didn't look surprised to see me at the door. He looked from me to Nate. I did the introductions.

"What can I do for you?" he asked.

"I wondered if we could go over one or two things from our conversation the other day," I said. "It won't take but a minute."

"Very well." He led us into the living room, made a gesture towards the chairs, and sat on the sofa.

"Professor Fishburne, you and Professor Hamilton spent quite a lot of time together, didn't you?" I asked.

"Yes, I told you. He was my best friend for thirty years."

"You were a part of his family, really, weren't you?" I asked.

"I'd like to think so," said Professor Fishburne.

"And the two of you had lunch together every single day, that right?" I asked.

"Weekdays," he said. "Weekends we did other things, with the kids when they were younger. Then we took up fishing. Until recently, anyway."

"How many years have the two of you been having lunch together five days a week?" I asked.

"Close to thirty years." His voice softened.

"You had a system, didn't you?" I smiled. "How did it go?"

"It changed over time," said Professor Fishburne. "Most recently, we had Millers All Day on Monday. Tuesday was Dell'z Uptown. Wednesdays we went to Jestine's Kitchen. Thursday was Asian. Our current spot was Xiao Bao Biscuit. Fridays we splurged a bit. We went to Magnolia's, sometimes 82 Queen. Again, what does any of this have to do with Murray's death?"

"You mentioned Professor Hamilton was worried about his weight," I said.

He shrugged. "Yeah, he'd put on a couple pounds. That's not what killed him."

"But he was worried about it, right?" I asked.

"He was," said Professor Fishburne.

"Did he mention what he planned to do about that?" I offered him a smile. "Was he going on a diet?"

Professor Fishburne looked away, at something to his right. "He talked about it."

"What sort of diet was he thinking about?" I asked. "Weight Watchers? The Mediterranean diet?"

"He was going to cut back," said Professor Fishburne. "What the devil does this have to do with his death?"

"Was he going to give up tea with Annalise?" I asked.

Professor Fishburne gave a bitter little half chuckle. "No, I don't think so. You'd have to ask her about that."

"You know what she told me?" I asked. "She said she doesn't eat lunch. She has a good breakfast, then works through lunch. Tea is her main meal of the day. I had tea with her myself the other day. I have to say, it was fabulous. I was thinking to myself, if she put together a spread like that for me every day at four, I'd probably give up lunch too."

Professor Fishburne's eyes glittered with something that approached hatred.

"Is that what Murray Hamilton was going to do?" I asked. "Give up your traditional lunches together?"

He glared at me, didn't answer.

"I was admiring that photo the other day." I looked at the framed picture from the aquarium. "That must be a happy memory."

Pierce nodded. "It was."

"When was that taken?" Nate asked. "It looks recent."

He lifted his chin a bit. "In May. We spent the day together."

"It's interesting," I said, "because Flannery said her Uncle Murray had the only copy."

The professor shrugged. "Guess not."

"It must've been really hard for you, when Murray started dating Annalise," I said.

"What do you mean?" He scowled.

"Murray was your best friend. You spent all your time with him, for decades. The two of you were thick as thieves. Annalise moves in, and in a couple of months, everything changes."

He looked down at his lap, didn't say anything.

"It was bad enough when he started internet dating," I said. "But that never amounted to much, did it?"

"I told you that," he said.

"But Annalise, she was entirely different. Murray spent a lot of time with her, didn't he?" I asked. "But the last straw was when he told you he was going to give up your lunches together. It was tradition. That hurt you badly, didn't it?"

One side of his upper lip curled up just a bit. He nearly snarled at me. Then his lip quivered. Maybe it wasn't a snarl after all. His gaze returned to his lap.

"Professor, do you remember when you were running from Murray Hamilton's house across the street, right after you set the explosion?" I asked.

"You're out of your mind," he said.

"You were nearly hit by a car, a red convertible," I said. "You were clutching that picture to your chest." I pointed to the frame.

"We have three witnesses," said Nate.

"You meant the poison for her, didn't you, Professor?" I kept my voice soft.

He looked up, misery in his eyes. He stared at me for a long moment, looked away, then back. Then he nodded. His voice broke. "I loved Murray like the brother I never had. I would never have hurt him, not in a million years. You have to understand. He and Tyler and Flannery, they were my family. All the family I had. And she...she changed everything. Suddenly, I was nothing but a bit character in someone else's story."

"You must've tried to slip her something earlier," I said.

He was shaking. He nodded. "I...I think I must've snapped a little. They had tea every day. Murray must've felt bad for me. He invited me a couple weeks before and I went. It was awful. Watching her prance around with her fancy cakes and sandwiches. I have no idea what Murray saw in all that. He invited me back the next week. It was a Thursday, a week and a half before he died. They were fiddling around in the kitchen and I put some antifreeze in her teapot, at least I thought it was. But it was the wrong teapot. I couldn't tell him not to drink it. I knocked over the pot after he'd only had a little bit.

"I had a key to her house. Friend of mine used to live there before he died. Stupid woman didn't have the locks changed. I went in and put the antifreeze in her juice. I knew Murray would never drink that mess. He told me. He swore up and down he would never, ever drink her damned green juice.

"But then I called him, the morning he died, and he told me was having the green juice Annalise made him with his breakfast. Laughed about it. I told him he shouldn't drink that stuff. I didn't know what to do. I went running over there. But it was too late. He was gone."

"And then you overheard Flannery or Tyler talking about the cameras in Murray's house?" I asked.

"Before that I had no idea. He never told me there were cameras. But I knew I'd be on film running over there, seeing him dead, and leaving. I panicked. I just couldn't face the idea of prison. I did what I had to do."

"And you couldn't resist taking that photo with you when you left?" I asked.

"It was such a happy memory."

Nate called Sonny, spoke in a low voice. "You get all that?"

TWENTY-NINE

None of us knew what to think. It was Sunday dinner, and Mamma had grilled chicken, steamed vegetables, and salad on the table. She prayed over it, just like every other Sunday dinner. When we all said "Amen," Daddy and Blake looked at the table like maybe they were having a shared dream. Not exactly a nightmare, but not a particularly good one, either.

Daddy had been bouncing from surly to happy grandfather-to-be and back so fast it was making everybody's head spin. Chumley whimpered loudly in the den. When Daddy was unhappy, Chumley was unhappy.

"Oh, for goodness sake," said Mamma. "We can't have Poppy eating all those fried foods. It's not good for my grandchild. Poppy, you want me to fix your plate?"

"No ma'am, thank you," said Poppy. "This looks delicious."

We commenced passing food and fixing plates.

Blake stared at a piece of grilled chicken suspiciously as he put it on his plate.

"This will be better for all of us." Nate might've been the happiest one in the room aside from Poppy, who honestly loved everything Mamma put on the table.

Daddy glared at him. "Speak for yourself. This situation is causing my blood pressure to go sky high, I just know it."

"What has my blood pressure up is that crazy hound dog of yours," said Mamma. "I haven't slept in days."

"What's going on with Chumley?" I asked.

"He likes little Daisy next door," said Daddy. "She's in heat."

"Those dogs howl and moan at each other all night long," said Mamma.

"Are y'all ready for your trip?" I asked Merry.

"We leave a week from Saturday." She piled salad on her plate. "I guess we're as ready as we're going to get."

"And you come back when?" asked Nate.

"December fifth." Joe grinned. Normally he might've mourned Mamma's fried chicken under the circumstances, but he was on the verge of becoming a married man and an official member of the family.

"All my babies will be married when you get back." Mamma was all teary-eyed. She held Merry's hand, squeezed it.

"You sure y'all are good with the twenty-first?" asked Nate. "You'll just be back from a three-week trip."

"Sure," said Merry. "We're in. But you sure are awfully mysterious about whatever it is you have planned."

"Monday, December 21, through Monday, January 4. Nobody make any plans." Nate looked around the table. "All right?"

Everyone said sure and all that.

"I can't imagine what it'll be like not to plan Christmas," said Mamma. "I always put up a tree right after Thanksgiving. I'll still do that, I guess." She looked at Nate with a question.

"Of course we'll have a Christmas tree. What's the matter with you?" Daddy looked scandalized at the suggestion there might not be a tree.

"After the Halloween fiasco, you have no say in decorations whatsoever," said Mamma.

"What the devil are we going to do for two entire weeks?" asked Daddy.

"We're going to celebrate," said Nate. "We have quite a lot to celebrate, don't we? The twenty-first is our first wedding anniversary. Blake and Poppy just got married. A baby's on the way. And Merry and Joe will be newlyweds." Nate grinned.

"Can we eat normal?" asked Daddy.

"Frank, you can eat whatever Carolyn lets you get away with," said Nate.

"Hmmpf." Daddy winced.

We did have so much to celebrate. I was truly grateful for every smiling face and sour puss at that table. I had no idea what Nate had planned by way of a celebration. He wouldn't even give me the teensiest hint. But even as I reveled in all the joy in the room, a part of me couldn't help but grieve. I hung on to Colleen's words. Even if I couldn't see her, I imagined her sitting on the buffet the way she'd done so many times before at Sunday dinner.

I knew she was still alive, somewhere. But I missed her, and I knew she missed me, and Nate too. She'd rebuilt her life here in Stella Maris, become re-entwined in the ins and outs of our small-town life. I knew it must've hurt her something awful to have to leave, to lose home all over again. She'd freely given up everything because she loved me and knew what losing Nate would do to me.

Somehow, I was going to have to figure how to keep us all safe without her help from now on. I figured I had at least five years before my biggest challenge.

Susan M. Boyer

Susan M. Boyer is the author of the *USA Today* bestselling Liz Talbot mystery series. Her debut novel, *Lowcountry Boil*, won the Agatha Award for Best First Novel, the Daphne du Maurier Award for Excellence in Mystery/Suspense, and garnered several other award nominations, including the Macavity. The third in the series, *Lowcountry Boneyard*, was a Southern Independent Booksellers Alliance (SIBA) Okra Pick, a Daphne du Maurier Award finalist, and short-listed for the Pat Conroy Beach Music Mystery Prize. Susan loves beaches, Southern food, and small towns where everyone knows everyone, and everyone has crazy relatives. You'll find all of the above in her novels. She lives in Greenville, SC, with her husband and an inordinate number of houseplants.

**The Liz Talbot Mystery Series
by Susan M. Boyer**

LOWCOUNTRY BOIL (#1)
LOWCOUNTRY BOMBSHELL (#2)
LOWCOUNTRY BONEYARD (#3)
LOWCOUNTRY BORDELLO (#4)
LOWCOUNTRY BOOK CLUB (#5)
LOWCOUNTRY BONFIRE (#6)
LOWCOUNTRY BOOKSHOP (#7)
LOWCOUNTRY BOOMERANG (#8)
LOWCOUNTRY BOONDOGGLE (#9)

Henery Press Mystery Books

And finally, before you go...
Here are a few other mysteries
you might enjoy:

PUMPKINS IN PARADISE
Kathi Daley

A Tj Jensen Mystery (#1)

Between volunteering for the annual pumpkin festival and coaching her girls to the state soccer finals, high school teacher Tj Jensen finds her good friend Zachary Collins dead in his favorite chair.

When the handsome new deputy closes the case without so much as a "why" or "how," Tj turns her attention from chili cook-offs and pumpkin carving to complex puzzles, prophetic riddles, and a decades-old secret she seems destined to unravel.

Available at booksellers nationwide and online

Visit www.henerypress.com for details

BOARD STIFF
Kendel Lynn

An Elliott Lisbon Mystery (#1)

As director of the Ballantyne Foundation on Sea Pine Island, SC, Elliott Lisbon scratches her detective itch by performing discreet inquiries for Foundation donors. Usually nothing more serious than retrieving a pilfered Pomeranian. Until Jane Hatting, Ballantyne board chair, is accused of murder. The Ballantyne's reputation tanks, Jane's headed to a jail cell, and Elliott's sexy ex is the new lieutenant in town.

Armed with moxie and her Mini Coop, Elliott uncovers a trail of blackmail schemes, gambling debts, illicit affairs, and investment scams. But the deeper she digs to clear Jane's name, the guiltier Jane looks. The closer she gets to the truth, the more treacherous her investigation becomes. With victims piling up faster than shells at a clambake, Elliott realizes she's next on the killer's list.

Available at booksellers nationwide and online

Visit www.henerypress.com for details

CPSIA information can be obtained
at www.ICGtesting.com
Printed in the USA
BVHW061345190820
586728BV00001B/1